US MOB

HISTORY, CULTURE, STRUGGLE:
AN INTRODUCTION TO INDIGENOUS AUSTRALIA

MUDROOROO

Angus&Robertson
An imprint of HarperCollins*Publishers*

In memory of Kevin Gilbert (1933-1993)
who told it how it was. We miss you Bro.

This project has been assisted by the Commonwealth Government through the Australian Council, its arts funding and advisory body.

Angus&Robertson
An imprint of HarperCollins*Publishers*, Australia

First published in Australia in 1995
Reprinted in 1996
by HarperCollins*Publishers* Pty Limited
ACN 009 913 517
A member of the HarperCollins*Publishers* (Australia) Pty Limited Group

Copyright © Mudrooroo 1995

This book is copyright.
Apart from any fair dealing for the purposes of private study, research, criticism or review, as permitted under the Copyright Act, no part may be reproduced by any process without written permission.
Inquiries should be addressed to the publishers.

HarperCollins*Publishers*
25 Ryde Road, Pymble, Sydney, NSW 2073, Australia
31 View Road, Glenfield, Auckland 10, New Zealand
77-85 Fulham Palace Road, London W6 8JB, United Kingdom
Hazelton Lanes, 55 Avenue Road, Suite 2900, Toronto, Ontario M5R 3L2
and 1995 Markham Road, Scarborough, Ontario M1B 5M8, Canada
10 East 53rd Street, New York NY 10032, USA

National Library of Australia Cataloguing-in-Publication data:

Mudrooroo, 1938– .
Us mob: history, culture, struggle: an introduction to indigenous Australia.
Includes index.
ISBN 0 207 18818 1.
1. Aborigines, Australian — Social conditions. 2. Aborigines, Australian — History. 3. Aborigines, Australian — Politics and government.
4. Aborigines, Australian — Ethnic identity. I. Title.
305.89915

Internal illustrations by Bronwyn Bancroft
Printed in Australia by Griffin Paperbacks, Adelaide

9 8 7 6 5 4 3 2   96 97 98 99

Contents

Preface..................iv

Lecture 1
Our Indigenality........................1

Lecture 2
Our Family Ways....................18

Lecture 3
Our Spirituality..................33

Lecture 4
Our Languages............................56

Lecture 5
Us Mob and Politics....................75

Lecture 6
The Master's Law........................92

Lecture 7
Our Education.....................112

Lecture 8
Our Health.........................126

Lecture 9
Seeing and Reading Us Mob................................142

Lecture 10
Selling Our Culture....................154

Lecture 11
Our Histories......................175

Lecture 12
Our Struggle for Our Lands........................193

Lecture 13
Reconciling Us Mob............................220

Conclusion...................235

Index.....................240

PreFaCe

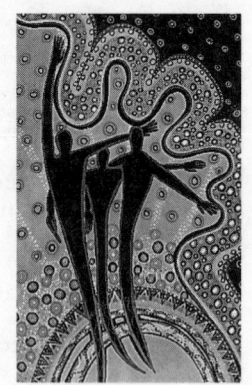

AUSTRALIAN INDIGENOUS STUDIES ARE ESSENTIALLY THE study of Australia, not the Australia constructed for us as a historical continuity beginning two hundred odd years ago with the arrival of the first wave of European invaders, so pregnant with contradictions and constant rewritings, inscriptions, rubbings out and pencillings in of what, after all, are perhaps mundane events in the history of European imperialism. To Us Indigenous Mobs, the arrival of the first wave of invaders (those who came to settle and take up land, dispossess and deprive us of our inheritance, so that what we once owned, what had passed down to us from our ancestors, no longer belonged to us) is but an interlude in our long possession of Australia. It is a traumatic period which needs healing, and perhaps 'Aboriginal' studies may be seen as part of that healing process. During this suffering period, we were forced to live on land doled out to us by a faraway foreign government; we were then deprived of those parcels of land when they were needed by the invaders. We then had no 'native title'; we were seen as savages, somewhat above the animals, and if seen as humans were to be civilised and absorbed into a foreign culture.

We were overcome by these events; our blood was mixed; and we were forced to struggle and debate our very identity as human beings. We were defined and rendered by others in books such as this one. Once we inscribed ourselves on our bodies, on our land; now we were inscribed into books, made the subject of a discourse, a way of talking which was not with the tongue but with the sharp points of sticks dipped in charcoal and marked in lines of strange symbols in a strange language. We had to learn those symbols; we had to learn that they represented a strange language which we also had to learn. We men and women, Us Mobs, had often to forgo our languages; had to forgo our culture; had to plunge into the new pools of fright. Still, we are learning about the devils living in those pools; and we shy away from them, while dancing out new ceremonies of healing. A new word for us, that word 'shy', from the action of that new animal, 'horse', him with the hard hooves that pounded at our earth. Our animals hopped, or crawled, or scuttled; the new animals had few of these natural movements. They galloped, they trotted; the land echoed with new sounds; the very trees were uprooted, torn out root and trunk to be replaced by high waving grass, by plants which did not grow in clumps but all over the land, just as the invaders spread all over us. But we exist on changing and adapting. A tree grows shaped by the wind, by the rain, by the earth; and so we have grown and been shaped by the winds rushing in from the whole world.

We are many mobs with many countries, but we have become mixed up. We were put together without thought for our differences and our attachment to our countries. We were taken here and there; sometimes we went voluntarily; other times we were like cattle rounded up, slaughtered and bought and sold. We were made into what are called 'Australian Aborigines', or now 'Aboriginal Australians', though we were never a single mob. We are many, as many as the trees, as the different types of animals. We are Nyungars, Nangas, Yolngus, Kooris, Murris, et al, all different, but all forming the indigenous people of Australia.

And so this book, these words put down on paper — not as marks of contention — is about the indigenous people of Australia, who are like the different species of trees all belonging to different families. Us Mobs are like that — different families, different cultures, and the blossoms of these families of trees spread their pollen to fertilise the great tree which is Australia. Us Mob are many mobs, but we all come from that great tree which is Australia. Without that great tree, we cannot grow in our own ways. He orders us, and without knowing that Grandfather Tree we fall into dissension, we say 'our mob is better; your mob is no good'. But as all families of trees have their natural growth around that Grandfather Tree so do we. We are a singularity in diversity, and that singularity is Australia..

Our InDigenaliTy

Lecture 1

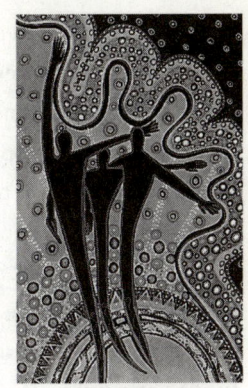

US MOBS OVER THE PAST TWO HUNDRED ODD YEARS HAVE been forced to adapt, have been placed in a position so that we have had to come to grips with the world and its many other peoples. Before this, in our old days, we related mainly with each other. We lived as extended family groups next to each other, and squabbled, fought, intermarried and came together in peace at regular intervals, at such places as the bora circles where we held joint ceremonies. These were inter-family gatherings that kept us together in a harmony, though we should not forget those family squabbles. All was not peaceful and harmonious among us, but there were ways to heal the quarrels. At the joint family gatherings, we managed to settle our differences, for we knew that families must cooperate for survival and well-being.

So, did we know only other Australian extended families? This is not exactly true. In the north of our land and along the coasts, people did come to visit. Our culture was never unchanging: these visitors brought in new ways and ideas which we could adapt. The Baijini and Macassans came to the land of the Yolngu extended families; other peoples came to what is now known as the Kimberley. Our oral traditions and songs record these visits. Some visitors stayed and became members of our families; others departed. These were different sorts of relationships to those into which we were forced when the first wave of Europeans came. These came to stay, and not only to stay but to conquer, to take over our lands, and then to attempt to change us drastically. Theirs was not a gentle way — it was violent, and this became a time of sadness and disruption for us. Our culture was not enough for humans to live in, our languages were not enough for humans to speak by, our methods of oral transmission were not enough for continuance. Our very being had to be inscribed and imprisoned on the pages of books. It was as if our souls had to be imprisoned in another language in another way of recording and other ways of formation. Not only had our bodies to become settled, but so had our spirits.

To survive, we had to become educated in the conquerors' ways, and when we became educated we found others in the same predicament as ourselves. We began to learn about these other peoples, and discovered that we had become colonised and been transformed into the Native, the Other, and that our very dignity as human beings necessitated that we struggle. And so to effectively struggle we had to acquiesce in becoming the one mob of the colonisers, though we knew that before we had been many and are still many. Still, education made us become the Native, the Other; opposed to the colonisers, the Masters, who were themselves more than one mob. They themselves had inscribed and written down themselves as one mob. Against You Mob, we became Us Mob.

And so some of us became educated and read Albert Memmi, Frantz Fanon and Trinh T. Minh-Ha. A man from a mob called Jews in a country called Algeria, a black fellow from the French colony of Martinique, both of whom wrote about the psychological and physical effects of colonialism on oppressed people, and, lastly, a Woman of Colour from Asia who wrote about the oppression of women and the 'native' who became seen as the different *Other*. What were we, but the good, the bad and the ugly. Weren't we always being broken down into good, noble savages and bad ugly savages, good, clean and civilised and bad, dirty and savage; and eventually even divided into real and unreal? It was a way of control and governance. Also a way that the mind of the Master worked. Often what they saw as good was opposed by what they saw as bad. The good woman (wife and mother) was opposed to the whore; the traditional (the real native) was opposed to the unreal, the non-traditional, one of Us Mob who writes this book; or, if it is to be extended back to the Masters' oppositions of all oppositions, nature was opposed to culture (or precisely Us and Them). And the Other? Well, there is the tame Other, the ones who say, 'Yes, Master', and the unknown Other (the ones the white man exclaims about in exasperation: 'I don't know what these people want.').

To educate the Woman, the Native, the Other is to put into our hands and minds a weapon. The Master wants us to be educated into his ways of seeing things, of thinking things, of doing things; but we want to be educated so that we can do things our way, think our own thoughts, and see with our own eyes. We do not want to continue on in this uneasy colonisation of the spirit, of the body, of the material, of the land, and we do not want him to become like us either. We wish only that all trees remain and continue their natural growth around that great Grandfather Tree which is Australia, to respect Australia and its ceaseless and unending variety.

Australia may be seen to be made up of Indigenous people, those who belong to the earth, and those who came from other lands where they too belonged to the earth and slowly became attached to their new countries. Until they did so, they suffered nostalgia for their own womb places. This nostalgia caused them to dismiss not only our trees, but the very earth itself, comparing it to their sad old granny, Europe. Yearning for her withered breasts, they sought to establish our country, Australia, in her image. Their cities imaged her body as they sought to make their granny young again, even as they sighed for their own earth of Europe and her trees and climates. But Australia is not Europe and was often seen as a harsh mistress, another woman, and thus coupled with the Native, the Other. The Master constructs stereotypes of the *Other* as Woman, as Native, and all he is doing is building on his own emotions, his feelings, which want everything to conform, to be controllable, to be amenable to his own well-being. The sad Master discourse continues to seek to imprison the *Other*, in love: 'You are not like the others,' or in hatred: 'You are just like the rest.' Or the *Native* in assimilation: 'You must see yourself above that pack of bludgers, or what have you,' or even: 'He is not a real native.' When the Master fails to assert his authority, or to possess, he turns sour. If the Woman, the Native, the Other does not accept his possession, then the Woman, the Native, the Other is not really

Other, is refusing to remain under his gaze. She or he is seen, in effect, as a person in conflict with the Master for possession, thus:

MR HINZE: Would you say that Senator Bonner is an Aborigine?

DR SCOTT-YOUNG: No, Senator Bonner claims to be an Aborigine.

MR HINZE: Do you think he might be an Indian or an Afghan?

DR SCOTT-YOUNG: I do not know. He claims to be an Aborigine.

(Tatz, *Race Politics in Australia*)

The Master refuses to see the Other, the Native, as being equal, as being capable. It is a colonial discourse, a way of speaking which seeks to disarm, a way of removing a threat. Examples of such a discourse abound, and it is little wonder that in Australia those in control find it easier to accept the Native as an artist, a musician, or a writer, but as a politican, as an equal vying for a sharing of power, never. For the Native, the Woman, the Other to have equal power may mean a loss of possession, control and conformity, and the Master is ever the conservative, the Father in absolute control, for if he was to lose control, was to share his power, then this might in effect mean that he would lose control of himself. When a plurality of voices and power-sharers emerges, then other means of ordering are necessary, and these other means of orderings — or should I say negotiations? — mean the death of authority as structured by the Master.

Perhaps there may be some questioning about how this fits into an introduction to Australian Indigenous studies. Are we to discuss the whole of Australia and its political structure(s), and perhaps expand outwards to cover the whole of race and gender politics and the place (or lack of it) of Indigenous peoples throughout the world? I reply that it is difficult to discuss any family without discussing other families and their relationships — that a forest is composed of trees of many types, that even in the desert there are the brushings of the individual particles of earth to consider, and in any social or national set-up the Other, the Native in our case, does not exist in isolation, no matter how remote the settlement or camp site and no matter how much it is repeated: 'They should be left alone.' It is impossible to be left alone, to exist as an isolated culture in this Australia. For better or worse, everyone is bound up in a system of personal, social and political relationships, and these now cannot be avoided, if they ever could. Even when reserves were set aside for the Native and entry strictly regulated, the outside still penetrated, and even when Australia was Indigenous Australia, there is enough evidence in our traditions to suggest that our land was never the isolated continent as established in the Master texts. In fact, whatever the past position, it is impossible for Us Mob to remain in or reconstruct a splendid isolation, for now our very beings and cultures are part of Australia and the world.

The topic of this lecture is Indigenality. 'Indigenous' is a word which has come into prominence over the last few years in order to give a common term to Us Mob. In our languages there is no common word for all of the Indigenous people of Australia, or even of Australia itself, and every English word which has been used is but a term to render us into a commonality. I too am guilty of this, but until the time comes when we have our own word for Us Mob, I use Indigenous, which simply means originating in or from a country and thus is descriptive of Us Mob. Still there is the word 'Aboriginal' or 'Aborigine' which I should write about.

Aboriginal (that is, a member of Us Indigenous Mob seen as a totality) was for many years used as either an adjective or a noun, though in recent times there has been a tendency to use Aborigine as a noun, and Aboriginal as an adjective. But what is this word but an ideological construction which is part of the historical process of the naming of the Other in Australia? In the journals of those on the First Fleet, and Captain Cook before them, the Australian Other were discussed as 'Indians' if not 'savages', sometimes modified by 'noble' or 'abject'. We then became 'aborigines' with a small 'a', as well as 'natives'. 'Myalls' became fashionable for a while — usually augmented by 'savage' — as a term for those Indigenous people outside the boundaries of the Colonial domain, opposed to those seen and treated as tamed remnants struggling to keep their connection with their land within that domain. The latter became the objects of the whites' compassion and attempts to 'civilise' them, which eventually led to these Kooris, Murris, Nangas and Nyungars being incarcerated in separate settlements and missions where the imposition of Christian values could proceed unhampered by so-called exploitative forces (another Other, but one of class) lurking in the colonial centres. By now, with the gradual framing of government policies, we had become Aboriginals, or Aborigines, until in the 1960s the politicised Other, seeking a subjectivity within the International Black movement (to some extent read 'American'), seized on the term 'blacks', which has endured in Queensland (where there are other 'blacks') and in the newspapers. Again, 'blackfella' remains popular among some groups, though there are other Aboriginal groups who dispute any term signifying blackness.

As for women, from the first they were designated by the bastardised 'Aboriginal' words 'gin' or 'lubra'. It was as if the position of the female Other (coupled with the native Other) became doubly removed: an unknown Other. It was as if the European Master could only see this 'naked Eve' through the native language, or through the male Other, gazing at the male native who then directed his gaze at the female native. She was doubly opaque, almost a material object. Women did not exist except though the Master text, and had to be mediated through maleness. It is easy to see that the European position of women fastened on the black woman and rendered her able only to be seen and designated through the male. If the black male was inferior, the black woman was doubly so. The white male gazed at the black man who gazed beyond at the black woman.

The Native, the Indigenous person, the Aboriginal, is, I believe, as much a construction of the Master text of the European as is the Master himself. We are dealing with a hierarchical structure of order, of power, in which the Master constructs his own text, one in which he positions himself and his subordinates; or, we might even say, himself as subject and others as objects. His is the all-powerful gaze and consciousness. Thus, it is a difficult task in historical texts to find true representations of the Other, the object which is defined and described by the all-seeing gaze of the Master. The Other becomes lost in the Master text which continues to write on and about —

what else? — how the Native, the Aboriginal, appears to him. There is a whole, almost completely white organisation, the Australian Institute of Aboriginal and Torres Strait Islander Studies (AIATSIS), devoted to the study of the Native, and often the study is concerned not with the Native but with the structure of the Master text, which now has been changed to include the Mistress. As ideological shifts have occurred in the Master culture, the text must now be broadened to include the Mistress. Anthropology, that Master text limiting the Other, has thus become bisexual. The European woman has taken her place beside her Master and now produces studies that ape his text, or at least add to the Master text and give it a certain bisexuality. Thus, because the Master subject has bifurcated into male and female, so has the Other, the Native, and the Native female has entered anthropology as a legitimate concern of study, so that we now have books on such topics as 'women's business'.

The construction of the Indigenous person in Australia is in the main a matter of discourse, of language, and if we are to gain a glimpse of the reality existing as a trace within the language we must seek to deconstruct it. Even if we accept the proposition that language is value-free, the problem Indigenous people have with the texts of Anthropology still have to be explained. If we accept that language echoes reality, and turn to what is termed 'prehistory' to find the Other in a state of pristine wholeness before the arrival of the European, what do we find but the Master text in which are embedded the phantoms of the past as seen by the Master. Prehistory is the domain of the Master European subject and it is through his discourse that we are condemned to reconstruct any past. In the Master text the Other reflects no consciousness or subjectivity. The Other is only a trace in Master discourses which have other concerns (as any examination of nineteenth-century documents will reveal) than to present a true picture. Discourses about the pristine prehistorical native only lead to more Master discourses of the pristine prehistorical Native. To reconstruct Indigenous life and society before what has been termed pre-Cook is to risk being trapped by a mishmash of interpretations of the various discourses found in documents. Any contemporary Indigenous project then is to seek in these documents, texts and discourses those traces from which we might try to reconstruct a pre-Cook Indigenous existential being which will aid our present and give us strength. In this way we will pay homage to our ancestors and resurrect them in the present. This is all we can do, realising that there are very few documents stemming from the Other. In other words, our ancestors do not speak through these documents but are only a presence in them, and if Indigenous people use such documents to establish a pre-Cook life then they must remain aware that they are entering into an anthropological or ethnological discourse and that to find our ancestors we must follow their traces through the ideological assumptions of the Master subject. Thus, recognising the enormity of the problem, in this book I do not attempt to construct the pristine past of the Indigenous people of Australia. It would take up the rest of this volume to seek out the traces of our ancestors in such texts and so I keep to the contemporary, our present which is held within memory, rather than the distant past. In this present, our scattered families are seeking to bring their members together, are daring to hope and aspire, and are returning to Indigenous people a family identity. My problem is how to speak and write about Us Indigenous Mobs, who are only just coming out from under the gaze of the Master.

How do I speak, how do I write about Us Mob and our Australian Indigenality? What after all is an Indigenous Australian, a person of many names, too many of which have been unwarrantably imposed? To name is not only to define but to own, and so 'counter-names' are being used by Aborigines, such as Koori, Goori, Boori, Yolngu, Yamadji, Nyungar, Nanga, Anangu and Murri, which signify a regional Indigenality. We do not have our own name for Us Mob, the complete Indigenous people of Australia, though we continue to seek our own name; but this urge for wholeness, a total Australia-wide expression of our Indigenality, too often and too quickly breaks down into regional and local differences. Our identity does not rest in an imagined Australian Aborigine, but in regionality — for example, Nyungar — and beneath that, at the local level, there is the tribal title — such as in my community's case, Bibbulmum — which is itself often a reconstruction, or closer still a collection of family names making up the local Nyungar identity.

There are problems when we seek to isolate this local identity implied in a tribal name. Once upon a time the Masters came, saw and named, and then began to discuss their whole naming process. They continue to do so, and there is even a map of tribal areas and boundaries created by a Master. It has some sort of historicity, but the question remains: Did local Aboriginal families or collections of families have a common name for their collectivity? Did they need one? We know that the Masters invented tribes as they perhaps invented language groups as a way of ordering their world. Each thing had to be named, and to be without a name, a patronymic, the name of the father, was to be bastardised and without a legality. It is difficult to apply wholeness, unity or oneness, even to a single region, or what appears on the surface to be a single community. If we seek to do so, we are swiftly disillusioned when we find ourselves amid a welter of families, clans, social groupings and factions, and even different traditions. But then, why should we expect a common purpose when we have passed through such a terrible history and are still attempting to come to some agreement among ourselves, to forge some common Australian Indigenality without giving up our local freedoms? Nonetheless, to attempt some sort of understanding and show how such a process of Australian Indigenality is beginning to be formed, I discuss a close friend of mine who died some years ago.

In some of our cultures it is not permitted to speak or write the name of one deceased, and so I give my friend the pseudonym Kevin Jones, which in itself sets him among those Indigenous peoples (here Kooris) who bore the full brunt of the British invasion and thus have English names. I base the account of his life on a manuscript which includes an interview conducted with him shortly before he died.

Kevin Jones spent his boyhood in the Sydney suburb of Balmain and was thus a Sydney Koori, though he was part of another mob — the group who live in the NSW country town of Minimbah, which he always regarded as his country. Naturally, with someone's identification with a particular country area, one enters what may be considered a whole complex of Indigenality, or 'Kooriality'. One must take into account a number of factors — to which family does he belong; whether that family are the landowners of the area; what language was/is spoken there and what state it is in today; the living conditions of the community and even the factions within it, such as the Land Council. Kevin Jones states in the manuscript that his full-blood paternal grandmother lived in Minimbah. 'Full-blood' is a word used to mean someone who through heredity is close to what is termed 'traditional', though without further information it is impossible to know how processes of culture and life have adapted or been changed by the presence of British settlers. I do not believe that the mere fact of 'blood' denotes a possible plenitude of an original Indigenality, for though resting on heredity and descent, Indigenality includes a learnt portion, and to stress degrees of 'blood' is in effect playing the Master's game, which is always one dealing with possession, legality, paternity and caste.

Kevin Jones declares about his grandmother: 'She lived on a small settlement with an unbroken Koori tradition near a 40,000-year-old midden.' The small settlement is not identified as either an ex-mission or a government station. Kooris were incarcerated in such areas and eventually, with the passing of the NSW Land Rights Act of 1983, these areas became Koori land. Often people were collected and shipped off to such places, but here the settlement is modified by an 'unbroken Koori tradition'. What that tradition means is further explained in the text:

> He travelled with her to the settlements and missions around
> Forster, visiting relatives, and she instilled in him a sense of
> being Aborigine, a feeling for the land, an awareness of the
> old ways and customs, an idea of a community.

Travelling over the land corresponds to the old rites of passage when the boy was taken over the land to get to know it. It is interesting to note that it was the paternal grandmother who did this, whereas in the old days it was the job of the males, principally the maternal uncle, and the education process ended in the ceremonies of the Bora circle; but by Kevin Jones's time this is no longer so, and the paternal grandmother has taken over the role of educating the boy into his land and society.

'Visiting relatives' is an aspect of Us Mob culture which has been part of Australian Indigenous society since the beginning, as has the love of one's country, an awareness of the old ways and customs and the ideas of belonging to an extended family, here glossed under 'community'. It was only after he learnt about being an Indigenous person, a Koori, from his paternal grandmother that Kevin Jones was ready to move beyond his area and embrace an Australia-wide Indigenality.

This awareness of nationwide Indigenality may be seen as an urban phenomenon. Cities tend to break down small communities and establish larger and looser groupings. In some remote settlements no-one is ever alone, no-one is allowed to go off by him- or herself, but it is in the city that we come across solitary Kooris and individuals. Here we have government policies, housing commissions and anti-squatting laws, and there is not a trace of the old Us Mob camping areas. Many Kooris and Murris who have come to Sydney live in Redfern, but I doubt that Redfern can be broken up into discrete Us Mob local communities. There are Murris from Queenland and Kooris from all over NSW, as well as families and individuals from other States. District and regional affiliations endure, but the closeness of a small, tightly knit community is absent, and even the feuds that occur do not reflect old rivalries. The city skyline dominates all, but in this hotchpotch of Us Mob individuals, there rises a sense of being Indigenous above being Koori or Murri.

Born of what is termed a mixed marriage, Kevin Jones arrived not in Redfern but Balmain, which was still a working-class suburb at the time. He won a scholarship and dreamed of becoming a doctor; but there was no money for school uniforms. His father decided that he was to become a tradesperson. He revolted against this and ended up in prison.

Here we have what could almost be said to be a typical Us Mob Koori youth story of today; for as I write this, too many Nyungar youth in Western Australia are languishing in gaol. But it is not just the younger generation which finds itself imprisoned. For many adult males, a gaol sentence may be accepted as an indicator of Indigenality. Many of Us Mob, among them the well-known Koori writer, the late Kevin Gilbert, have served goal sentences, and it is in the prisons of Australia that many of Us Mob develop a consciousness of nationwide Indigenality which is overtly political.

After his spell in gaol, Kevin Jones's life took a sudden and unexpected turn. He left the 'typical' childhood of one of Us Mob, became an actor and somehow made it overseas. He did commercials, modelled clothes in Europe and the US and finally, in New York, decided to become a serious actor by enrolling in Stella Adler's studio, eventually becoming her 'adjutant' and a dedicated student and teacher of 'Method' acting. He became part of the Open Theatre and performed both on and off Broadway, as well as in regional theatre. In Atlanta, Georgia, he even played in Noel Coward's *Blithe Spirit*, and being relatively fair-skinned, the audience in the segregated South of the early sixties did not realise that he was black. Talking about this, he says: 'If they had known, they would have killed me.'

Kevin Jones eventually returned to Australia, not as a successful Australian triumphantly coming back from abroad, but as an Indigenous person who had never forsaken his land. He returned eager to add his experience and knowledge to the common pool of expertise and knowledge which Us Mob were accumulating.

He acted in and directed the first Indigenous plays such as *The Cake Man* by Robert Merritt, and in association with other Kooris organised an Indigenous Playwrights' Conference which was to have led to the establishment of a national Indigenous theatre. An organisation emerged from this conference, the aims of which were to be a focus of indigenous productions, provide networking and continuity, and to provide the foundation for an ensemble of Indigenous theatre artists, but after only a short life it collapsed. From this, Kevin Jones went into film production and not long before his death made a film which involved a struggle with the Masters who controlled the Australian Film Commission. In their view, films about Indigenous people should portray them as victims — that is, the Other as victim, an object of pity framed by the camera lens. Kevin Jones, on the other hand, wanted to make a film which told the story of an Aboriginal woman who became a successful fashion designer — that is, a subject beyond the Master's stereotype of 'poor bloody Mary'. The Koori community rallied in his support and the AFC, after being threatened with a law suit, agreed to fund it. The film may have been a love story, somewhat glamorous and

Hollywoodian, but it gave Kooris experience in feature film-making and laid the foundation for better things.

The life of Kevin Jones may thus be seen as the story of a Koori who moved from a basic and local awareness of Indigenality to that of a broader Australian indigenous identity and then beyond to the national and global, though still continuing to be based on three elements: descent, love of country and attachment to community.

FURTHER READING

Davis, Jack, *Kulkark and The Dreamers*. Sydney, Currency Press, 1982.

Fanon, Frantz, *The Wretched of the Earth*. Melbourne, Penguin Books, 1973.

Gilbert, Kevin, *Living Black: Blacks Talk to Kevin Gilbert*. Melbourne, Penguin Books, 1984.

Memmi, Albert, *The Colonizer and the Colonized*. London, Souvenir Press, 1974.

Minh-ha, Trinh T., *Woman, Native, Other: Writing, Postcoloniality and Feminism*. Bloomington, Indiana University Press, 1989.

Mulvaney, D., 'The chain of connection; the material evidence' in N. Petersen (ed), *Tribes and Boundaries in Australia*. Canberra, Australian Institute of Aboriginal Studies, 1976.

Simon, Ella, *Through My Eyes*. Melbourne, Collins Dove, 1987.

Tatz, Colin, *Race Politics in Australia: Aborigines, Politics and Law*. Armidale, University of New England, 1979.

OUR FAMILY WAYS
Lecture 2

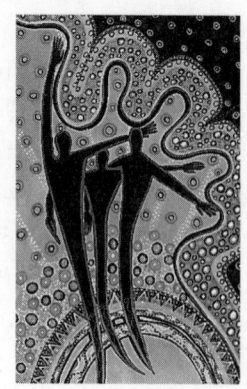

WHEN I TRAVEL THROUGH OUR COUNTRIES, WHEN I pass through the temperate rainforests, through the too often lacerated lands of the south, when I stand in the arid regions, head northwards towards the very tip of our continent, towards Cape York, and gaze across at the islands linking us with New Guinea, I become conscious of the whole of our land. My consciousness becomes Australia, the diversity of our land, and beneath the diversity is the underlying singularity, the earth which makes us Australian. The huge trees of the southern countries, huddling into themselves because of the coldness, change into drier and stringier types as I go inland from the eastern coastline. As I proceed further north, the trees continue to undergo change. Their leaves broaden, their trunks shed the hanging bark with which I am familiar and their roots stretch out across the earth, but they are still the same beneath their changed forms. I admire the resiliency of the countries through which I pass; I mourn the passing of the great forests; I lament over the cleared paddocks of mallee scrub; I stand before the small white trees of the arid regions and admire them in their daintiness. I see the diversity of Us Fella Tree; and in them I can see and understand the diversity of Us Mobs.

For days I travel across the land, even in these days of the Toyota. So why in the old days should there have been a singularity termed 'Aborigine' spread far and wide across the land in an awful sameness of conformity? To experience is to understand, but the Masters came and essayed to see a singularity. They who believed in the singularity of Europe perceived a singularity in faraway places and across wide terrains. They saw Indians and Aborigines and whatever else they might care to construct.

We should exult in diversity, not try to impose one system, one ideology, one philosophy, one vision of sameness on all. It is a problem for us and for all those who do not want to be part of a totality. It is possible now to go from city to city in an aeroplane, and experience nothing but sameness: the sameness of plane, the sameness of airport, the sameness of city, the sameness of language, of television program; the diversity is gone. But when I travel over the land, through our countries, the changes come sometimes slowly, sometimes abruptly, but constantly. Over the land of Australia, Us Mobs order our families in different ways, speak our different languages, and conduct our different ceremonies, but for all this, underneath is the basis of family and kinship.

And this is the unity which underlies the diversities of Us Mob — the family, the kinship patterns which I find in all the countries I have visited. This is the enduring structure of Us Mob which continues to survive, though it has been constantly under threat from the Master, who sought to destroy it and replace it with his type of family in which he was the ruler, the father, the protector, the station owner, the missionary, the police sergeant, the premier, the prime minister, the king. He was the All-Father and he saw us as children to be raised in his image; in most cases he failed, though in some he succeeded and thus strife arose between our family structures and his singular structure. Thus Us Mob males were photographed often in his image, standing above the women, or above the owned single wife and children in solitary, clothed splendour. How lonely it must be to be a solitary God ordering from on high His universe. How pleasant it is to be our ancestors coming up from our land, or coming from the sea to create Us Mob in a kinship of reciprocity. Our network of kinship was inscribed on the land, on the environment, on the skies. Nowhere was there a singular All-Father; for we had many fathers and mothers and many relations. We were never that solitary figure which was only pictured and made by the master in his image.

The original Master, Governor Phillip, invaded Australia at what they called Port Jackson, and what were we to make of the strange family which came to take without recompense? They were ordered by a king, by a governor, by Masters in a pyramid based on class, on the governor, on the free settler, on the soldier and the convict, in an ordering unlike our own. Against this pyramid we had a tree structure which they did not understand; and so, against our families and kinship structures they ordained what we might call the anti-family, in which everyone was ordered to do things without any discernible tradition. No-one cared for other people without being commanded. Alien structures were built on our land, like gaols, barracks and orphanages. These structures, anti-family as they were, were soon transferred from them to us. Suddenly, we no longer belonged to each other or could follow the ways of our ancestors; no longer could even the trees be trees. Our tree shape was not the pyramid of the Master, our placements were not his placements; our thoughts, our ways, not his thoughts or ways. Us Mobs were to renounce our very thoughts and think in other patterns; our tree was to be cut down and carved into a pyramid. The father, the Master at the apex of the pyramid, knew what was best for all, and especially for us. He took us from our camps and put us in these gaols and orphanages where our kinship system was completely ignored. He sought to render Us Mob futureless by cutting away our tender shoots — our children. Some were even taken away to his country, Britain, where they died far from family and country. A terrible future was forced on us without a qualm, for the Master knew what was good for us. Many of our children were placed in those orphanages he had constructed for his own bastards, and even had special places constructed for them where they might be far from us. They were to be disciplined and educated in what was called 'civilisation'.

Perhaps our ways were as rude and shapeless as our trees, but they were our ways, and if they were all bad, then how come we had survived for so many thousands of years? It was because our ancestors had fashioned us into kinship systems which ensured that we continued from the past, through the present and into the future. These systems worked well until You Mob came and decided that they did not — that they were brutish systems not based on the scripture of the All-Father. The Master came and saw and hacked and chopped. Adults were killed or rendered powerless, and the children suffered far away from us under the care of the Master who knew what was best. And even today this continues. Children knowing only the despotism of the Master grow up neither as Masters or one of Us Mob. How many of them roam your spaces belonging to no-one? How many who have adopted your ways are used to govern us and how many are discarded when they try to be like the Master and talk back to him as equals? The bureaucratic bodies set up over the years, like the various Departments of Aboriginal Affairs, the Aboriginal Development Commission and now the Aboriginal and Torres Strait Islander Commission (ATSIC), include many of those who have entered the Master's structures of power, often directly from those institutions. Under the gaze of the Master and under our gaze, they too often suffer in their position. They return the gaze and try to please both the Master and Us Mobs. They try to do the best they can from their position, not quite part of the pyramid, not quite part of our tree. They are considered 'Aborigines', which is different from Us Mobs. They try to see Us Mobs as one people and try to help us by implementing the policies of the Master, to whom they are accountable. But often the politics and policies of these Master organisations are wrong, owing to a lack of understanding of our kinship and family ways, and lead to a wastage of funding, which other Masters then attack. Master contrives against Master, while we look on and continue striving to keep our family and kinship structures together in the face of Master plans which seek to destroy us.

Our extended families are different from the European extended family in that ours are based on classificatory relationships, part of our general philosophy whereby everything — human beings, animals, plants and inanimate objects including the stars in the sky — is seen as forming one vast universal family. In many respects this way of seeing the universe has been destroyed, but we still remember it and yearn for its comfort.

Our classificatory kinship system is so called because it applies the same term to a whole group or class of people rather than a few individuals supposedly related by 'blood' as in the European 'descriptive' system. It came from our remote ancestors and they constructed it so that every person could find his place in the universe. There were no strangers — only people we regarded as brothers, sisters, aunts, uncles, fathers, mothers, grandfathers and grandmothers.

In my Nyungar mob, as among many others, all our communities were divided into two groupings, called 'moieties' in European parlance. These were Crow and Cockatoo, or in our language, *Wardangmaat* and *Manitjmaat*. The root *maat* here means leg, symbolising the fact that just as human beings have two legs, so did the Nyungar people, who saw their society as being arranged like a huge human body. These moieties were essential to the social cohesion of our people, especially by providing the basis of our marriage law, under which a member of the Crow moiety must marry a Cockatoo, and vice versa. In some parts of our country a baby when born took the moiety of its father, in others that of the mother.

The moieties were further divided into four sections: *Ballarak*, *Tondarap*, *Nagarnook* and *Didarak*, with the first two belonging to the Crow moiety and the second two to the Cockatoo. There was some variation between those following the father's or the mother's line of descent. Where the father's line was followed, Cockatoo men adhered to the following marriage rules. A *Tondarap* man married a *Ballarak* woman and the resulting child belonged to the father's section, *Tondarap*; a *Didarak* man married a *Nagararnook* woman and the child was *Didarak*. With Crow men, *Ballarak* married *Tondarap* and the child was *Ballarak*; *Nagarnook* married *Didarak* with the child being *Nagarnook*. In those areas where the mother's line was followed, the marriage was simply across the moieties with a Crow woman marrying a man from either one of the Cockatoo sections, with the child belonging to the mother's moiety and section and with a Cockatoo woman marrying a man from one or other of the Crow sections, with the child belonging to the mother's moiety and section. A marriage within the same moiety was not allowed and was seen as *mootj* (wrong). Any transgressors were sternly punished.

How this system worked to unite the Nyungar mob may be seen from the following example. A *Tondarap* Cockatoo woman would regard all *Manitjmaat* (Cockatoo) people as her *nganning* (family) and wherever she went she met family members and found a welcome at their fires. The oldest people were her *demmamaat* or *marrangar* (grandparents); the next generation of women were seen as her *ngangamaat* (mothers) and their brothers as *kongamaat* (maternal uncles); the men and women of her generation were her *ngoondanmaat* and *jookamaat* (brothers and sisters) and their progeny were her *nobab* (children). All these she considered as her own family, her *nganning*.

Our Family Ways

In regard to the Crow moiety, the *Tondarap* Cockatoo woman saw its members as being her relations-in-law, her *noyyangar*. The oldest people were her *demmamaat* and *marranmat* (grandparents); the next generation of men she regarded as her *mammamaat* (fathers-in-law) and the women as her *mangarmaat* (fathers' sisters, or aunts). She also saw her mother's brothers who had married Cockatoo women as her *kongamaat* (mother's brothers' stock). The young men and women who were the sons and daughters of her mother's brothers and her father's sisters were her *kordamaat*, *ngooljarmaat* or *deenammat* (husband stock, brother-in-law stock and sister-in-law stock). The children of these were her *moyerman* (nephews) and *kumbartmaat* (nieces). She accepted all the Cockatoo women of her mother's generation as *nganga* (mothers) and their sons and daughters as her brothers and sisters, and their offspring as her children. These were seen as her very own family.

Where the father's line was followed, a Cockatoo woman with a Crow mother and a Cockatoo father would accept all the Crow women of her mother's generation as mothers and all the Cockatoo men of her father's generation as fathers. Classification was made somewhat differently, but still as part of the family system which bound all the Nyungar people together.

Our Nyungar system of ordering the universe began to come apart when Captain Stirling sailed up the Swan River and established a settlement there. More and more land was taken and if we protested we were ruthlessly suppressed. Incidents like the massacre of Pinjarra in 1834 severely damaged our kinship system and over the years the classifications gradually disintegrated. Nevertheless, our large extended families still survive and when a family member dies we come together in our hundreds to farewell them.

But our extended families are often under attack by the Masters, and by those who listen to them. Archie Weller has written about the effect of this on us Nyungars and our families in his 1981 novel, *The Day of the Dog*:

> Yeah, well it's none of 'is bloody business. The Greyboys just 'appen to be my cousins, as well as your nephews and nieces. Ya forgot about our black 'lations, Mum, ya so 'igh and mighty now.

Not only does he write about our extended family structures, but also the tension now existing within them caused by threats from without. Our families provide a sure haven of relief and identification against the Masters threatening us with a world view based on individualism and the nuclear family. The nuclear family is all-pervasive in Australia, at least as an ideology, for even in Western Australia it is so unstable that 30 per cent of such relationships end in divorce. In contrast to this, we always have a whole mob of relatives and 'mothers' to relieve the pressures on individuals.

In the old days, the male had little to do with the rearing of infants. His role, at least in the care of the male children when they reached a certain age, came later. In fact, even then the biological father did not train his child into the duties of adulthood. This was left to an uncle, usually from the mother's side. With the invaders came the ideology of the nuclear family, and the placing of the male, the biological father, at the head as boss. His supposedly natural role was the breadwinner and that of the woman the nest-maker, the home-maker. This was not so in our society and Master texts have even been written arguing that the father's role in the conception of a child was not accepted in Aboriginal society, that spirit children waited to enter women at certain significant places and that men had little to do with creating them. Babies and infants belonged to the women, and it was only later that men more or less came to adopt them. In fact, certain men's ceremonies seem to be based on the birth process, and male children have to be 'born again', as it were, before they can become men. The male role in the extended family was that of supplementing the protein portion of the diet by hunting, and if this job was lost, then the man's role was also lost, as was his 'fathering' role when the initiation ceremonies stopped. All in all, with such reservations in mind, it is extremely difficult to construct an accurate picture of our contemporary family structure: in fact, it is sometimes seen as a matriarchy in which the women have the larger role in family affairs, as Sally Morgan, one of Us Mob from Western Australia, has claimed. But whether or not this is so is, perhaps, not as important as the existence of an extended family structure which removes the pressure from individuals and in which children are not seen as problems in themselves.

Unfortunately, our extended family structures are often seen as barriers to our entering the so-called 'mainstream', and as hindrances to the westernisation of Aboriginal institutions, which are family-oriented and dominated. They are also blamed for keeping many of us at the same level of social well-being, or ill-being, by clinging to a sharing system which is outside the Master norm. The Master does not share, but indulges in charity, which often is used as a bait for those outside the system to be drawn into it. The rise of so-called philanthropy in the nineteenth century occurred not so much to help a wretched working class, but to 'uplift' the wretched working class — not to mention fallen women and 'natives' — to a symbolic level which conformed to the ideological beliefs of the Master. I use 'symbolic' here because the aim was not to raise the Other to the Master's level and to share his power, but to draw the Other into an ethical system in which he or she could have a productive role in the economy, while the Master retained his power and control. This is the same today with job-production schemes. They have nothing to do, for instance, with producing leaders of industry or entrepreneurs or politicians, but tradespeople and cheap labour for the service industries. We are taught that to be without a job is a misfortune but, in fact, in a more benign social system, it would be better to teach those without jobs, if they desired it, how to make use of their free time, rather than to instil in them the idea that there is something wrong with them because they are without a Master whom they must beg to give them a job, a purpose in life. Again, it might be better to seek to restructure Australian society along lines akin to our extended family, rather than to try to prop up a system which is failing many Australians and which is also causing them to regard themselves as failures.

An extended family in which the members insist that they have a legal right as relatives in a kinship grid to share in the circulation of goods and wealth, that they have the right to enjoy what other better-off family members have accumulated through hard work and energy, is seen as an archaism in this day and age. It is believed with ideological fervour that the individual Master (and his immediate nuclear family) alone has the right to enjoy the products of his labour and wealth. This is taken to the extreme that sometimes the alleged right of the father to enjoy the products of his labour, wealth and power is withdrawn from his children, especially when they reach an age where they are supposed to be constructing their own lives in their father's image. As against this, especially where the old ways still hold sway, the members of our extended families, even if unproductive, still have claims on a share of the products of the labours of the productive members. Because this is contrary to the Master's beliefs it is regarded as a serious problem. Still, by pooling and circulating resources, such as social service payments, the extended family can manage to keep its structure intact and survive in a dominant social system tied, at least ideologically, to the nuclear family.

The strength of our ways and our lack of aspiration to be like 'them', plus our refusal to accept their Master plan, are what forces us to the fringes of cities and towns. In Perth, for instance, we end up in Homes West (public) housing in suburbs which quickly become identified as 'black' areas. The Australian city sprawls in disarray and its centre is the abode of the rich, while those the Master does not want to see are dumped on the outer edges of the city in public housing which is similar to our old fringe camps. Out of sight is out of mind, and if the bus fares are raised enough and the services limited, then we remain out of sight. In Perth, where I am now living, movement is based not on public but on private transport. Not to have a car is to be socially isolated, especially with a Master policy which houses us Nyungars and

Yamadjis in different suburbs. To get from one to another to visit family members without a lengthy detour to the central city area is often well-nigh impossible, for the transport system is designed not for social use but for the Master's use, to move masses of workers in and out of industrial areas or offices in the city centre. We have a problem to get from one point to another, and if a family member is not available with a car, what do we do? In Perth, Nyungars have found two ways to solve this problem. One is to steal a car, the other is to take a taxi. We are not discussing morality (which is a complex issue far beyond the Master text) here, but simply the problem of getting from one social area to another, especially after business hours when public transport slackens off and few connecting links operate. But then, the system was never intended to facilitate social meetings.

So, on pension day or pay days, people in predominantly Indigenous areas like Maddington make use of taxis. I remember talking to a taxi driver who expected me to enter into a dialogue about 'them' and why they used taxis. I suppose if you are Indigenous, poor, or old, you are supposed to rot in your suburb, or only move about in daylight. Of course, other taxi drivers know that this is a good time for business, and I doubt that few, if any, taxi drivers have been assaulted by Nyungars in Perth. After all, we both need each other, and those of you without the prejudice of the Master race know this — in fact, too much so and sometimes to an exploitative level. Taxi drivers in country towns are often eager to provide services for us, such as grocery or grog runs, for which they overcharge us, though if they are honest it may be only to ensure a continuing source of income. It works both ways, a satisfactory arrangement for us and them.

The maintenance of extended family ties is of tremendous importance to us, as Archie Weller's novel again brings out:

> He flings himself disconsolately onto the squeaking bed that takes up almost the entire room. The mattress is lumpy and there is a depressing air about the place. All his own. He has no-one to share things with ... Sometimes this room has been crowded with as many as seven people, black and brown bodies all over the floor and bed ...

Our extended families are a source of our strength and durability, but the Master plan does not see them as the most essential feature of our culture, only as useless social structures getting in the way of remaking us in *their* image. But if Us Mobs want to establish an Indigenality from the grass roots up, we must use the extended family as its political foundation. If cries of lack of unity emerge, and if against the family are posed the demands of the Indigenous totality labelled 'community', then we are entitled to ask exactly what is this 'community', and why it should differ from our extended family, which most of us would acknowledge as our basic social unit.

Further Reading

Bates, Daisy, *The Native Tribes of Western Australia*. Canberra, National Library, 1985.

Berndt, R.M. & C.H., *The Aboriginal Australians: the First Pioneers*. Melbourne, Pitman, 1978/83.

Keen, I., (ed.), *Being Black*. Canberra, Aborigines Studies Press, 1991.

Stockton, Eugene, *The Aboriginal Gift*. Sydney, Millennium Books, 1995.

Weller, Archie, *Day of the Dog*. Sydney, Pan Books, 1981.

OUR SPIRITUALITY

Lecture 3

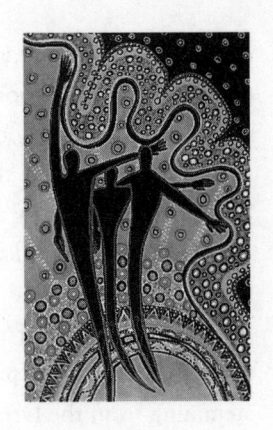

OUR SPIRITUALITY IS A ONENESS AND AN INTER-connectedness with all that lives and breathes, even with all that does not live or breathe. It is not a matter of this religion or that religion, of traditional beliefs or non-traditional. It is a feeling of oneness, of belonging, as Bill Neidjie declares in his book, *Story About Feeling*: 'Must keep it. You must keep im story because e'll come through your feeling.'

Most authorities on Indigenous spirituality write about ceremonies and rituals, totems and dreamings and their social implications. It is a materialist view of what spirituality is, and although they speak about 'religion', they do not seem very concerned about the deep innermost feelings which give rise to religion in the first place. Many also completely ignore how this spirituality changes and adapts. Some even ignore the influence of Christianity in Indigenality and write about what they think once was, rather than what is. They are more interested in the structures of what they call 'Aboriginal religion' than in the spiritual beliefs underlying those religious practices. It is because of this that I wish to examine some of the books which have been written about Indigenous spirituality and beliefs.

The first is *Creation Spirituality and the Dreamtime*, edited by Catherine Hammond, one of the few books which refer to 'spirituality' instead of 'religion' in their titles. It is very sympathetic towards Indigenous spirituality and particularly traditional beliefs stemming from the Dreamtime, though it seems to dwell overmuch on what is wrong with European spirituality rather than seeking to explain our Indigenous beliefs. Hammond evidently equates the Dreamtime with Indigenous spirituality, though there are some problems with the term which I will go into later. She reproduces an interview with an Indigenous person, Eddie Kneebone, from which I would like to quote:

> CH: How would you describe Aboriginal spirituality — the Dreamtime — to someone unfamiliar with it?
>
> EK: How can I answer that in a few moments? . . . But I'll do my best. Aboriginal spirituality is the belief and the feeling within yourself that allows you to become part of the whole environment around you — not the built environment, but the natural environment . . . Birth, life and death are all part of it, and you welcome each.
>
> Aboriginal spirituality is the belief that all objects are living and share the same soul or spirit that Aboriginals share. Therefore all Aborigines have a kinship with the

> environment. The soul or spirit is common — only
> the shape of it is different, but no less important.
>
> Aboriginal spirituality is the belief that the soul or
> spirit will continue on after our physical form has
> passed through death. The spirit will return to the
> Dreamtime from where it came, it will carry our
> memories to the Dreamtime and eventually it will
> return again through birth, either as a human or an
> animal or even trees and rocks. The shape is not
> important because everything is equal and shares the
> same soul or spirit from the Dreamtime.
>
> Aboriginal spirituality is not the equal of the
> European ideology of reincarnation. The Dreamtime
> is there with them, it is not a long way away. The
> Dreamtime is the environment that the Aboriginal
> lived in, and it still exists today, all around us.

Eddie Kneebone's explanation of the Dreamtime is how many Indigenous people describe the concept, which they declare lies at the basis of Indigenous spirituality. It is encoded in various Indigenous words which have been translated for a long time as 'the Dreamtime'. I mention this here because the terms 'Dreamtime' and 'the Dreaming' are considered by some so-called authorities to be mistranslations of the Indigenous words.

The anthropologist W.E.H. Stanner discusses the term in some detail in *On Aboriginal Religion*, an interesting account first published in the 1960s of the religious life of the Port Keats and Daly River Indigenous communities (whom Stanner calls Murinbata) in the Northern Territory. Its main weakness is that he fails to treat positively spiritual developments in the two communities which were occurring at the time he conducted his study. His description of the Dreamtime is worth comparing with Eddie Kneebone's.

> Things began. How or whence no-one knows. But there is a state of life that, though differently, contained all that now exists. Strife divided it into different parts. The parts remained connected by a common source (The Dreaming) but were made distinct, separate and in some cases opposed. The mysterious transformation (*demnginoi*) led to the fact, constitution and appearances of all the entities now recognised as totems (*mir, ngakumal*). They are distinct from men, but as brothers (fathers, sisters, friends) to them because of connections through places of marvel (*ngoiguminggi* and *dambit*). Powers immanent in those places are still available to men. The Dreaming that was, still is: *demnginoi* still happens. Because of that many remarkable events now occur. Child spirits enter the corporeal world, and survive it. Pure spirits and creature-spirits that 'did not start anywhere' but 'found themselves' persist and may intervene in men's lives. Men of mystical ability draw special powers from the existent Dreaming. They do so not by thought (*bemkanin*), which is 'like dream in the head', but by dream (*nin*) itself.

Despite the differences in their approach, there are certain common features in Eddie Kneebone's account and Stanner's observations from his Northern Territory experience. It is interesting to note that the two communities he studied, which once were Catholic missions, have now split apart. Daly River is still connected closely to the church, while Port Keats has retreated into a traditionalism which is very apparent in its art and culture.

OUR SPIRITUALITY

Australian Stations of the Cross, by Miriam-Rose Ungunmer-Baumann, shows how the community of Nauiyu Nambiyu (Daly River) has adapted Indigenous spirituality and art to Christian religious beliefs. This is an account of a quite remarkable series of paintings which depict the passage of Jesus Christ towards his crucifixion and demonstrate how traditional art styles, as well as philosophy, have been employed to indigenise this central aspect of Christian belief. When I visited Nauiyu Nambiyu, I was quite taken by the religious syncretism which had influenced the artistic tradition, so much so in fact that I used one painting as the cover illustration on my volume of poetry, *The Garden of Gethsemane* (1992). The painting, which depicts Christ undergoing his moment of doubt in the garden of Gethsemane, came complete with a narrative explaining the subject matter in the manner of Papunya Tula art pieces. The way in which Indigenous people make use of Christian stories and symbolism is often seen as an anomaly and condemned as an alien influence, but since so many Indigenous people have been in missions and been subjected to such pressure by missionaries and evangelists, it would be absurd to pretend that these influences did not exist. In fact there have been recent efforts by Indigenous people to take Christian beliefs and make them more responsive to Indigenous spirituality.

In 1983, playwright Jack Davis, Marlene Jackamara and myself organised the first national Indigenous writers' conference at Murdoch University in Perth. This was very successful and the proceedings have been published by the Australian Institute of Aboriginal Studies under the title, *Aboriginal Writing Today*, which is somewhat of a misnomer in that oral literature was very much to the fore at the conference. At the conference, Daphne Nimanydja told the well-known myth of the moon, Ngalindi, which concluded:

> It's [the] same thing when Jesus died on the cross he rose again, the same way that Ngalindi when he dies he comes back, you know, he came back in the [full] moon — same thing happened for Ngalindi, like Jesus died on the cross and he rose again. And that's the story we use, for the R.A. [united] community at Milingimbi.

What is interesting here is the parallel drawn between Ngalindi and Jesus. It shows how some Indigenous people do not see any contradictions between accepting both Indigenous and Christian spirituality and mythology.

The influence of Christianity on the Indigenous people of Australia is documented in *Aboriginal Australians and Christian Missions*, edited by Tony Swain and Deborah Bird Rose. This is a typical academic book in which non-Indigenous experts discuss and dissect Indigenous people almost in a parody of what has came to be called the 'discourse of Aboriginalism', which is described by Bob Hodge and Vijay Mishra in *The Dark Side of the Dream* as follows:

> Aboriginalism insists that Aborigines as the Other cannot [be allowed to] represent themselves, cannot even be supposed to know themselves as subjects or objects of discourse. This tactic deprives Aborigines of the possibility of authority, of being authors of their own meanings able to monitor and influence the meanings that circulate about and among Aborigines.

And so in Swain and Rose's book we seek in vain for an Indigenous voice and find none. Our culture, spiritual beliefs and the influences upon them must be defined for us by specialists who have little use for 'spirituality' in general.

One of the papers in the volume, by Robert Bos, discusses the problems inherent in the use of the term, 'the Dreaming'. It is pertinent here to refer back to W.E.H. Stanner and what he has to say about the term and its use in the areas where he conducted his fieldwork. He, at least, accepts a spirituality where others accept merely a sociality. He writes:

> Evidently the use of the English word (which is in universal currency from Central Australia to North Australia, and doubtless has passed from tribe to tribe) is an attempt by metaphor based on analogy, to convey the mystical quality of the relation as being like the relationship of dream-life to waking-life. At the same time one must note that, to the aborigines, an actual dream-experience is agentive and prophetic. Their choice of the English word seems to me a brilliant economy of phrase, covering both the denotations and connotations of the mystical conception of totemism within the ontology.

What is important here is that he does not say that it is a direct translation of an Indigenous word, or an accurate term in itself, but is merely a way by which Indigenous people try to get a spiritual concept across to non-Indigenous people. It is this spirituality which is often lost sight of by experts who use purely linguistic analysis to dismiss the term.

When in *The Dark Side of the Dream* Hodge and Mishra dismiss 'the Dreamtime' as implying an a historicity, they come close to falling into the very trap of Aboriginalism of which they accuse other academics, though it must be added in their favour that they do pay heed to Indigenous voices.

> The place of the concept of 'the Dreamtime' or 'the Dreaming' in contemporary Australian discourse is now a complex product of the conflicting forces involved. It is widely accepted shorthand to refer to the whole of the traditional culture that has been threatened by a variety of attacks from non-Aboriginal agents of cultural policy. It has been authorised by anthropology, the discipline that has been assigned the task of understanding and mediating Aboriginal culture to the rest of Australia and the world. Those who use the term use it to signify not simply an object (traditional texts and beliefs) but also their own very positive orientation to that object. The term is also part of Aboriginal English, used by many traditional people to refer to such texts. However, the many Aboriginal words in different languages that are now automatically translated as the Dreaming normally have no semantic connection to 'dreams' or 'dreaming'.

Much of what they say is open to debate and in the foregoing quotation from W.E.H. Stanner he makes no claims of its being a translation, or one imposed on Indigenous people by anthropologists. I also note that there is no discussion of any 'spirituality' underlying the word. Instead we have 'culture', which also has been taken into Indigenous English and really has a different meaning from 'the Dreaming' or 'the Dreamtime'. 'Culture', in Indigenous English, encompasses the whole material and spiritual life of Indigenous people whereas 'the Dreaming' or 'the Dreamtime' indicates a psychic state in which or during which contact is made with the ancestral spirits, or the Law, or that special period of the beginning now past which is still heavily pervasive in the present and can be contacted in a 'dreaming' state. Indigenous words such as *bugaregara*, *alcheringa*, *tjurgurba*, *ngarangani*, etc, are often simply glossed by such English words as 'law', 'business' and the two villains 'Dreamtime' and 'Dreaming'. We are not dealing with a simple word to word translation such as *yonga* equals 'kangaroo', but with a complex metaphysical and spiritual concept for which there is simply no adequate English rendering.

Even then, if the concept is difficult to render into English, I might ask why has such a monumental misrendering been able to endure and why have so many Indigenous people accepted it? I know there is a state of dreaming and that during this state one can enter, or at least commune with, other levels of the brain and some would say other levels of the universe. I remember Daisy Uttemorrah telling me that she had dreamt a ceremony especially for us Nyungar people so that we would not be without 'culture', and it is said that Butcher Joe Nungan of the Kimberley dreamt a ceremony or series of ceremonies. Many Indigenous people dream 'culture' and recently I came across an explanation which I had not known before for how it happens in Arnhem Land. I had heard about it in the Kimberley and other regions, but not in the Northern Territory. I would now go so far to say that this is an Indigenous creative process and that it does not relate only to what is usually called 'traditional culture', for I have heard of one Queensland Murri Christian who dreams his religious songs.

The Arnhem Land dream, which has never been documented, is interesting in that it gives a full description of the process. The original account, by an elder of the region, was in Kriol, from which it has been adapted.

> Yeah *min-min* light, I call it, I call it that. It gets up and goes. I was looking at it, like, you know, I say in my language *Dalabon*. Bungridj-bungridj, he got up then that light on him. Balanjirri, he showed me the corroboree then; he showed me the *wongga*. I've forgotten that song. I've forgotten it now. I was singing it well, I was, was asleep and that light came from that direction. I saw it coming and I thought: 'Oh, this might be spirit coming.' I was asleep; I was watching. 'Boy,' he said, 'are you asleep? I'm coming up. Balanjirri and Bungridj-bungridj, we two are coming up.' Both of them came up. 'Get up, come here, we're going to sing for you.' that's what he said, in Ngalkbon, you know. 'Get up, we're going to show you that song.' *Min-min* light, it came from over there. That huge spirit, that dangerous one, he came up, that *min-min* light. 'We'll show you this one.' I might get that song today if I sleep. I'll think about it later. I got a good song and then I lost it.
>
> Yeah, Balanjirri showed me that song, together with that didjeridoo player. He looked at that light and then he followed that light. He followed it. It was Balanjirri that made me know when that light appeared. He followed it himself and it was dangerous because that *min-min* light was then at the same place he was. Yeah, he got that song; he got it from there for sure, then he came to me and said:

> 'Boy, you listen. You might be frightened father-in-law.'
> That's what he said. He said: 'Father-in-law, are you asleep. Come here, you. I'm looking at you,' he said. 'Well, we've got to show you this song, *min-min* light.' That's what he said to me. And I replied: 'You come out here, you come here. You sing it to me.'
>
> I go to it, yeah; but that Bungridj-bungridj, he sang too. Balanjirri and Bungridj-bungridj, they were together then. Balanjirri had these big corroboree sticks, long! Oh, I've lost it. I was so close. I was singing it well. I'll find it. And that didjeridoo player. He sat down. Balanjirri said that it was his son. His didjeridoo was very long and he plays right there for me. He played on that long didjeridoo . . .
>
> 'This one, don't lose this song,' he said to me. 'You keep this one. I sang this *wongga* for you. It's yours.'

A *min-min* light is a will-o'-the-whisp, a mysterious light which appears and follows people and sometimes cars. Indigenous people consider it a spirit and somewhat dangerous. This light appeared to the old man in his sleep and gave him a song, though it appears that this sleep, or dreaming state, is not deep sleep but is a state between sleeping and waking, for the elder's account continues:

> Yeah, I was awake. He was singing a good song too . . . He showed me that *namortho*, *min-min* light, that *gowehbon*, that light. It led him and that's the one he followed. Perhaps one day it will want to kill me . . . Balanjirri appeared and followed it. He came to me. He showed me that *min-min* light. Oh, it was a good song, a good song. I sang it once and that was it. I fell asleep. If only I could have kept on singing it, it would have been alright; but I lost it, I fell asleep.

What the elder is talking about here is the transmission of a song from spirits, or ancestral beings while in a dreaming state; and it is such a dreaming state which relates to the metaphysical concept of the Dreaming and Dreamtime. It is during ceremonies that the *tjururba*, or dreaming state — a state of trance, or what Stanner calls 'mystical states of being' — overtakes the participants and they connect with the ancestral beings of the Dreaming, or Dreamtime.

In his book, *Aboriginal Men of High Degree*, the anthropologist A.P. Elkin examines the concept of the *maban*, or shaman, and discusses certain states of being or consciousness which overtake postulants during ceremonies in which they are brought into contact with the souls of the dead, or ancestral beings. In this unique work he fully accepts Indigenous spirituality and describes many of the practices which give it structure. Indigenous people who have read this book in the main agree with what he says about the ceremonies and rituals of the shamans, though much has remained hidden from him. Again, he was more interested in traditional practices than contemporary ones and ignored Christian practices.

I recall meeting Auntie Eileen, an elder of the Bandjalang people of northern New South Wales, and accompanying her to a village where a man approached her with a problem. He was being haunted by a spirit every night. Naturally, if one is romantic towards Indigenous people and their culture, you would expect some novel Indigenous method of chasing the spirit away, but Auntie Eileen simply told him to place a bible under his pillow; if the spirit came he was to open it and read a verse from it. It has been said that northern New South Wales has little traditional culture remaining, but this is not true, for the mythology of the ancestral beings is still known, dances are still performed, the waterholes are still inhabited by spirits and the origins of the rivers are still remembered. Indigenous spirituality can co-exist along with Christianity, and among many strong Indigenous Christians a number of the old customs and beliefs continue, such as respect for the land and ancestral beings. They see no conflict in this.

Since the time of the invasion of the eastern seaboard, Christianity has had a marked influence on Indigenous beliefs and spirituality. When I lived in Queensland I became interested in this syncretism. Of course, being from Western Australia, where the tendency was less pronounced, I did not go along with what I felt was essentially a reformulation of Indigenous spiritual beliefs into what seemed to be a monolithic Indigenous spirituality with a single ancestor becoming predominant. I did some research on it and found it dated back to the 1880s, if not earlier, and in particular to William Berak, a Koori elder who was an 'informant' to the ethnologist A.W. Howitt, who mined him for material. It would be nice to think that perhaps William Berak, who has left no writings, may have similarly mined A.W. Howitt for information on his own beliefs.

It is rarely acknowledged that Indigenous people were not the passive victims of an overwhelming advanced civilisation in the face of which their beliefs and customs simply crumbled away. This is a racist belief which needs challenging, for there is ample evidence that resistance to cultural domination from Indigenous people was intense and that in response to the missionary impact they consciously modified their beliefs. Many of them did not become Christians, but succeeded in accommodating their beliefs to the new Christianity. One response to Christianity was the acceptance of an Indigenous All-Father deity, Biami. How this happened may be seen in the works of one of the greatest Indigenous thinkers of the late nineteenth and early twentieth century, David Uniapon.

David Uniapon was born in 1872 at the Point McLeay Mission in South Australia and went on to become, among other things, the first Indigenous writer. His account of 'native' legends was put together by 1929, but never saw publication. One of his stories appears in the 1989 anthology, *Paperbark: A Collection of Black Australian Writings*. When we read this piece, 'Narroondarie's Wives', we are struck by the synthesis of Indigenous and Christian spirituality. This is apparent from the very beginning:

> Narroondarie is the name of one of the many good men that were sent among the various tribes of the Australian Aborigines. Now the name Narroondarie is better known among the Narrinyini tribes of the lower Murray, Lakes Alexandrina and Albert, and the Encounter Bay, South Australia. Before he came to South Australia he was known or called Boonah, hence the initiation ceremonies. Narroondarie and Boonah are names by which he is known as a good man, as a Sacred Man who is endowed or guided by the will of the Great Spirit, the Nhyanhund or Byamee, the Our Father of all, His messenger and teacher. After coming from the Northern part of Australia down into the various parts of New South Wales and Victoria, he found his way into South Australia.

Byamee, or Biami, has a continuous presence in Indigenous writings from the Eastern States and his importance is stressed in the writings of Oodgeroo of the Tribe Noonuccal, Custodian of the land Minjerribah. Towards the end of her long and eventful life, she expounded her beliefs in the All-Father (or in the All-Mother) in a staged performance at the Brisbane Exposition of 1988. This was *The Rainbow Serpent*, which she composed with the help of her son, Kabul.

The dramatisation begins with the stage lighting up on an Indigenous elder who says:

> Well, gidday, all you earth fullas. Come, sit down, my country now. I see you come into sacred place of my tribe to get the strength of the Earth Mother. That Earth Mother . . . We are different you and me. We say that the earth is our mother — we cannot own her, she own us.

This is similar to Bill Neidjie's exposition of Indigenous spirituality in his *Story With Feeling*, in which he expresses these sentiments: 'Earth . . . exactly like your father or brother or mother because you got to go to earth, you got to come to earth, your bone . . . because your blood in this earth here.'

This spirituality is preoccupied with the relationship of the earth, nature and people in the sense that the earth is accepted as a member of our family, blood of our blood, bone of our bone, and to show it disrespect or wilfully harm it is tantamount to patricide, matricide or fratricide.

The scene in Oodgeroo's exposition shifts to show a rock shelter as the elder states:

> This rock and all these rocks are alive with her spirit. They protect us, all of us. They are her, what you fullas say now,

temple. Since the Alcheringa, that thing you fulla call Dreamtime, this place has given man shelter from the heat, a place to paint, to dance the sacred dance and talk to his spirit.

Or as Bill Neidjie says:

> And that way they left that story. They said . . . 'Well, we'll be dead' and they can see our painting because behind us all the children . . . right back. They can keep on look at this painting and bone. They can see if they behind us. This country for us.

And the elder in Oodgeroo's exposition continues:

> How does one repay such gifts?
>   By protecting the land.
>   This land is the home of the Dreamtime. The spirits came and painted themselves on these walls so that man could meet here, grow strong again and take his strength back into the world.

This refers to how some ancestral spirits or beings painted themselves on the walls of rock shelters and caves such as the Wandjina in the Kimberley. Oodgeroo might have been influenced by the late Daisy Uttemorrah, who was very concerned to pass on aspects of her culture, and by Murri beliefs in general. However, it is difficult to know if such aspects are conscious borrowings or are received in the dreaming state, for there is a similarity of Indigenous spirituality across Australia which makes for similarity of belief, as we find in Bill Neidjie:

All that painting, small mark . . . they put cross, cross and
over again. White, yellow and little bit of charcoal, little bit
red clay . . . that's the one all small meaning there. They put
it meaning. They painted fish . . . little mark they make im,
you know. That's the one same as this you look newspaper.
Big mob you read all that story, e telling you that meaning.
All that painting now, small, e tell im you that story. That
meaning you look . . . you feel im now. You might say . . .
'hey, that painting good one. I take im one picture' — That
spirit e telling you . . . 'Go on . . . you look.'

In *The Rainbow Serpent* the deity appears and the elder introduces Oodgeroo's totem, or Dreaming:

This my totem, Kabul. You know her as the Carpet Snake.
She my tribe's symbol of the Rainbow Serpent, the giver and
taker of life. Sometimes she is called Borlung, sometimes
Ngalyod. She has many names, that wise one.

Belief in this snake deity is spread all across Australia. It is connected with many things including magic. Many of her ceremonies and rituals are a secret beyond a secret and are not to be disclosed except to an initiate of equal status, though she may also be a personal and tribal totem. W.E.H. Stanner, following in the footsteps of the anthropologist, A.R. Radcliffe-Brown, writes this about our snake deity:

It has been long recognised that aboriginal mythology in
many parts of Australia gives great prominence to a being . . .
The Rainbow Serpent. Certain elements of the belief about

> that being are so widely distributed that they might 'very possibly be practically universal' and form a conception 'characteristic of Australia as a whole and not of any part or stratum of it.' The elements 'more essential' are:
> 1. a conception of the rainbow as a huge serpent which
> 2. perennially inhabits deep, permanent waters
> 3. is associated with rain and rain-making, and
> 4. is connected also with the iridescence of quartz-crystals and mother of pearl. He [Radcliffe-Brown] was inclined to represent The Rainbow Serpent as a sort of guardian-spirit.

Stanner goes on to remark that the myths told about the deity among the people he was studying were not connected to any rite or ceremony. This probably means that he was not told of any, that they were kept from him. Anthropologists readily accept what their informants tell them as having validity for a particular community and go on to construct theories about all Indigenous people. But it should be borne in mind that Indigenous persons do not tell everything to such outsiders and that it is anthropologists and not Indigenous people themselves who are most interested in recording Indigenous culture and customs. Reverence for the Rainbow Serpent is very much a part of contemporary Indigenous spirituality, even if due to Christian influence positive aspects are reversed, as Miriam-Rose Ungunmer-Baumann does in her *Australian Stations of the Cross*:

Fourteenth Station: The burial of Jesus

The body of Jesus is being carried away for burial. Along Jesus' body is a snake, a mysterious and frightening being for Aboriginal people. As the power of evil, it tempted Eve

in the Garden. Its power can be overcome, if we
really be ve that Jesus is God.

The Rainbow Serpent continues:

> When the spirits of men have been made strong again by
> Kabul, she'll come back to earth.
> But we are not strong now. We are too tired from
> fighting time, machines and each other.
> But she send her spirit ones with message sticks to help
> us take time. To remember. To care for her special things.

These 'spirit ones' are what in the old days would have been totemic animals used in ordering society. Now they are given a new role as protective spirits to the Earth Mother. Even with this transformation, it is similar to how Bill Neidjie sees the roles of ancestral beings who set up certain laws and customs for us to follow. It can be argued that these days the main law is to protect and look after our Earth Mother and all else is secondary:

> First there is Dooruk, the emu, with the dust of the red
> Earth Mother still on his feet. He come to remind us to
> protect the land, to always put back as much as we take.
> Then there is Kopoo, the big red kangaroo, the very
> colour of the land. He come to remind us to always take
> time for ourselves.
> And Mungoongarlie, the goanna, last of all because his
> legs are short. He bring the news that we, his children, are
> forgetting to give time to each other.

But the animals of our Earth Mother come to say more than this. They come say that our creator, that Rainbow Serpent, she get weak with anger and grief for what we are doing to this earth.

The interconnectedness about Indigenous spirituality relates everything into a kinship system which identifies itself with all that is, that lives and grows. There is no separation or alienation, which are the main factors responsible for us hurting the earth, the environment and ourselves. As Bill Neidjie observes:

What for you cutting it land? Because tree going down and that road go. Soon as bitumen there e don't grow any grass there. Side's all right but middle of it nothing. You drive, you look lumber-stick there, big log there, big dozer pull it out . . . well, your body you feel. You say . . . 'Oh . . . that tree same as me!' I look tree but I say . . . 'Just like mother, father or brother, grandma.' Cause your granny, your mother, your brother, because this earth, this ground, this piece of ground e grow you.

One of the main features of Indigenous spirituality is to keep the earth and the environment in good repair, to look after it, and this obligation has been passed down as Law from the Dreamtime. The Dreamtime is always present within us. We are there at the beginning of creation and it is our very selves which continue the processes of creation and preservation. So Oodgeroo summons the Dreamtime:

But here now you fullas. You come sit down by my fire. Warm yourselves and I will tell you the story of how this

> world began. In the time of Alcheringa, the land lay flat and
> cold. The world, she empty. The Rainbow Serpent, she
> asleep under the ground with all the animal tribes in her
> belly waiting to be born. When it her time, she push up.

Here the Rainbow Serpent is equated with the All-Mother as a female creator being. The Rainbow Serpent can be either male or female. There is a strong feeling of androgyny about this deity and either male or female attributes can be emphasised. I remember when I used to visit Oodgeroo at Moongalba on her island of Minjerribah, we would sit around the fire and discuss these theological questionings. In Oodgeroo's words above it is interesting that the Rainbow Serpent is seen as being under the ground. Similarly, Bill Neidjie says:

> Something under here. E listen to you. E listen for us.
> Might be Rainbow . . . but e listen. That way they told
> me. 'No matter you walking around, that's the one
> just like your mother.'

This means that the Rainbow Serpent is equated with the mother as creator who in turn is equated with the earth, which is somewhat different from the anthropologists' contention that the Rainbow Serpent is always connected or associated with water. However, snakes — especially the rock python, which is the visible symbol of the Rainbow Serpent — live among the rocks and crevasses of the earth, so that there is clearly a Rainbow Serpent/Earth Mother analogy as well as a connection with water. The logic of spirituality works differently from the logic of science and to expect spiritual facts to fit scientific theories is to misunderstand the nature of spirituality.

The spirituality of the Indigenous people of Australia is an affirmation of the spirit of humanity and the earth. There is no myth of a severance between humanity and nature, or between deity and person. The earth is a vast dreaming organism; the environment is a community or family arranged in kinship patterns across her skin. As Bill Neidjie says, this living spirituality is there for us to experience: 'This story e can listen careful and how you want to feel on your feeling. This story e coming through your body. E go right down foot and head, fingernail and blood . . . through the heart, and e can feel it because e'll come right through.' Those who espouse an Indigenous form of Christianity do not see any conflict between Christianity and Indigenality. To quote Bill Neidjie again:

> That missionary e telling bible there . . . 'Oh, you got to remember up there and you got to become good.' Same thing Aborigine of lot of story. I used to go church but I hang on this because I can't say liar . . . e's true. E's very true this story.

FURTHER READING

Davis, Jack and Hodge, Bob, *Aboriginal Writing Today*. Canberra, Aboriginal Studies Press, 1985.

Davis, Jack, Muecke, Stephen, et al (eds), *Paperbark, An Anthology of Black Australian Writing*. Brisbane, University of Queensland Press, 1989.

Elkin, A.P., *Aboriginal Men of High Degree*. Brisbane, University of Queensland Press, 1977.

Hammond, Catherine (ed), *Creation Spirituality and the Dreamtime*. Sydney, Millennium Books, 1991.

Hodge, Bob and Mishra, Vijay, *Dark Side of the Dream*. Sydney, Allen & Unwin, 1991.

Mudrooroo, *Aboriginal Mythology*. London, Aquarian Books, 1994.

Neidjie, Bill, *Story About Feeling*. Broome, Magabala Books, 1989.

Oodgeroo (Noonuccal, Oodgeroo and Kabul), *The Rainbow Serpent*. Canberra, Australian Government Publishing Service, 1988.

Stanner, W.E.H., *On Aboriginal Religion*. Oceania Monograph 36, Sydney, University of Sydney, 1989.

Stockton. Eugene, *The Aboriginal Gift*. Sydney, NSW, Millennium Books, 1995.

Swain, T. and Rose, D. B. (eds), *Aboriginal Australians and Christian Missions*. Adelaide, Australian Association for the Study of Religions, 1988.

Ungunmer-Baumann, Miriam-Rose, *Australian Stations of the Cross*. Daly River, 1985.

Our Languages
Lecture 4

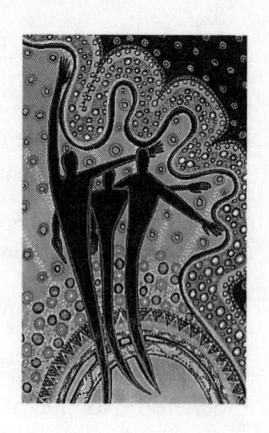

As the shape of a tree might serve as a model of our Indigenous communities, so too it might of our languages and dialects. Perhaps, as some linguists tell us, there was a common Indigenous language of Australia, Pama Nyungan, and from this trunk the numerous dialects and languages of Us Mob developed; but like much else it is a mystery of the Dreaming. Now we are only aware of the branches making up our hundreds of languages and dialects. We took pride in these languages, for they came from our ancestors and were to be kept and spoken forever, but like so much of our culture, many of them have been lost as a result of the European invasion, and only twigs of words remain. But alongside our language tree another has been planted with many strong branches. It is English and we cannot ignore it, for it is the language of the Master and whether we like it or not, whenever we deal with him we have to speak, or attempt to speak, his language. When we were collected together into those concentration camps called reserves or missions, we of the many languages had to learn English to communicate even with each other, as well as those over us, though the English we learnt differed from the language they spoke and has remained distinct until this day. So we ignore the language of the Master at our peril, as one of our stories, which I heard in Broome, reminds me:

> Tis woman now, she bin go ta court. Tis fulla bin standin tere, and tat fulla, e got long air down ta ere. E come out now, an tat sarjint, e say im to tat woman: 'What your name?' Tat woman, tat fulla, she tell im name. He sayim to tat woman: 'What your address?' Tat woman tell im: 'Tis dress, I bin ave on.' An ten tat judge, tat fulla with the air down ta ere, e aks im tat sarjint, what tis woman bin in court for. E tell im, and tat judge fulla, he say: 'How you bin plead?' She tellim tat judge: 'I bin pleed from me ead, tat udder fulla, he bin it me tere.' Judge den tellim, tat woman: 'I fine you five dollars.' An she appy, an she say: 'Oh tank you, I bin lose um tat five dollar last week.'

So when we use our kind of English, we often have problems, and when we use our own languages no whitefellas can understand us. We are caught in a double bind. We have to learn a type of English, the official dialect which the Master understands. We must remain speakers of many languages, and even if a variant of English is our first language, this must change when we speak to the Master. We have to use different languages in different situations — an Indigenous language or our variant of English in the cultural and social, and the Australian standard of English in the economic.

For us, the acquisition of a standard English is a matter of economic importance in that to function effectively in the Master's world we have to understand and be understood by those with whom we come into contact, though among ourselves we may use the language with which we are most at home. In many places this is what is now called 'Aboriginal English', an English dialect often interspersed with Indigenous words. Thus in New South Wales the police are known as 'gunjees' and in Nyungar English 'monaitch', and so on. Many Aborigines use two brands of English, and switch from one to the other as occasion demands. There is the formal language of the economic situation and the informal of the social. Problems often arise for someone who has not mastered the economic language. He or she will be at a disadvantage, which the speaker of standard Australian English may exploit to assert personal or political power.

On the other hand, those who become fluent in standard English are at a distinct advantage, especially in a number of remote settlements where the communities have become increasingly reliant on them to conduct business and financial negotiations on their behalf. More and more, as young people go off to such places as Bachelor College in the Northern Territory and learn the subtleties of economic English, they are the ones who rise to positions of power on the local councils and organisations. Is this good or bad? It depends on the results, but although it is obviously necessary to understand the 'economic' language, this is only one form of communication available to Indigenous people, many of whom may be multilingual, or at least bilingual, and at home in both worlds.

Our Indigenous communities form what may be called speech communities, which may use any or all of the following languages:

- Standard Australian English;
- Indigenous English;
- Kriol;
- Indigenous languages

Standard Australian English is, of course, the language of power and economics, while the last three are social languages, with the Indigenous languages having not only social but cultural and ceremonial importance. The other two are also important as spoken languages of communication. Kriol (which may also be seen as shading off into Indigenous English) is now regarded by linguists as a separate language rather than a dialect of English. It has become a subject of academic study and been given an alphabet. Often, this has occurred without consulting the Indigenous speakers, or only in ways which serve the ends of those wanting to utilise these English language variants for their own purposes: for example, the Bible has been translated into Kriol. The creation of a written language from a spoken one is not a neutral act. Its aim may be to create a means of identification, or to provide an aid in teaching Indigenous students a level of English which is necessary for them, especially when the alphabet differs markedly from that of standard English. Thus the origins of this dialect of English — which it surely is — are disguised, and make the transition to standard English more difficult. One has not only to relearn an alphabet, but another spelling. As an oral social language, Kriol has its place; but its status as a written language must be open to doubt.

Kriol is a fine example of what happens when an orthography is constructed for a spoken language. The word 'Creole', from which it obviously derives, originally referred to persons of French or Spanish parentage in the Americas, gradually extending to those of mixed French, Spanish or African descent. Then it became the name of dialects of various European languages spoken by such people, which often became first languages or, as in the case of pidgin English, the main means of communication between speakers of different Indigenous languages. In Australia, this occurred when different language speakers were herded together into missions or when they were employed as stockmen and domestic servants on the vast cattle stations which were established on their lands. Over time, this common language became the first language of many in the community, with the ancestral languages being relegated to the background. I regard it as a dialect of English, as do other Indigenous people, who refer to it as broken English, or even as a 'rubbish language'. The word Kriol in itself typifies how English or European words become corrupted in the process of literating a language. Kriol, in the new orthography, is the variety of Creole spoken in Barunga (formerly Bamyili) and Ngukurr (Roper River), and among Indigenous people over the Northern Territory. The term itself is normally used to refer only to the speech of people from Barunga and Ngukurr, although some people apply it more widely. In Western Australia there is a Creole at Fitzroy Crossing which is sometimes called Fitzroy Valley Kriol.

The question remains of whether there is one language, widely spoken throughout Northern Australia, which may be called 'Kriol', or whether there are varieties of Creole. Perhaps we may answer, does it matter, except possibly to linguists? However, there are language varieties which are so close that I would call them dialectal varieties, but which for certain political and ideological reasons are declared to be different languages. At other times, and for other political reasons, they are said to be very similar. We are in the realm where alleged scientific reality comes into conflict with actual social reality. In western thinking, the dominant intellectual and ideological paradigm, or discourse, is the 'scientific' and this paradigm concerns itself with what it claims are scientific 'facts'. Only scientific 'facts' have any validity, or at least more validity than social facts. Thus science, and even linguistics, which is often seen as the only science of the humanities, tends to ignore the socio-political factors which have more importance to the people involved than the cold analytic 'facts' of science.

Thus, the people in the Daly River area do not consider that they speak Kriol, even though they acknowledge that their dialect and Barunga Kriol are mutually intelligible. I could take a 'scientific' position and dispute their claim, but if I did so I would be adopting an approach to knowledge and science which should be questioned before we impose it on others. The dominant, colonising culture accepts the scientific method as determining the truth or falseness of a proposition, but the subject group does not. If we seek to impose it on the group, it is to engage in that process of colonising which has been inflicted on the Indigenous peoples of Australia since the invasion.

The way in which this so-called scientific approach sweeps aside social and human considerations is a problem for all these Creoles, and not only Kriol. It is not Aboriginal people, for example, who are in charge of determining educational policy in the Northern Territory, but linguists. The decisions of these experts on language affect not only the status of the Creole languages in the communities, but also the ancestral languages. Furthermore, the Northern Territory government, which to a degree supports bilingual education, has shifted its emphasis from ensuring the survival of ancestral languages to that of promoting the learning of the mainly economic standard Australian English. Of course, if the situation in what I term 'speech communities' was a simple bilingual one, then the choice would be relatively simple, as in what has been called 'Both Ways' education, about which Bakamana Gayaka Yunupingu, the principal of the school at Yirrkala, says:

> The school is the place which can do a great deal to help children become successful in language use, but it will work best when the community is consulted about how language is used. This is because Yolngu draw on the philosophies that will help to sustain sensitive components of Yolngu knowledge through the pedagogy of 'Both Ways' education . . .

In other words, the acquisition of both standard English and ancestral languages is the ideal. But in many Indigenous communities, born from forced collectivisation, more than one ancestral language is spoken, and by choosing to use one rather than another, the school discriminates against certain languages and, by implication, the status of certain social groups within the speech community. In fact, this language rivalry may have been a factor in the rise of Creoles in the first place.

To complicate matters further, Kriol is now being raised to the status of a 'language' through the work of linguists. Only one speech community, Barunga, has had an official Kriol language component. At Ngukurr, Kriol is used only orally, although there is some informal Kriol literacy. Both these speech communities have groups speaking different ancestral languages, and there are substantial differences between the status of Kriol and the Aboriginal languages. For example, no-one identifies him- or herself as a 'Kriol' person. People refer to themselves by the name of their ancestral language, even though they appear not to speak it. I use 'appear' here because, as a result of the incessant research conducted on them by white academics, Indigenous people are asserting their right to privacy. Some of what I say here should be viewed in this light. Against this may be placed the value to Indigenous people of having a *walypela* (white person) studying their languages. The walypela confers status on some Indigenous communities, and if the walypela linguist selects a particular language to study, it achieves status, possibly at the expense of other languages. An example of this is Walmatjarri which among other reasons has become a strong language because it has been extensively studied and given status.

The use of Kriol as a first language or as a lingua franca is widespread throughout much of the school-age population in the Northern Territory, as well as parts of the Kimberley and northern Queensland. These youngsters inhabit a linguistic desert between standard English and the ancestral language. In fact, they are often treated as if they spoke standard English badly, and there is no provision for them to be taught English as a second language. They are also often treated as if they should be speaking an ancestral language. At the same time, children who speak a Creole often live in communities where the establishment or continuation of a bilingual program in an ancestral language has been refused on the grounds that the children do not have such a language as their first language. They thus miss out on both counts. They have no adequate access to standard English, since they are not taught it in ways appropriate to second language learners, and they receive no instruction in the Indigenous language and culture because it is assumed to have disappeared.

At Barunga, because of the Kriol program, it is acknowledged that the children do not arrive at school as English speakers. Moreover, due to a possibly unique combination of committed Indigenous teachers and white teachers with a background in linguistics, ancestral languages are not totally ignored. Of course, this is a somewhat ad hoc solution and is vulnerable to changes in school personnel and the controversy about the status of Kriol.

In Ngukurr (Roper River), where Kriol is widely spoken, the school does not have an official bilingual program, although Kriol is used informally in the classroom. There are two reasons for this: firstly, written Kriol has been used in Christian religious contexts, and secondly, a majority of the school staff are Indigenous, most of whom are Kriol speakers. However, Ngukurr does not want to use the bilingual materials produced by Barunga. The issue here is control of the literature used in the community and language ownership itself. The use of Creoles as oral languages is less contentious than writing them down. For example, at Nauiyu

Nambiyu (Daly River) there is antagonism towards Kriol, possibly because it is seen as a threat towards the local languages, Ngan'gikurunggurr and Ngan'giwumirri.

What place, then, has a written Creole outside the school room, especially with a different orthography? It appears very little, and if access to standard English is essential in today's Australia it might be better to use a modified English spelling together with the standard alphabet to help children acquire a necessary grasp of English, with other resources being used to develop an increasing bilingual program based on both English and as many local Indigenous languages as possible. In this way, the Creoles would continue to play their social role, while standard English would be used officially outside the communities and Indigenous languages would maintain or regain their primary place in the ceremonial and social spheres.

What I have said about Indigenous communities being multilingual speech communities in which ancestral languages still play an important social and ceremonial role holds true for the whole of Australia in that the ancestral languages are present in every community, even if only a few words are used. Even then, they continue to exist in a deep and abiding sense of loss. This is something native English speakers can probably never feel or understand, unless they be Irish without Gaelic, Welsh without Welsh, and Scots without Scotch. Language loss for Us Mob is marked by an enduring sense of grief.

The Indigenous languages of Australia came from the ancestors and were developed in the environments of Australia to give it a voice and to sing its praises. Here is an example from a song in the

Ngiyambaa language, owned by the Wangaaybuwan people of central western New South Wales, north of the Lachlan and east of the Darling Rivers: *Walung-gula:y dhun-lugu yuga-yuga-nha walu*, which may be translated: (He/she) flirts his/her tail like (a) walu.

One word here is given in the original — walu. What is, or are, walu? Ngiyambaa nouns, as in other Australian languages, are not specifically either singular or plural unless a number suffix is added, the meaning otherwise being clear from the context. The image from the song is of a red robin, so what we have to work out is what the motion of the robin's tail is compared to.

The simile can only be translated by a paraphrase, as there is no single word in English which directly corresponds to walu. Outside my window I see a gum tree on which the bark peels and hangs in narrow strips. In Ngiyambaa, these narrow hanging strips are called walu. As I watch I observe a walu hanging by a thread, which suddenly catches a current of air and vibrates as if it has a life of its own, like the twitching of a robin's tail. The word 'walu' stayed in my mind from the first time I came across it, so that when I was writing my poem cycle, *Dalwurra, the Black Bittern*, I thought about it and translated it as 'the shredding bark shreds'. I used it as an image of homesickness. Although the aptness of the original simile may now be clear, it is not immediately obvious as an image of the movement of the robin's tail. The vocabularies of our languages spring from their origins with the ancestors and the environment of our country, and develop over time with the cultural preoccupations of their speakers, revealing among other things our ways of seeing our environment. They are uniquely Australian.

I am always surprised to read how the first English speakers in Australia reacted to our hospitable environment. For example, during his brief visit with the *Beagle* in 1836, the famous evolutionist Charles Darwin was dismayed by the uniformity of the bush, particularly by the bark of the trees which hung dead in long strips and swung about in the wind, making the bush seem so scruffy and desolate to him that he left the country without regret. Forty years later the novelist Marcus Clarke found the bush equally unfriendly. He wrote about feeling a 'weird melancholy', and walu is felt to be part of that feeling: 'From the melancholy gum strips of white bark hang and rustle.'

The poet Judith Wright uses the walu concept in a different way. In 'Gum Tree Stripping', she writes: 'The hermit tatters of old bark split down and strip to end the season.' Here the bark of a tree is compared to the tattered rags of a traditional European hermit, so that the walu represents his garments being rent as if to signal the end of a season. I am not sure which season is referred to, for the walu I have been observing for over a year still survives, although now that it is towards the end of summer and the beginning of autumn it is becoming a little thinner. But Judith Wright's poetry shows the way in which modern non-Indigenous writers in Australia are trying to come to terms with the essential differences between our landscape and that of Europe. At first, what occurred was the use of familiar English names such as 'robin' to render the Other familiar, or by borrowing words from Aboriginal languages as if to stress the exotic, such as *galah* and *beelah*. But as for the 'shredding bark shreds', walu, there is no handy word, and so the attempt ultimately falters and the mood comes to rest between the familiar and exotic and ends in melancholy.

To return to Marcus Clarke, who further expressed his alienation from our landscape as follows:

> In historic Europe ... every rood of ground is hallowed by legend and in song ... But this our native or adopted land has no past, no story. No poet speaks to us. Do we need a poet to interpret Nature's teachings, we must look into our own hearts, if perchance we may find a poet there.

This is writing the Indigenous people out of the Australian landscape with a vengeance, for when we do appear, says Clarke: 'From a silent corner of the forest rises a dismal chant, and around a fire dance natives painted like skeletons. All is fear-inspiring and gloomy.'

One can only conclude from this that the writer is unconsciously making comparisons with his beloved Europe, and because Australia is not Europe, he condemns it and us. In European literature there are many examples, starting with Ovid, if not before, about the melancholy pinings of exiles, and this is what we have here — an Ovid gloomily gazing upon the Hellespont. He has no, or little, interest in the foreign Other, be it land or 'native'. They are but vehicles for his feelings, and he never leaves his heart to consider that the 'natives' are chanting words with meaning, possibly about the very earth on which he is standing. That is, that the poets are not in his heart, but in front of him, singing songs of the land which he dismisses as dismal.

Clarke's attitude reflects the general settler beliefs that Indigenous languages and the oral literature were of little value in comparison to those of Europe. Even today, the social and cultural significance of Australian Indigenous languages is derogated in favour of those of other countries which are considered to be important to the Australian economy. It is sometimes even said that the fault is ours for having too many languages, and that if only we spoke one language — supposedly like the Maoris in New Zealand — then the problem would be solved. It could be taught in schools and everyone would be able to know the rudiments of this language so uniquely Australian. Unfortunately, however, human beings do not organise their affairs so easily. Just as they form into societies which fight and struggle for supremacy, so do their languages struggle until one achieves a dominance of sorts before it fades into oblivion again, as happened, for instance, with Anglo-Saxon in England. Yet in other countries, such as Australia before the white invasion, many languages may develop side by side and happily coexist. In India, for example, there are at least twenty-one official languages enshrined in the Constitution, and more clamouring for recognition. In fact, a plurality of languages could be said to be the natural human condition and the dominance or existence of a single language a comparatively recent development. Given the opportunity, other languages will begin to be heard.

This official ideology of singularity rather than plurality affects most aspects of our lives. Thus when I was considering Nyungar as a language to be taught at Murdoch University, it appeared easy, as there was supposedly only one regional language. However, this is not the case. The southwest of Australia was divided into a number of speech groups, each of which owned a dialect or language. When, following the massacre of Pinjarra, the political and social cohesion of the Nyungar nations was broken and the people began referring to themselves in the collective Nyungar, or Nungar, this did not mean that all traces of the nations or groups vanished. In fact, they went underground, and when I begin considering Nyungar as a single language to be taught, not only did the question arise of what Nyungar actually was but also which dialect or language should be used. This is a problem yet to be solved, and is often the case all over Australia. Under regional names like Koori or Murri, for instance, there are many local landowning groups which still own their language or dialect, even if the majority no longer speak it. The problem is so great that it is best to put it aside for a time, lest we assume parameters which simply do not exist, except possibly in suspect translations.

In March 1977, *The Bulletin* magazine asked a number of white critics and writers which people they considered were the most undervalued authors in Australia. The prominent settler poet Les Murray led off by stating: 'Our most serious undervaluation is Aboriginal poetry . . . the poems set down, in say, Ronald Berndt's recent *Aboriginal Love Poetry*, mostly from Arnhem Land, and Strehlow's classic *Songs of Central Australia*.'

What this says is that Indigenous poetry is that which is translated as poetry from an Aboriginal language by an accepted authority such as Professor Ronald Berndt, who I might say is no poet but an anthropologist, although he and his late wife have been arranging and translating Aboriginal poetry from the 1940s. Les Murray thinks highly of their translations of the *Moonbone Cycle*, first published in the anthropological journal *Oceania*. Naturally, it is poets like Les Murray who make choices not only about what Indigenous poetry is but also its worth, and are in a position to have what they consider Aboriginal poetry included in anthologies. It is interesting that in an anthology of Indigenous poetry put together by an Indigenous poet, Kevin Gilbert, none of Les Murray's examples appear, nor do any of the songs published by linguists in such anthologies as *The Honey Ant Dreaming*. Such work produced by linguists and anthropologists immediately raises the question: how Indigenous is it? Few answers come from the people who are equally at home in the language and culture of both the original and its translation. This is the same with the Arrenthe speech community songs, translated and annotated by Strehlow in his *Songs of Central Australia*. Without knowledge of the language, there is no way of knowing the relationship between the oral text and the translation derived from it.

All records of oral literature require extensive documentation regarding performance, composition and transmission, and who it is who is doing the collecting, the recording, the writing down, the editing and so on. The problems associated with Australian Indigenous oral literature lie not so much in the literature itself but in the collecting, translating, explaining, editing and publishing of it. The authenticity of a text stemming from an Indigenous person rests as much with the listener and eventually the transcriber and editor as with the speaker. The problem with putting oral literature into book form is that it ceases to be oral literature and becomes written literature.

When I was speaking before about the place of standard English in Indigenous speech communities, I described it as an economic rather than a social language. The emphasis in today's Australia is towards a monolingual economic language in keeping with the dominant Anglo-Celtic community who mostly use only one language and often feel threatened by polyglot speakers. By contrast, in Indigenous Australia there exists a multiplicity of languages and dialects, and even after two hundred years of language genocide, a number of these languages and dialects are still the first language of Indigenous people, many of whom often have more than one Indigenous language. In some places there is a Creole which has replaced the ancestral languages as the common means of communication, even though those languages still survive to some extent. Then there are forms of Aboriginal English which in some cases serve to identify particular communities and are spoken socially within them.

It may be said that ancestral languages are property, in the sense that they have been given by an ancestor to a particular group along with their ownership of land. Thus an ancestral language and land are owned along with the cultural products of that land and language. There are two types of ownership. Perhaps the major one is collective and associated with ownership of land. Ownership of religious narratives together with their associated songs detailing ancestral dreaming journeys may extend across a wide band of linguistic and landowning borders. Songs telling of these dreaming tracks with more or less identical words may be sung in ceremonies by people who otherwise speak a different language socially. The second type of ownership is individual ownership, as by the composer of a song. Songs owned in this way are, or were, often traded over large areas, with people sometimes setting out on long journeys to collect new songs. They were learnt verbatim in the languages in which they were composed, sometimes with pronunciation changes in line with the learner's sound system. In the late nineteenth century, for instance, there was a new corroboree dreamt which travelled extensively throughout Indigenous Australia. The *madlunga*, said to be a ceremony detailing the whitefella and his ways, arose in central west Queensland and moved from group to group, nation to nation, as people learnt the songs and ceremonies and dances from neighbouring communities and passed them along the dreaming tracks.

These travels of songs and ceremonies are important when discussing Indigenous languages in that words found in language groups may not be seen by some as markers of similarity and divergence of a basic language, but as reflecting the adoption of words from other languages over a considerable period of time. If we make the mistake of seeing Aboriginal speech communities as being isolated groups or families without much contact with other such communities, then we are bound to form an entirely erroneous view of Indigenous society and culture.

FURTHER READING

Barnes, John (ed), *The Writer in Australia: A Collection of Literary Documents, 1856 to 1964*. Melbourne, Oxford University Press, 1969.

Blake, Barry J., *Australian Aboriginal Languages*. Sydney, Angus & Robertson, 1981.

Donaldson, Tamsin, 'From speaking Ngiyampaa to speaking English', *Aboriginal History*, 9 (1–2), 1985.

Eagleston, R.D., Kaldor, S. and Malcolm, I.B., *English and the Aboriginal Child*. Canberra, Curriculum Development Centre, 1982.

House of Representatives Standing Committee on Aboriginal and Torres Strait Affairs, *Language and Culture — A Matter of Survival*. Canberra, Australian Government Publishing Service, 1992.

Thieberger, N. and McGregor, W., Macquarie *Aboriginal Words*. Sydney, The Macquarie Library, 1994.

Walsh, M. and Yallop, C., *Language and Culture in Aboriginal Australia*. Canberra, Aboriginal Studies Press, 1993.

Us Mob and Politics

Lecture 5

How many times have Us Mob said that everything in Australian Indigenous affairs is interrelated? Yet it doesn't seem to have registered with those politicians who keep creating new government organisations to deal with us and think they have solved everything. It is said that we are the most studied race in the world, and it may be said that we are also the most governed. Now there is the Council for Aboriginal Reconciliation, which is preparing Us Mob for 2001 and the Republic of Australia. Will its efforts result in a new start, or will it be more of the old assimilation tactics of ignoring political solutions for the social? At least in its submission to the Commonwealth Government in March 1995, *Going Forward: Social Justice for First Australians*, the Council asks for constitutional guarantees acknowledging our prior possession of Australia. It also urges that specific Indigenous rights be included in any general Bill of Rights and calls on all political parties to formally endorse the principle of a 'treaty' or some other form of 'reconciliation' with Us Mob. At the time of writing, the government has not yet made an official response so we will have to wait and see.

What is usually given to us is a hierarchical government structure based on European thought and practice. Our tree is replaced by a pyramid and our 'leaders' are virtually chosen for us and then take their place at the apex of the pyramid. We are supposedly given the chance to elect our own federal organisation with its regional councils, but less than thirty per cent of Indigenous people in Australia voted for the Aboriginal and Torres Strait Islander Commission (ATSIC), and it is this percentage which elects people to the so-called regional councils. The ATSIC electoral process is tied in with the Australian electoral process. To vote for Indigenous regional councils, one has to be on the government electoral role, but some Indigenous people do not vote because they do not accept the legitimacy of the Federal and State governments. There have been no treaties of accommodation made or overall political solutions offered, and this means that Indigenous people continue to oppose by whatever means at our disposal the illegitimate structures we are supposed to accept. Political problems are seen as social problems and the social welfare state seeks to coerce us into accepting what they regard as the prevailing norms of the Australian community.

'Community', with its derivation from 'common', implies a single social entity, thinking and acting along the same lines through some mysterious process of consensus. The word is too often applied to a supposed unity of individuals or groups, without taking due account of differences of class, race, or sex. In particular, when we examine the Indigenous community we find that instead of forming a bland amorphous and anonymous mass, it is as diverse and complex and fractious as any other. But, and I stress this, if the commonality of Indigenality is ignored or lost sight of, if each Aboriginal group asserts its individuality and independence and moves away from a common purpose, then this can be and is used by the Master who promotes divisions for his own ends and in order to control the individual groups.

This can be seen in two Federal Government policy papers which offer solutions which, it is claimed, will alleviate, if not overcome, any problems in Indigenous 'communities'. In 1988, in a submission to the House of Representatives Standing Committee on Aboriginal Affairs, the Department of Aboriginal Affairs (DAA) evaluated its own policy of Aboriginal self-determination. It acknowledged that the Federal Government had encountered practical and philosophical difficulties in delivering services to Indigenous people while, at the same time, affirming Indigenous self-determination. The DAA admitted that because of the differing social structure of many Indigenous groups, its theories did not work and as a result many Indigenous communities were not making the political and administrative progress which had been hoped.

According to the DAA, self-determination policy was based on the recognition of the right of the Aboriginal people to determine their own future within the Australian community. It explicitly acknowledged that Aborigines were a distinct cultural group, as well as recognising the worth of Aboriginal culture and the right of

Aborigines to pursue lifestyles in accordance with that culture. Self-determination, the department said, also sought to improve the social and economic circumstances of Aborigines by encouraging them to take charge of their own affairs. This is all fairly straightforward, stating the political parameters within which Indigenous groups will be allowed to determine their own future though it should be noted that the term 'community' seems to have been used where really 'nation' is intended.

In regard to self-determination, the submission went on to say that the policy 'means that Aboriginal people should identify their needs, plan programs to meet those needs, manage projects and assume responsibility for the outcomes achieved'. Incorporated Aboriginal associations, of which there were then no more than 1500, were essential to this program, 'not just for legal purposes (acquiring property, entering agreements, conducting business) but also to ensure a structure for individual community participation'.

Actually, there are all sorts of contradictions here. The term 'Aboriginal people' remains vague and undefined; incorporated Aboriginal associations are structures used to contain Aboriginal needs within a legal framework under the *Aboriginal Associations Act*, which is similar to the overall Commonwealth legislation dealing with associations and how they should be managed. There is no provision for Indigenous organisations to be structured and operated differently — for example, according to kinship ties. The term 'community' is used again, but with a further shift in meaning. It appears to mean 'groups' and these 'groups' must participate in the programs through associations. However, only a few pages later the submission stated that part of the DAA's policy was to encourage 'the establishment of community councils and executive management infrastructures within Aboriginal communities'. 'Communities' here seems to refer to fixed settlements with a stable population, waiting, as it were, to be colonised by the DAA. There is no room here for legal organisations based on kinship affiliations, which are apparently subsumed under the rubric of 'community'. It is interesting that the DAA itself noted that its policy and practice on self-determination were often contradictory.

What this meant was that Murri, Koori, Nyungar and other such ways of doing things were outside the scope of the DAA, and that in order to get DAA funding, Indigenous communities were obliged to set up replicas of western-style organisations which cut across existing kinship and family structures and undermined them. Such structures have little place in this kind of self-determination, and when Indigenous people enter into funding relationships with government organisations it is on the government's terms and according to the way the government wants to structure Indigenous people's lives. In other words, self-determination means government-determination, and until economic self-reliance is gained there seems little chance that Indigenous social structures will be strengthened, or even used. The Master still continues to colonise, but now frames his fine words in a rhetoric which means little to those outside his control.

And so when Indigenous and Master ways clash, it is usually the Indigenous ways which must change and adapt, for the Master's ways are the right ways and he has the means and the power to enforce them. This was also acknowledged in the DAA paper we are discussing. It said: 'Community development sometimes undermined the preservation of "traditional cultural patterns".'

In response, the House of Representatives Standing Committee on Aboriginal Affairs sought clarification on a number of points, specifically for the following:

- Did not dependence on government funding allow self-determination in only a limited sense?

- Were there not their cultural impediments to self-determination, such as the conflict between administrative impartiality and kinship obligations, the perception that administrative systems, accounting and inter-agency liaison were 'whitefella business', and the 'alien' nature of the concept of elected representation and delegated authority?

- If so, what alternative was there but to encourage the Aboriginal communities' movement towards self-management by getting rid of these impediments?

- Was it true, as it seemed to the Committee, that the DAA's criteria for judging a community's attainment of self-management were the extent of its reliance on welfare payments, educational profiles, employment levels, and the degree to which the community was able to manage antisocial and socially destructive practices?

It might have been better for Indigenous people if the debate had broadened to include the Indigenous people themselves and their organisations, but it remained confined to the Committee and the bureaucracy continued to flounder in its own policies. In fact, like many government instrumentalities, the emphasis was on the smooth running of the department rather than on any reformation of its policies and grants system. Not only did it seem unable to deal with Indigenous social organisations, but its own concept of self-determination made no reference to any Indigenous social concerns and goals, such as the effective transmission of knowledge of 'country' and the opportunity to determine the use to which such knowledge was put. Land Rights were seen as problematic, with what was needed being in line with the rest of government policies for all Australian citizens: high levels of employment (and low levels of welfare dependency), high rates of educational achievement, and effective control of what were seen to be anti-social and socially destructive forces. Such policies were advanced by many government departments and did not reflect much credit on the DAA, which was after all primarily concerned with Indigenous affairs. In particular, of course, they had nothing to do with the key question of self-determination, but were overall policies directed by bureaucracy at Australian society in general. Similar policies could be found in all such government departments dealing with Indigenous affairs. What needs to be asked is: Does the 'Aboriginisation' of such bureaucratic structures produce anything but bureaucrats beyond the pale? In 1988, for instance, about thirty per cent of the staff of the DAA were Indigenous and of the Aboriginal Development Commission, under Charles Perkins, about forty-five per cent.

In 1977, the professional Aboriginalist, Dr H.C. 'Nugget' Coombs, drew attention to 'an emerging intelligentsia of politicians, administrators, writers and artists, a source from which . . . an ideology may before long emerge to unite and give common purpose to Aboriginal aspirations and political action'. What should be noted here is that Coombs was postulating that the outcome of what I assume to be westernisation was a 'totality of purpose and aspiration' which simply has not and might not come about, because of powerful countervailing pressures. Chief among these is the fact that the emerging or emerged 'intelligentsia' are precisely those who have achieved a certain accommodation with the Master and have the most to lose if a common purpose and aspiration were to develop and bring about drastic change. Perhaps it was merely wishful thinking on Coombs's part, for by 1984 he had shifted his position to accord with those Indigenous people who saw that a 'black bureaucracy will come to identify itself progressively with the white bureaucracy and to accept its methods and ways of thought, ceasing in any real sense to be an instrument of Aboriginal self-management or self-determination'. But he went on to modify this by adding: 'In this role they can help the Governments and their agents understand Aboriginal aspirations and help Aborigines frame their demands in ways most likely to be understood and sympathetically received by white authority.'

Of course, when we use a blanket term like 'black bureaucracy', it tends to obscure the individuality and even class of the persons grouped under the term. Perhaps it might be better to focus on individuals and see what happens to them when they find themselves in opposition to a government minister and the white bureaucracy by refusing to be assimilated into its structure. White may be right, but there is a place for black bureaucrats if only because Indigenous people generally prefer to deal with other Indigenes when they have to approach a government department. Also, senior Indigenous bureaucrats tend to have greater credibility in coordinating with other government departments, and in dealing with the media and Indigenous people themselves.

But the so-called 'Aboriginalisation' of government departments will be nothing more than window dressing if the control of departmental policy remains in the hands of senior white bureaucrats. Black faces may be seen around the department, which in itself is an advance, but at the same time the traditional public servant rules of protocol and accountability restrain their ability to function at not only departmental level but on statutory bodies supposedly set up to ensure greater flexibility and independence. In 1988 Charles Perkins, the most senior Indigenous bureaucrat in the Federal Government, who has been fighting to change the bureaucratic mindset, fell foul of these strictures and was forced to resign, although he has since re-emerged into public life and controversy. Perkins has been connected with the DAA from its inception and thus forms a black link between such government instrumentalities as the DAA, the Aboriginal Development Commission and finally ATSIC.

The Department of Aboriginal Affairs was formed in December 1972 under Gordon Bryant as Minister, with Barrie Dexter as permanent head. It was an amalgamation of previously existing bodies such as the Office of Aboriginal Affairs, the Department of Internal Affairs, and the Northern Territory Welfare Branch. There were four divisions: Policy, Planning and Research, Economic Development, General Programs and Consultation and Liaison.

Charles Perkins was appointed head of the Consultation and Liaison branch and immediately proceeded to 'Aboriginalise' it. However, he was always hindered by economic priorities determined by the bureaucratic structure around him, having to report to the Policy division which then informed the Economic Development branch of the department's priorities and goals. Economic Development, which was staffed by whites, took the major decisions, distributed funds and worked to its own agenda. Bryant and Perkins got on well together, and Bryant often bypassed Economic Development by distributing funds without consulting the department. This provoked the ire of the professional bureaucrats whose guiding principle was 'accountability' — that is, to themselves — and pressure was exerted on Bryant to mend his ways.

Government policies made for Indigenous people never proceed by continuous development but are inevitably disrupted by a series of starts and turns, restarts and returns, which occur with changes of governments and Ministers of Aboriginal Affairs. The Fraser government ended the heady Whitlam era, with Ian Viner as the new Minister, later succeeded by Fred Chaney. New Government meant new Government body — the Aboriginal Development Commission (ADC) came into being in 1980 and would last for the next eight years. With the DAA now being seen as a lame duck, the new Commission's tasks were to assist Indigenous people by buying land, issuing housing grants and loans, and lending or granting the money for business enterprises. The ADC superseded such bodies as the Aboriginal Land Fund Commission, the Aboriginal Loans Commission and the DAA's enterprise program.

At first Indigenous organisations feared that this was an attempt to rein in the powers of the Land Fund Commission permanently. They queried why there had to be white commissioners; why the commissioners were to be appointed by the Minister; why they could be dismissed for 'misbehaviour'; why there was not an iron-clad guarantee of continuing finance for the all-important capital fund; what powers the Minister would have to instruct the commissioners; why the ADC should be allowed only to fund incorporated organisations; why it could make grants to housing associations, but only lend to individuals; in what ways the commissioners' powers would be limited by state law; and whether there should be a provision for a treaty between the white settlers and the Indigenous people.

Chaney, who by then was the Minister, took some of the objections seriously and over fifty amendments were accepted during eighteen months of negotiations. The board of directors would all be Indigenous, and employees would not come under the Public Servants' Act, so that Indigenous people could be employed at senior levels almost immediately.

The *Aboriginal Development Commission Act* was unique in the powers it conferred on the commissioners. It began with a challenging statement: 'The purpose of this Act is to further the economic and social development of the Aboriginal race of Australia . . . and in particular (as a recognition of the past dispossession of such people) to establish a Capital Fund with the object of promoting their development, self-management and self-sufficiency.' Shirley McPherson, the ADC's second chair, described the Act as the envy of Indigenous peoples throughout the world.

The Capital Fund was an immense step forward, but its potential was cut short by the drying up of appropriations which would have made the ADC independent of Treasury appropriations. In 1981 and 1983 the housing grants program was transferred from the DAA, and the Commission took on the work of the National Aboriginal Sports Foundation. It also combined with the National Aboriginal Committee (NAC) to hold conferences on land needs, compiling a confidential register of properties which the ADC would eventually purchase.

The Director was Charles Perkins and for the first few years, what with its all Indigenous commissioners, it appeared that at last executive power had been placed in the hands of Indigenous people. Perkins himself saw the ADC as a means of salvation for Indigenous people from the vicious circle of 'welfare'. As he put it:

> A sound economic base will help us to cut the welfare umbilical cord that binds us. Increasingly, we must become active producers, instead of passive users, in the context of the Australian economy. We must develop sound economic and social infrastructures . . . in order to take control of our own destiny. Unless these imperatives are achieved, Aborigines will continue to be gripped by a counter-productive 'hand-out' mentality, and destined to be a race of economic cripples and perpetual dependents.

But against this brave new thrust towards Indigenous independence, as the following table shows, housing consumed much of the Capital Fund. This was to house Indigenous families rather than 'rental' property; a provision prevented the accumulation of housing as a capital asset and an income derived from rent. This emphasis on housing meant that funds were taken away from other programs, especially those with the charter to purchase properties and businesses for the generation of capital for further investment. The drain of housing on the budget of the ADC may be seen in the following table.

EXPENDITURE ON FIVE MAIN ADC PROGRAMS FROM 1980–88		
PROGRAM	$ MILLIONS	PROPORTION OF TOTAL
Housing Grants	243.6	53%
Housing Loans	131.2	29%
Enterprise Grants	40.5	9%
Enterprise Loans	27.5	6%
Land Grants	15.6	3%
TOTAL	458.4	100%

Thus the welfare nature of other government bodies concerned with Indigenous people was maintained by the ADC. There was also the constant need to be accountable in the use of public funds, which partly explained the emphasis on housing. This inevitably placed a strain on the departments and commissions set up to formulate policies along the lines of what the government saw as fit and necessary for Indigenous communities. It reflects a 'western' attitude and methodology which decides on programs and objectives which can only lead to assimilation and the continuing colonisation of the Indigenous people of Australia.

By this I mean the way in which people with their own social and economic structures are incorporated into those of a conquering state. Colonial expansion is a process which continues until its power is total, by a combination of coercion and assimilation. An integral part of this colonisation is welfare, which only perpetuates the subjugation of the Indigenous people, whether they recognise it or not. The only way out is to join the mainstream of Australian society — that is, unless conditions change and a secure alternative economic base can be created.

The Hawke government's coming to office signalled the establishment of a new centralised organisation, the ATSIC, which would incorporate the functions of the ADC and DAA. Indigenous Australia was to be divided into twenty-six regions supposedly responsible for their own administration. The regions would combine to form six zones (although this was subsequently amended in the final Act, as was the number of regions), mainly following state boundaries, which would each elect their own commissioner. Twelve commissioners, five (subsequently reduced to three) of whom would be appointed by the government, would decide funding priorities and financial allocations for each of the zones. A preamble to the Act included the acknowledgement of the Indigenous people's prior occupation of Australia and their dispossession without compensation. It was quickly noticed that the Minister had a significant degree of control over the Commission, which was unusual in that the shift of responsibility from a ministry to a statutory body implied greater flexibility and freedom from control. It was no wonder that, before long, people were saying that ATSIC stood for 'Aborigines Talking Shit in Canberra'. Although some changes were made in the final Bill before it passed into law, the Minister's power remained, and this caused many Aborigines to have misgivings about the whole setup, with only thirty per cent voting in the first election for the commissioners.

In 1990 the House of Representatives Standing Committee on Aboriginal Affairs brought down a report entitled *Our Future Our Selves: Aboriginal and Torres Strait Islander Community Control, Management and Resources*. Unfortunately, there was not much evidence of the 'Our' of the title in the extent to which it drew on anthropological studies and submissions to review the difficulties of delivering 'support services' to Indigenous 'communities' while keeping faith with Indigenous self-determination. But it did make a useful distinction between 'self-determination' and 'self-management'. The latter, it said, referred to efficient administration, while the former 'goes beyond this and implies control over policy and decision making, especially the determination of structures, processes and priorities'.

The report made four important points:

> 1. It upheld the importance of 'resource agencies' as instruments of self-determination;
>
> 2. It advocated negotiation, rather than consultation, as the government agencies' method of interaction with Indigenous representative bodies;
>
> 3. It called for government agencies to coordinate their negotiations by working through ATSIC field staff and to make the formulation of a community plan the objective of such negotiations;
>
> 4. It promoted the importance of training in various aspects of 'self-management' for Indigenous people.

The report was thorough and raised many valid proposals which are now being implemented, but it failed to come to grips with those aspects of culture which might be abruptly changed by the adoption of its host of recommendations. Furthermore, there was no discussion of what would happen with the transfer of power within Indigenous communities.

Australian Indigenous culture, like many other cultures, depends on the transmission of knowledge from older to younger people, and with the transmission of knowledge go power and prestige. The House Committee recognised this method of cultural self-reproduction, but its recommendations were to do with western educational practices and what they were really advocating was a reversal of the normal process of knowledge transfer. Where once the training of youth was entirely in the hands of older people, with knowledge now being geared towards self-management of resources a new method of power transfer is coming into operation. Young Indigenous people are picking up scraps of new information deriving from the technological age which they are able to translate into power through the training and careers that go with it, which in turn enhances their status and authority to an unprecedented level. In other words, the acquisition of knowledge is undermining the very basis of Indigenous social structure. The once-powerful elders whose authority has been steadily eroding since the invasion are finding that their power is shrinking further and being confined to the ceremonial field, while the bright young technocrats assert themselves in the councils and other social organisations. Thus all the policies and shifts in policy of the government organisations involved in Indigenous affairs result in tensions and conflict which are subtly changing the culture and society from within. This can be seen as either a disaster or 'natural' in the sense that as cultures and societies are never static, neither are 'communities' — those clusters of kin and family groupings which make up the Indigenous people of Australia. It is up to us to ensure how we may accommodate and respond to these changes while retaining our Indigenality.

FURTHER READING

Bennett, Scott, *Aborigines and Political Power*. Sydney, Allen & Unwin, 1989.

Fletcher, Christine, *Aboriginal Politics*. Melbourne, Melbourne University Press, 1992.

House of Representatives Standing Committee on Aboriginal and Torres Strait Affairs, *Aboriginal People and Mainstream Local Governments. An Issues Paper.* November 1989; *Our Future Our Selves: Aboriginal and Torres Strait Islander Community Control, Management and Resources.* August 1990; *Mainly Urban: Report of the Inquiry into the Needs of Urban-Dwelling Aboriginal and Torres Strait Islander People.* November 1992, Canberra, Australian Government Publishing Service.

Reed, Peter, *Charles Perkins: A Biography*. Melbourne, Viking, 1990.

THE MASTER'S LAW
Lecture 6

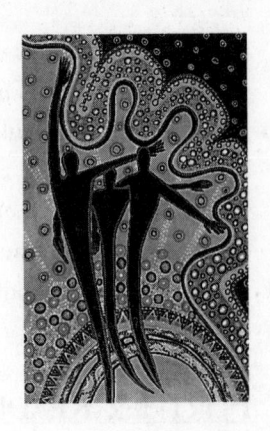

HOW MUCH OF THE GREAT FORESTS ARE LEFT, HOW MUCH OF the woodlands? Over the the last two centuries our land has been treated harshly, as harshly as we have been treated. Whole forests have disappeared and whole branches of the Dreaming Tree of Life have been ruthlessly lopped off. Genocide is not a fancy word. Indigenous people still whisper of those killing times when the law of the Master was the Law of the Rifle, and men, women and children were slain in their thousands. Wherever I go in Australia, one of Us Mob will come up to me and point out this massacre site and that massacre site. The Master may laugh at our sacred places and our efforts to protect them, but he ignores what happened at many places where we were mercilessly slaughtered. Among those who led the slaughter were the *gunjee*, the *monaitch*, the policeman, and after the pitiful remnants were rounded up and kept on a mere patch of their own land, again it was the policeman who was master over us, handing out meagre rations of sugar, flour and tea. The police were the force that kept us segregated, that enforced the curfews that made us get out of the Master's towns at sunset. How many of us have been incarcerated and driven almost if not actually to suicide in squalid cells under the malevolent gaze of the policeman's eye? Is it any wonder that we have no respect for the Master's law, that treated us less than animals, that told us to our very faces that we were worse than animals, and then flung a rope into a cell and told us to get on with the job — to kill ourselves and rid the world of Us Mob. Yes, we remember all that, and the story is only now just being told. And still, and still they wonder why we rebel and why we have no respect for the law.

If we are to understand Australian Indigenous people, we must be aware of the immense disruption caused by the incursion and subsequent dominance of European settlers over the last two hundred years. This is nowhere more apparent than in the split between Indigenous law and whitefella law. It is often said that the difference between Indigenous law and whitefella law is that 'Our law is forever, is never-changing', whereas whitefella law is ever-changing, unfixed and unstable, and when it is necessary it will be changed to satisfy the Master's needs. But then, is our Indigenous law so fixed and unchanging? We may wade through the realms of works by anthropologists and fail to find any clear definition of Indigenous law and how it works and how it endures. Texts abound with the Master's theories discussing law in broad philosophical terms, but for the most part avoiding any attempt to apply it to Indigenous practices. What is Indigenous law and how was it propagated? What gave it its enduring nature? How was it encoded from what has been loosely termed 'the Dreamtime', that period long ago when men and women were not yet men and women but ancestral beings, and formulated the rules by which people must live? Indigenous ideology postulates clearly that all our laws come from the Dreamtime, when they were laid down by our ancestors. My question is, how did they continue on from then into the present?

Oral literature, especially the genres termed 'Dreamtime stories' is too often relegated to the status of children's stories and hacked to pieces by collectors and editors who do not pause to think why they existed and what they signified. It is easy to say that they reflect the primitive creative meanderings of a savage mind or part of a universal construct based on some such thing as the collective unconscious, rather than as social products forming part of the very fabric of a community. Western critics constantly interpret Indigenous culture from what I would like to call a 'primitive' viewpoint, but which I will call only an unsophisticated one. Entering the social and ideological arena, I would like to suggest that these so-called stories or myths were never primitive attempts to understand the universe, but were narratives which had encoded within them the divine sanction of law, the law itself and a commentary on how the law was to be enforced.

In contemporary 'non-primitive' theory, these stories may be seen as social sign systems which comment on the law; extending this, the entire physical environment is made to refer to the various stories and the laws. Indigenous people used objects in the natural environment as signs to order society. Everything, in fact, was related to the operations of the law and the proof of these laws, the signs, is to be found in the environment. For example, a Ngarinjen story says that the hair of a widow must be cut. The law is encoded with commentary in the narrative. Superficially, the narrative is in the familiar genre of how such and such animal or bird received certain markings (in children's stories, the story would end there and produce a nice fable), but in the complete Ngarinjen version, the marking — in this case the black head of the python — is a sign of the law ordering that a woman who has lost her husband should cut her hair and cover herself with charcoal. We are not so much concerned about how the python got the marking, but how the marking itself encodes the law. It is a visible sign, not only of the law, but of the origin of the law. It is there for all to see.

To illustrate further how narrative encodes law, I would like to refer to another story by a well-known Kimberley elder, 'Djaringalong the Eagle who Ate Babies', published in Hugh Edwards's anthology, *Aboriginal Legends of the North West*. The title itself is suspect, as is the editing of the story, but it still serves my purpose. It is a Dreaming story about a 'giant eagle' named Djaringalong who lived near the sea and ate babies and small children. Two young boys of the Djanbir community named Walumba and Dagudal found her nest, then decided to return and kill her. Once she was dead, they plucked the down from Djaringalong's breast, made a ball of it, and blew it into the air. The wind caught it and whirled it on high up and up into the sky where Djaringalong became the Southern Cross.

Djaringalong is a mystery and I have not been able to find out much else about her. She obviously has a social role as well, for the eaglehawk is important in the social ordering of communities, but this is not given in the text. I suspect, however, that this would be explained in other stories, for many of these narratives are linked together and one narrative leads into another. But as far as the two boys are concerned, Walumba became an owl living in a hollow tree, and Dagudal became the sand-bird, expert at camouflage and evasion. The story states that Walumba is the lawgiver of the Ngarinjen and all the tribes of the north, and it was the bird-men who set the marriage classes which govern the tribes. And the reason for this story is precisely this — to give sanction for the marriage laws; the owl and the sand-bird ancestors are visible signs of the ancestral giving of these laws. If they are queried, the birds are pointed at as visible signs of the origin of the laws — laws stretching back to the Dreamtime and never-changing.

This was when Indigenous communities or extended families were intact and operated under these laws. But what happens when the laws are no longer followed and the stories encoding the laws no longer have this social purpose? What happens to these narratives, and what is their importance now? I suggest that they become socially meaningless, except as signs of a diffuse Indigenality. That is, they become merely stories, though Indigenous stories.

In his collection of texts titled *Gularabulu*, Paddy Roe gives a truncated version of the Djaringalong narrative to editor Stephen Muecke in which, although it is set in the Dreaming and the divine attributes of the eaglehawk are emphasised, it becomes only a story of two men killing the being which is like — but not actually — an eaglehawk. The killing loses its significance and a quasi-meaning is supplied to the effect that with the death of Djaringalong ended the genus of the giant birds. This pseudo-scientific explanation for the absence of giant eaglehawks only serves to render the narrative meaningless. Its point and rationality are lost and the social content disappears. Even when Stephen Muecke asks the obvious question: 'But he's in the other world now?' the only answer he gets is: 'He finish now.' Which might as well refer to the narrative.

Nonetheless, Paddy Roe's Djaringalong still illustrates the social significance of the story, but this time the emphasis is on the discontinuity which occurred with the invasion and the disruption of Indigenous laws and customs, at least in that area of Australia. And what happens when Indigenous law becomes a crime under European law and cannot be carried out? The policeman is the all-powerful lawgiver and it is through him that the Master's law must be upheld, or else the Indigenous lawgiver is punished when he is morally and socially obliged to enforce Indigenous law and punish a lawbreaker.

Paddy Roe's story Mirdinan, in the same volume, is a social text in that it shows how Indigenous law can be upheld and carried out even under the Master's domination. As it can no longer be done in straightforward fashion, subterfuge must be employed.

Mirdinan is a narrative about a wife-murderer, and how he is brought to justice — in this case, both Indigenous and Master justice. In cases like this, it is the brother of the dead woman who is bound under Indigenous law to avenge her death. Mirdinan's wife has committed adultery, and he takes the law into his own hands and kills her. But he has broken the law in two ways, for he is not the right person to inflict punishment on her, and the offence is not one for which the death penalty is prescribed. Mirdinan has murdered his wife and thus become an outlaw not only in the eyes of his community, but in the eyes of the Master as well. Now it is the duty of the wife's brother to execute him, but this would result in the brother being seen as a murderer in the eyes of the Master. To overcome this, he hands Mirdinan over to the police, but Mirdinan is so strong and determined that it is only through the joint efforts of the police and the Indigenous people that the outlaw is finally captured and executed, and both laws satisfied. In this text, the message is clear, that it is only through cooperation, or by the use of the Master's law, that Indigenous law can be upheld, at least in such serious cases.

This underlines the severity of the social disruption caused by the European invasion, which Indigenous people have been seeking to cure ever since. It is difficult to keep practising Indigenous law when the Master's law is the only law acknowledged, or Indigenous law is unknown by whitefella judges, or if known is only regarded as a mitigating factor in certain circumstances.

When Indigenous people come before the Master's court, they sometimes find themselves in an incomprehensible situation, often extremely distressful. The British legal system, with its arcane rituals and procedures from an alien culture, makes for unease, not for ease, not only among Indigenous people but many other Australian citizens who fall victim to it. In the case of Indigenous people there was a real need for an organisation to provide a buffer against this system, and for all the criticisms directed at it, the Aboriginal Legal Service (ALS) has managed to do this. In fact, without the ALS, many Indigenous persons would be at the complete mercy of the court (which means pleading guilty), rather than being able to begin to understand its complex rules and regulations and how they function.

Because it filled a real need, the Aboriginal Legal Service quickly became accepted by most Indigenous people and helped them to grasp the workings of the legal system. Some idea of how things were in the inner-city suburb of Redfern, an Indigenous enclave, before the formation of the ALS in Sydney comes from the third scene of Robert J. Merritt's *The Cake Man*, first performed in 1977.

This scene could be a brief film sequence. Evening. A street in Redfern, outside a pub. We hear traffic, a juke box from the pub, voices and laughter and all the pub noises.

SWEET WILLIAM *walks along quietly and stands outside the pub door. He has a battered suitcase in his hand. He pauses, looking in. Out the door staggers a drunk. He is an Aborigine. A few others like him are pushed out of the door. The* **PUBLICAN** *appears behind them in the doorway.*

PUBLICAN: Now g'wan, get on your way! Back when you're sober. (*They mutter and mumble and call abuse. They bump into* **SWEET WILLIAM** *and crowd about him.*) Go on, piss off. (*Warning*) The police were rung for five minutes ago. Better get.

(*They give him some more abuse, and linger. We hear the roar of a police van pulling up. The* **PUBLICAN** *nods. The Kuris look on in alarm. Two* **POLICEMEN** *run on with batons.*)

POLICEMAN: This the trouble, Mr Pott?

(*The* **PUBLICAN** *nods. He turns and goes inside his pub. The* **POLICEMEN** *proceed to arrest the lot. They run them off to the van, and at last the pair rush back at* **SWEET WILLIAM**.)

POLICEMAN: Right, you, get your arse in that wagon.

WILLIAM: Who, me? Oh, no boss, I'm down from the bush.

POLICEMAN: Don't you bloody well answer me back!

(*They grab* **WILLIAM**. *They give him the bum's rush off stage. We hear the wagon door being slammed and locked. Doors slam. The motor starts, roars and fades. The* **PUBLICAN** *appears in door. He smiles, satisfied after the wagon. Music: 'There's a Happy Land Somewhere.'*)

As this scene depicts, some Indigenous people were regularly arrested in Redfern without cause, and unfortunately this situation still occurs there and throughout the rest of Australia today, though the ALS has done what it can to alleviate the situation. Until its establishment, Indigenous persons were routinely brought to court, tried and sentenced without legal representation, and often without knowing that there was such a thing. They came, pleaded guilty and went off to gaol. With the ALS, legal representation and the knowledge that it was there to be used at last began to spread throughout the Indigenous communities.

The ALS was not a government initiative, but came from the Indigenous community and concerned lawyers. With the assistance of a panel of lawyers willing to do voluntary work, a group was formed to provide representation for Indigenous people living in Sydney. From this came the Sydney ALS, which has remained under Indigenous control ever since, although until recently all of the lawyers were white. It is now headed by the Indigenous lawyer Paul Coe.

When the Whitlam government came to power in 1972, one of its promises to Indigenous people was that legal services would be expanded to places where they were needed. ALSs were established in New South Wales country areas, Queensland and other States. In 1982 a conference was held resulting in the formation of the National Aboriginal and Islander Legal Services Secretariat (NAILSS), which appears to function only intermittently, however, owing to funding difficulties.

The ALSs are governed by elected boards, because each service had to become an incorporated body in order to satisfy the conditions for government funding. Thus — and this is true of almost all Indigenous resource organisations — they are locked into structures and procedures stipulating annual general meetings, audited financial statements and so on, which necessitate a larger staff than would otherwise be required, using funds which might be better employed. Government funding also has another drawback in that the services are publicly accountable and are at the mercy of Governmental Review Committees, not to mention Parliamentary criticism. So there is much pressure from the top to operate within certain guidelines, such as concentrating on criminal law rather than expanding into all aspects of legal work.

Under the *Aboriginal Organisations Act*, the majority of the elected board of each ALS must be Indigenous. The board formulates policy and employs staff, with day-to-day management in the hands of an executive officer or office manager. This is a similar setup to that of many Indigenous resource or service organisations and despite its obvious positive features can cause certain problems in that it is difficult to get people to attend the annual general meetings without a considerable outlay of funds, especially in the larger States. This difficulty even affects government bodies like the Aboriginal Arts Board of the Australia Council. What happens is that such organisations tend to be dominated by urban-based people, and this leads to charges that they are not representative of all Indigenous people.

Another problem, though not one peculiar to the ALS, is the employment of expert white staff. As yet there are not enough Indigenous lawyers to go around, and friction may occur between the non-legal governing body and the white lawyers who may become de facto policy makers by claiming to know what is best for their clients and how to get the best results. A lawyer may persuade an ALS board that funds should be spent on briefing counsel to argue a point of law on appeal. If the point is won, the lawyer argues, then future clients will benefit. Against this, the governing body may think, especially if the point is lost, that the funds might have been better utilised on routine defence work. For the most part, however, there is a good working relationship between governing body and staff, both Indigenous and non-Indigenous.

The ALS also employs field officers who are the grass-roots contacts with their communities and form a bridge between clients and lawyers. Through experience on the job, they acquire a knowledge of the law which they can use to assist the community in which they work by offering advice on such things as rental arrears, domestic violence, or procedures to be followed in criminal cases. As a general rule they have no right to appear in court, although they may on occasions be allowed by magistrates to make bail applications, enter pleas, or seek adjournments. They are especially important in remote areas where clients have no knowledge of the legal process. The bulk of their work is conducted outside the court by channelling clients to the legal service, providing lawyers with relevant background information, operating bail funds, acting as prisoners' 'friends' and so on.

ALS offices are informal places, and their day-to-day work is flexible, in sharp contrast to the rigidity of the legal process. Clients are mostly Indigenous people, but non-Indigenous spouses are also eligible for help. There is no means test, because it is assumed that those using the Services have little money and that legal assistance should be available to all members of the community.

As resource organisations serving their communities, the Indigenous legal services have a holistic approach which avoids distinctions between legal and non-legal work, and offer assistance on a wide range of matters, including welfare problems. They need to maintain credibility in their communities, and someone who is refused help over pension entitlements, for example, may not return when he or she has a legal problem. But their main focus continues to be individual casework, especially in criminal matters. Day in and day out, ALS solicitors represent clients facing criminal charges, usually in magistrates' courts, with barristers being briefed wherever possible in more serious cases.

Despite the difficulties under which it labours, especially in assisting communities in remote parts of the country, the ALS has helped Indigenous people to gain some understanding of the complexities of the legal system and to realise that they need no longer stand alone against it. It has also been effective in opposing 'institutionalised racism', the whole entrenched alien system that still oppresses Indigenous people, often merely by its incomprehensible structure. This apparatus has often been employed against the ALS itself, especially when it dares to challenge the discriminatory status quo. The ALS is committed to representing individuals facing criminal charges in the courts, but it should also be interested in challenging and exposing those systems which bring people before the courts in the first place, though often paucity of funds means that the challenge cannot be taken up.

The ALS, as we have seen, had its genesis in Redfern, an Indigenous ghetto which is heavily policed. There is a well-known story about an Indigenous man who used to drive around Redfern in an expensive car, but was stopped so many times by the police that he traded it in for a cheaper model. It appears that if the police see an Indigenous person driving an expensive car they automatically assume that he or she must have stolen it. Another problem is that Indigenous people have different social habits, such as treating outside areas as social space, which is against the so-called mores of the Master community. A group of Indigenous people hanging out on a street corner, or in a park, for example, is often considered an unlawful gathering by the police and they move in to disperse it. Again, being drunk in a public place — or considered to be so — using 'unseemly' words, or so-called offensive behaviour are often charges which stem from rigorous policing of Aborigines. As one ALS lawyer commented:

> A chap charged with drunkenness or unseemly words or offensive behaviour or whatever might well be an example of a running sore in a particular area as regards, say, police behaviour. The Service may well see the defence of his case as of considerable general significance, so that you may see

a lot of time spent on a minor charge, but from the legal point of view it may be to a very serious end, particularly if you have a country area where the cops are playing up, as sometimes happens. Sometimes it becomes important to run some minor charges very hard indeed, and to take them through all levels of appeal, if necessary.

It is unnecessary to say that few country solicitors would do this. They are usually committed to preserving the status quo in the towns where they live and work, whereas the ALS lawyer is committed to the interests of one group and more prepared to go against the status quo to see that justice is done. Indeed, many ALS lawyers believe that legal channels can be used to effect significant social change. This is borne out in the area of police interrogation of Indigenous suspects.

Police interrogation has always been a matter of concern. Given the historically dominant position of the police in regard to Indigenous people, their aggressive language, intimidating uniforms and the enemy territory of the police station, as well as the ordinary difficulties of communication, it is little wonder that Indigenous persons may confess to crimes in order to escape the associated stress, or be bamboozled into signing a confession without fully understanding the contents, or simply be 'verballed'. In the interests of Aborigines who are accused of crimes, rules have been developed for the guidance of police conducting interrogations — most notably by the Northern Territory Supreme Court, although since the Royal Commission into Aboriginal Deaths in Custody the rules have been tightened in all

States. These were the direct result of submissions to the Northern Territory Supreme Court by the Central Australian Aboriginal Legal Aid Service. In South Australia, Queensland, Western Australia and the Australian Capital Territory, police are enjoined to follow special procedures when Indigenous persons are under interrogation or in police custody. In each case, the ALS has played a crucial role in shaping the rules that govern police practice when Indigenous persons are in custody. This has led to police antagonism, but such pressure is necessary to make the police obey their own rules.

One of the most far-reaching changes to which ALS has contributed is the treatment of Indigenous children by the courts and by State welfare agencies. The various ALSs have given high priority to providing legal representation in children's court cases, both where juveniles are charged with offences and where wardship applications are before the court. The ALSs have had considerable influence on the operations of children's courts, and on the practices and ideologies of State welfare departments. While they have sought to change criminal justice practices, the chief aim of their work has been to wrest control of offending 'at risk' or 'neglected' Indigenous children from the authorities — State welfare agencies and the courts — and to restore the care of those children to Indigenous communities, sometimes at the expense of considerable animosity from the general public. They vigorously represent Indigenous children in court hearings and have attacked attitudes long held by Master policy-makers. A major attitude is an abiding commitment to assimilation which has resulted and still results in the institutionalisation of many

Indigenous juveniles. A result has been that the 'Welfare' is feared as much as, if not more than, the police. To regain control of their children, Indigenous communities have relied on the ALSs firstly to defend charges and resist wardship applications, and secondly to suggest to the courts alternative ways of dealing with the children. The ALSs argue for children to be placed with stable, Indigenous families or in Indigenous hostels, so that they will not face the identity crises often experienced by Indigenous adolescents placed in Master welfare institutions or adoptive homes. They have called for a substantial shift in the thinking of magistrates, especially those sitting in children's courts, and in the official policies of State welfare departments. Because of its early and extensive involvement in child welfare issues — issues seen as being of paramount importance to Indigenous communities — the Victorian ALS in 1976 formed the Victorian Aboriginal Child Care Agency, which became the model for similar organisations in other States.

The ALS is thus doing a positive job in the face of a political system which follows the dictates of a government bureaucracy which holds on to controlling power through funding arrangements, and a legal system which necessitates being educated into the colonising institutions of the Master society. The legal process is one of the chief agencies of assimilation, and to work within its constraints is to run the risk of becoming assimilated into it. This is also an inherent danger in being an incorporated body with an established apparatus which is not Indigenous, but has been imposed. One must be aware of the deep contradictions that arise from working within such systems, but it is difficult to see how this can be avoided, or even how it is possible to develop a different structure. If the existing system is seen as a colonising tool and assimilationist device, then Indigenous people should opt out of it and form a counter-system of their own. However, given the number of Indigenous people who come before the courts and who need legal representation, this is essentially impracticable, unless an effective Indigenous legal policing and justice system comes into force. This seems almost impossible to envisage, considering the fragmentary nature of the Indigenous communities in Australia, and the fact that even if such an Indigenous justice system did come into existence there would still be areas of sanctuary for those who break Indigenous law, or refused to conform to its dictates. This is not a theoretical question, for even in a strong Indigenous law settlement, such as Jigalong in the Pilbara region of Western Australia, those who did not wish to live under Indigenous law have moved away to the outskirts of the mining town of Mt Newman, where they now live in a fringe camp. Then again the law of the Master, his police and legal system are everywhere in Australia. It is the dominant system and, as in the Mirdinan story, has to be made use of by Indigenous communities.

The future of any Indigenous legal system is in doubt, especially as, with the growth of a unified world system based on western mores, other legal systems which do not conform to what is regarded as universal values are under attack. If this is given due weight, then such organisations as the ALS have an important role to play, chiefly by forming a bridge between the Indigenous people of Australia and the dominant Australian legal system. It is across bridges such as this that Indigenous Aboriginal people will move towards an assimilation impossible to avoid in the long run. In cities such as Sydney, this process is well under way in that many members of the Indigenous population there are at home under the restraints and constraints of the dominant legal system. The role of organisations such as the ALS thus becomes one of accom-modation and reform. These would include the need to ensure that every Indigenous person enjoys basic human rights; the right of Indigenous people to retain their racial identity, subject to the constraints of the dominant society, of which they might eventually become a part by attrition and education; and equitable, humane and fair treatment under the criminal justice system.

There is little hope of Indigenous people being able to escape the Master's legal system. As I write, there is a heavy load of prisoners on my shoulders. We are the most imprisoned people in Australia and it is not changing. If the opposing canon of the Indigenous law system is invoked in court it is dismissed out of hand as being inconsistent with the Master's text. This happened to us a year or so ago in Kalgoorlie, and it was only in 1994 that Indigenous people and magistrates came together to discuss the problems of Indigenous people and the law. I went along and listened and joined in the debate. There was a general consensus among the magistrates that there was not room in Australia for two laws, so that Indigenous law could only be cited to plead mitigating circumstances. This position is borne out by a government report in 1994 on Aboriginal customary laws. It is worth quoting its recommendations to end this lecture:

- Aboriginal customary law should be recognised, in appropriate ways, by the Australian legal system;

- such recognition must occur against the background and within the framework of the general law;

- the creation of new and separate legal structures should be avoided unless the need for these is demonstrated;

- in most instances, codification or direct enforcement are not appropriate forms of recognition nor is the exclusion of the general law desirable.

FURTHER READING

Commonwealth of Australia, *Aboriginal Deaths In Custody: Responses by Governments to the Royal Commission* (two vols). Canberra, Australian Government Publishing Service, 1992.

Cunneen, Chris (ed), *Aboriginal Perspectives on Criminal Justice*. Sydney, Institute of Criminology Monograph Series, No. 1, 1992.

Edwards, H., *Aboriginal Legends of the North-West*. Melbourne, Nelson, 1976.

Hanks, P. and Keon-Cohen, B. (eds), *Aborigines and the Law*. Sydney, Allen & Unwin, 1984.

Merritt, Robert J., *The Cake Man*. Sydney, Currency Press, 1978.

Office of Indigenous Affairs, *Aboriginal Customary Law: Report on the Implementation of the Recommendations of the Australian Law Reform Commission*. Canberra, Australian Government Publishing Service, 1994.

Roe, Paddy, *Gularabulu* (ed Stephen Muecke). Fremantle, Arts Centre Press, 1983.

Our Education
Lecture 7

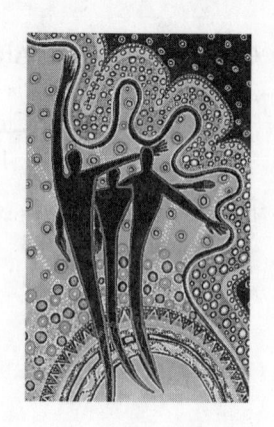

ONCE UPON A TIME, SCHOOLTEACHERS WERE CALLED school*masters* — an interesting concept which lingers and which is recalled to my mind when I hear about Indigenous kids who dare to contradict the Master (or Mistress) as to so-called 'facts' and are told to be quiet, as this is how it is in the textbook so what would a kid know about it. Of course, Us Mob have been living with such putdowns for a long time now, and can we help it if our own interpretations flow from generation to generation? In our connected family system, the Dreaming Tree of life and death, of culture and learning, kids are not isolated from adults, but learn by sitting in on our discussions, just as they learn by being part of our demonstrations. Our educational methods are far different from the Master's, but the result, when they are not taken into account or adapted using some alien theory, is that our kids flee from the schoolrooms.

Worse, Indigenous kids are often seen by teachers as candidates for failure and are tolerated in the classroom until they quietly disappear, and thus another stereotype is confirmed.

The education system in Australia is a socialising process. A kid enters it to be socialised into the dominant norms of the master society, and if he or she does not learn how to play the system, or refuses to participate, then it is too bad. Of course, the dismal dropout rate of Indigenous kids and the racism bedevilling Australia does lead to attempts being made to construct and implement Indigenous studies courses in educational institutions, but these courses are usually designed by Masters, perhaps with some input from Indigenous persons. Thus, when the Western Australian Department of Education began planning an Aboriginal Studies course, Nyungars, Yamadjis and members of other Indigenous groups in the State were invited to join an advisory committee. But they soon found that they were not being listened to — that the Masters knew better, and the course materials must reflect this bias. Of course, these complaints would flow from these branches of the Dreaming Tree to the twigs and kids would soon learn that the projected course was just another 'whitewash'.

Still, given the diversity of Indigenous communities and cultures, plus the underlying interconnection of Us Mob, the planning of an Indigenous course is difficult, but I feel there should be something other than an amassing of facts from Master texts of anthropology, social science and history structured by modish theories of curriculum development. In 1993, as part of a new Indigenous Studies course, the Western Australian Department of Education published the first volume of a projected trilogy of textbooks, *In the Beginning: A Perspective on Traditional Aboriginal Societies*. This book was compiled by Trevor K. Jacob and Robert Fleming, two Masters who, with the best of intentions, put together a volume which was received with unease by Indigenous people, though it is one of the more sensitive publications I have seen and is encyclopaedic in its coverage of Aboriginal communities and cultures; but then I too read the work with increasing unease. An initial concern was the use in the contents page of the personal pronoun 'our' when it is not the work of Indigenous people. Furthermore, although the present tense is used in the contents page, in the text itself the past tense is extensively used, so that we get the impression that much of the culture and the ways of ordering our communities are things of the past, which for Us Mobs in Western Australia is simply not the case. Even though there is an apology for this in the preface, one must still question why the use of the past tense was condoned when the so-called 'traditional' is far from belonging to the past.

For instance, the authors state that in part of north-east Arnhem Land, 'almost all things were divided into one or two categories: Dhuwa or Yirritja', instead of '*are* divided'. These divisions are not of a dead past, but still determine the social structure of Arnhem Land. Duwa and Yirritja are there to order not only Yolngu society but the whole universe, and will continue on into the indefinite future. Thus, what we are being presented with is a Master plan which will slot nicely into the curriculum — and give children the impression that Indigenous cultures and our ways of ordering our communities and the world are now of the past and have no relevance to the present and the future. My reservations about this volume have been supported by other Aboriginal communities who have rejected it on similar grounds, but as so much money and time has been put into its production it is unlikely that the objections will be heeded and an Indigenous work commissioned in its stead.

It has to be understood that the Indigenous education system is personal, not generalised, with information transmitted by experience and by being part of the Dreaming Tree of life and death. Thus in *My People's Life*, by Jack Mirritj — written in 1972 — we learn more about Yolngu life and culture from a Yolngu person than in this glossy production by the Western Australian Department of Education. It is true that from *In the Beginning* we may gain what is often termed 'objective' information, but this has been gathered from written anthropological sources, from those who are considered the expert Masters of Us Mob.

This reliance on the expert Master is evident from the outset of *In the Beginning*. He is the objective father explaining his children to his children. Thus our 'beliefs', and later our 'ideology', are opposed to 'scientific ideas' and 'theories', and there is no mention that 'scientific theories' may be as much a matter of ideology and opinion as any other system of thought. It is this ideology of science which is used to explain Indigenality — that is, if we grant that anthropology and archaeology are sciences — as if it was the only 'true' discourse. For instance, a chapter on 'Our Beliefs – Pervading All' does not refer to Indigenous beliefs at all but to the 'scientific' explanation of these beliefs, while once again the pronoun 'our' is used ideologically in that it does not refer to Us Mob at all, but to the Masters, the compilers of the text. This is a quasi-objectivity which does not pertain to Indigenality but to the discourse of anthropology and archaeology, to the discourse of the Masters.

Although the Australian education system supposedly supports innovation, the proposed Indigenous Studies course for schools in Western Australia simply uses existing curriculum models in the form of Master structures to order and classify Indigenality. No attempt is made to develop a holistic approach or any recourse made to Indigenous methods of categorisation, except in the sections on kinship, and even then kin sections are given as abstract categories and not as family groupings which extend beyond humanity to affirm a universal vision in which everything is simply 'family'.

As *In the Beginning* is a textbook, I would expect any indigenous educational methods would be emphasised, but there is nothing at all about them as such, although in the section titled 'A Lifetime of Experiences' much is made of the so-called 'initiation process'. It is not said, however, that this was a period of strictly imparted formal education and that the so-called initiation rites were used to drive the lessons home and were in the nature of exams.

The educational process in Indigenous communities is a system in which knowledge is passed from the experience and maturity of elders and adults to young people and children. This still happens, as any Indigenous source makes clear, and is a method which we are striving to maintain and strengthen. Our educational methods came under attack from the start by the Masters, who deliberately cut off the young twigs from our Dreaming Tree. Children were taken from us and thrust into the Master's system, but those who managed to stay with their families continued to receive an Indigenous education. Our culture and customs are best learnt not in the formal structure of the Master's schools but within our family groupings, and it is up to the mature adults of our communities to ensure that what should and must be passed on is indeed passed on.

However, there is no way of avoiding the Master's knowledge or ignoring its all-pervasive influence. With the increasing colonisation of Indigenous communities and the need to come to grips with the Master's technology and structures of power, a reverse flow of knowledge has occurred from the twigs of our tree back to the branches and even the trunk. These days the young often know more than their parents and grandparents, their uncles and aunts, about the non-Indigenous world, and this creates a conflict between generations which has yet to be resolved.

In the Beginning ends, as it were, with what are called 'Timelines', together with a huge Master bibliography. There are six such timelines: Aboriginal Cultures, Earth, Human Evolution, Technology, World Societies, and Geological Divisions. These are laid out in a linear timescale which gives the impression of being 'scientific', but in fact they are merely a juxtapositioning of various 'events' which western civilisation considers to be of the utmost importance and which are based on a simplified evolutionary theory. There is no common scale, although the timelines invite comparison, and Aboriginal culture is a blank filled in with the datings of archaeology and obscure 'facts' such as the extinction of the Tasmanian Tiger on the Australian mainland. It ends with 1788 and the invasion, called European settlement at Sydney Cove, with the implication being that Aboriginal culture ended there and then.

The Earth timeline begins at 4,600 million BC with the so-called 'big bang' theory (which has been criticised as a male ideological construct, though not here) and evolves nicely along to 10,000 BC when Tasmania separated from the mainland. Human evolution begins around 4 million BC with the earliest hominids and ends in 60,000 BC with the first scientific evidence of people living in Australia. The Technology timeline begins at 600,000 BC with the use of fire, and includes such things as people migrating to Australia on rafts in 80,000 BC — thankfully with a question mark — rock engravings, cave paintings and Marco Polo travelling to China, to end with Yuri Gagarin's orbit of Earth in 1961. The World Societies timeline begins at 8,500 BC with the domestication of animals, which is quite an interesting development which we might query as a starting point, and there follows a mishmash of things and events and people which ends in 1948 with the foundation of the nation of Israel. I do not understand the ideas behind these classifications, or the theory, if there is one, which mentions the first Crusade and Genghis Khan, the Dutchman Jansz meeting Aborigines in 1606, and in 300 AD mathematics, using decimals and zero, evolving in the Middle East. Geology, a 'real' science, timelines along from before 600 million years until today. It is divided into four eras — Protozoic (Pre-Life), Palaeozoic (Ancient Life), Mesozoic (Middle Life) and Cainozoic (Modern Life).

So end the Timelines which purportedly, though I might be missing something, will give the students of an Indigenous studies course the important facts of existence, minus the Buddha and, I think, Japan. Human and non-human process is laid out for us to contemplate, but what this has to do with the Indigenous people of Australia, who rate only a few honourable mentions, I do not know. I do know, however, that the rest of the Indigenous people of the world have been written out of human existence.

Indigenous people and their communities do not rate a mention. They have been wiped out of existence; they don't have human societies. They are the untermenschen of the world, the underlings unable to reach into history.

All in all, *In the Beginning* was an expensive waste of resources, as it has now been scrapped. My criticism of this volume and hence the whole projected Aboriginal Studies course in Western Australia is closely paralleled by a draft paper put out by the National Aborigines and Torres Strait Islander Studies Project, *Towards a National Philosophy and Guidelines for Aboriginal and Torres Strait Islander Studies, K12*, which stresses:

> The study of Aboriginal and Torres Strait Islander cultures and societies provides:
>
> • an avenue for understanding the values, attitudes, customs, beliefs and behaviours of a post-Cook society through identifying the features of a pre-Cook society and tracing their change during periods of exposure with other cultures and Government policies;
>
> • insights on important values, attitudes, customs, beliefs and behaviours of Aboriginal and Torres Strait Islander people and how these, combined with past events, have shaped current philosophy.

The emphasis here is on Indigenality and a development from Indigenous culture and societies, rather than an interpretation from the outside — and this emphasis is supported by the Coolangatta Statement on Indigenous Rights in Education, presented at the World Indigenous People's Conference on Education held in Wollongong in 1993.

Of course, it is easy to criticise the work of others without being able to offer any alternative. But as some sort of general counter-model for Aboriginal studies courses, I quote the work of Kevin Keeffe in what are called 'remote Aboriginal communities', although it must be said that owing to their very diversity solutions which are appropriate for one community may not be so for another. However, by discussing different ways of framing courses of Indigenous studies, we will hopefully be able to come up with one which fulfils its purpose as it should.

Kevin Keeffe was a Research Fellow in the Curriculum Development Unit of the Australian Institute of Aboriginal Studies (AIAS) and is well aware of the wide variation in systems, schools, year levels and attainments when framing potential curricula, as well as the diversity of Aboriginal communities and cultures. But a major aim of the AIAS research fellowship has been to describe and analyse efforts at local curriculum development in remote communities. This is in line with the National Aboriginal Education Committee's 1985 call that education for Indigenous people should recognise and build upon Indigenous culture and identity, taking into account Aboriginal ways of knowing and understanding while emphasising the importance of the growth of the person as a whole.

In March 1987, in conjunction with a group of Indigenous (Pinupi) teachers, Keeffe set out to explore Pinupi ideas about personal development and the school curriculum. Their school is at Kintore, or Walungurru, on the Northern Territory and Western Australian border, and was established in 1982 as an outstation school, following the return of Pinupi people to their own country after several decades of institutionalisation at Haast Bluff and Papunya.

The teachers are clearly ideologically committed, in that they recognise the intrinsic connection between school and community. They believe Walungurra school is part of Walungurra community and must be strengthened in order to consolidate Pinupi culture through the education of a child as a whole person. Unlike other curriculum developments, this springs from Indigenous initiatives. If it fails, blame cannot be laid on the *Walypella* (whitefella), and if it succeeds it is because of the strength of Pinupi culture.

Indigenous Studies were given the Pinupi word *Yanangu*, and from the outset differed from programs formulated by the West Australian Department of Education in its emphasis upon the use of the vernacular language. The cultural importance of language is clearly recognised by many Indigenous organisations, reflected in their efforts to find an Indigenous name for themselves. So the Pinupi teachers call Indigenous Studies *Yanangu*, which is defined in the Pinupi/Luritja dictionary as: 'People, body. Used of the body of other animals and objects. Used to contrast reality with unreal situations. v. *rringu*, to become a person, to be born.'

The word has been extended further to refer to 'Indigenous person', and can also be used to describe an initiated or adult member of society. In this sense, the significance of the term *Yanangu* for social maturity is central, especially as regards Pinupi concepts of the person. The word is in use throughout the western desert region with different dialectal pronunciation, but the complex of meanings associated with the word may be summarised as: 'Indigenous person, the people, the body, the real'.

The Pinupi teachers regard the complex of meanings of *Yanangu* as the essence of the educational process. They say that the experience of attending schools where their concept of the 'whole' person is disregarded can be painful and even traumatic, as the students' ideas about themselves and their personalities do not correlate with those of the school, and they become overwhelmed by a sense of *kunta* — shame, embarrassment, alienation — something which in my opinion happens to Indigenous youngsters all over Australia. It is worth noting that the teaching of conventional Indigenous studies to Indigenous students may also invoke such *kunta*. Instead of relating positively to the subject, they feel alienated and ashamed of themselves. Care must therefore be taken when drawing up these courses to ensure that they do not cause such unnecessary stress.

One way to structure a course might be first to distinguish clearly between what Indigenous people see as *Yanangu* ideas from *Walypella* ideas and then give due weight to both approaches in the final product. This would greatly help to break down such categories as 'traditional' and 'non-traditional', although in a properly constructed course the emphasis on the particular material to be studied could vary from community to community.

The Pinupi teachers selected a number of key concepts from *Yanangu*, or Indigenous culture. These were *ngurra* (place, camp, country, land); *waarrkaku* (work); *nintirrinytjaku* (to learn, become knowledgeable); *mayi* (plant food); *mani* (money); *kulintjaku* (to hear, to listen, to think); *walytja* (family, relations, one's own); *wilinyi yankupayi* (to go out in bush for food); *ngankari* (medicine man); *pikarrinyi* (fighting); *wankanytjaku* (to talk); *tjintu* (sun, days of the week); *pira* (moon, month); *kapi nintintjaku* (to learn where water can be found);

puutjingka (in the bush, all Indigenous business); *tulku* (things from the dreaming, songs, etc.); *kanyintjaku* (to have, hold and look after); *palypirrpa* (cards); *tjaatji* (church); *waala* (house); *tjurratja* (sweet bush plants, wine); *mingkulpa* (bush tobacco); *mutakayi* (cars).

It would be interesting to compare a corresponding list from urban Indigenous persons to see how similar or different it is. If we regard culture as a dynamic rather than a static process, it will be obvious that quite a few *Walypella* ideas and practices have been assimilated into *Yanangu* and become part of Pinupi, though this in no way detracts from the Indigenality of their culture. Far from being absorbed by a dominant culture and taking on its attributes, what has happened is that *Yanangu* has absorbed certain aspects of the dominant culture and made them Indigenous. This is how any culture works, not by remaining static and allowing itself to be destroyed, but by an endless process of adaptation and incorporation of new ideas. If this is not understood, then Indigenous cultures will be analysed according to their supposed degrees of purity or contamination, when in fact they are merely in a process of continuous change in response to the circumstances around them. This only underlines the fact that when Indigenous culture is excluded from curriculum development, schools will always be alien institutions in which students cannot identify with the choices offered them and we are back in the process of assimilation where Indigenous people must learn the alien methods of control in order to resist them.

It might be of interest to examine the items of *Walypella* identified by the Pinupi teachers as things which they think are of importance and with which many Aborigines collide. These are:

school, meeting, holidays, time, houses, shopping, money, budgets, clothes, education, bank, insurance, birthdays, parties, mining, cleanliness, washing machines, air conditioners, church, rent, power, telephone, alcohol, cigarettes, family, friends, sunburn, travelling, travel allowance, aeroplanes. As can be seen, many of them are common to both the *Yanangu* and *Walypella* worlds and it is these common aspects which might help to determine the material to be included in an Indigenous Studies course which would not be off-putting to Indigenous students.

An appropriate course must be designed to bridge the gap between the culture of the students and that of the school. Most, if not all, white students would be perfectly familiar with the timelines given in the course devised by the Western Australian Department of Education, as the conceptual framework involved comes directly from their culture. In the case of Indigenous students, this quite likely would not be the case, and both the items in the timelines and the content of the course itself would be greeted with suspicion. Course development is often based on processes of centralised, efficiency-oriented decision making with the emphasis on the imposition of selected knowledge, skills and values in a framework which is often an old model refashioned to fit the new knowledge. Little attention is played to the ideological and even political factors which influence the final shape of the program. Australian schools are embedded in a Western middle-class cultural tradition, emphasising not only particular ways of doing things and particular concepts, but also a particular structure. The subordination of education to this ideology often results in the alienation of students who come from a different class and society. It is significant that this is the effect which the projected Western Australian course has had on some Indigenous people. This indicates that if more thought had gone into the project in the first place to lessen the chance of this alienation occurring, there would not have been such an unnecessary waste of resources. In regard to the structuring of an Indigenous Studies course, the input of Indigenous people is essential.

FURTHER READING

Bourke, C. and E., and Edwards, Bill, *Aboriginal Australia: An Introductory Reader in Aboriginal Studies*. Brisbane, University of Queensland Press, 1994.

Deakin University, *Aboriginal Pedagogy: Aboriginal Teachers Speak Out*. Melbourne, Deakin University Press, 1991.

Fesl, E.M.D., *Conned*. Brisbane, University of Queensland Press, 1993.

Harris, S., *Two Way Aboriginal Schooling, Education and Cultural Survival*. Canberra, Aboriginal Studies Press, 1990.

House of Representatives Select Committee on Aboriginal Education, *Aboriginal Education*. Canberra, Australian Government Publishing Service, 1985.

Jacob, T. K. and Fleming, R., *In the Beginning, A Perspective on Traditional Aboriginal Societies*. Perth, Department of Education, 1993.

Keeffe, K., 'Curriculum development in Aboriginal studies: a Yanangu case study,' *Australian Aboriginal Studies*, 1, 1989.

Mirritj, Jack, *My People's Life*. Millingimbi, Literature Production Centre, 1972.

OUR HEALTH
Lecture 8

IT IS SAID THAT THE HEALTH OF US MOB DEPENDS ON THE health of our land, that if the land suffers, so do we. Thus if sacred sites are destroyed, if the Dreaming tracks of our ancestors are severed, it affects our bodies. For the Indigenous person, life and land are intimately connected, and if the land is harmed so is the person. Over the last two hundred years so much of the land of Australia has suffered, so many of our sacred sites have been desecrated, that the health of Indigenous people is in as bad a way as the land. If the Indigenous people are to regain their health, their countries must regain their health. Tending and caring for the land is tending and caring for not only humans but all that lives, and when the land is exploited and ruined, so are the humans, the fauna and flora.

It is not only the degradation of the land which affects the health of Us Mob, but also the politics of the country, the control exercised over Indigenous people and the fostering of programs in which they have little say, especially at the grassroots level. It is the lack of power, the feeling of powerlessness, the overall direction of Indigenous affairs in Australia which also affect the health of the people. It is the constant struggle and battle to keep a place on the land and to feel that our place is secure that causes ill-health. It is the all-pervasive racism that strikes us almost each and every day, unless we can retreat to a homeland. Indigenous health is too often considered on only a material level. Expensive health programs are foisted on us, but the health of our souls is ignored. Recently, on the gold fields of Western Australia, the Indigenous people there were dying like flies. The number of deaths was so alarming that the media took up the story and concern was expressed by the government, who stepped in to create health programs on the typical western model. Indigenality, except for the employing of Indigenous persons, was not taken into account. The many deaths of Indigenous persons were seen as a 'health problem' to be solved by conventional health means. What was not considered was the lack of any capacity for the people to gain control of their lives. Those affected were essentially a traditional people living close to their roots, but Kalgoorlie is noted for its complete lack of regard for the land and for its pernicious racism. Land and the riches it contained were there to be exploited, the Indigenous people to be kept as far as possible from the *Wadjelas* living there. Unwanted, unneeded and unaccepted, seeing their very earth being excavated beneath their feet, is it any wonder that many of them simply gave up the struggle?

It has only been through the efforts of the people themselves and the help of a few sympathetic white doctors that a certain degree of Indigenisation has occurred in the area of health, which is jealously guarded by the Master's medical personnel. The Aboriginal Medical Service (AMS) was one of the first resource organisations to be formed by members of Indigenous communities as an expression of their determination to manage their own affairs. It took shape in the early 1970s as a result of the adverse experiences of Indigenous persons when they came into contact with the mainstream health system.

Early participants in the establishment of the first Indigenous community health clinic, out of which the AMS grew, were Gordon Briscoe, Shirley Smith (Mum Shirl), Professor Fred Hollows, Ross McKenna (a legal aid officer), Eddie Newman and John Russell. This was a storefront medical clinic in Redfern to which, after it had been in operation for a year, the Government gave a small grant to pay the salary of a full-time doctor. The Redfern clinic was the model for Indigenous health services which began to spring up across the country, although mainly confined to the larger concentrations of Indigenous populations in the cities and towns.

In 1971 the New South Wales Health Commission decided that it had to take some form of positive action in regard to Aboriginal health and employed an Indigenous person, Liz Doolan, as a health worker in Moree. It also established an Aboriginal Health Section and created three positions, moving in a non-Indigenous male clerk to fill one of them. His job was to order equipment for community health nurses who were beginning to be employed to cater for the needs of Indigenous communities. Simultaneously, the new Aboriginal Medical Service began to make field trips. Doctors, nurses and Indigenous liaison personnel travelled around the State, bringing medical care to communities and to Indigenous families in their own houses.

With the appointment of community nurses and Indigenous health workers, conflict arose over the respective roles of the Health Commission and the AMS. There was concern that they would in effect provide duplicate services, but what was overlooked was that many Indigenous persons preferred to deal with medical personnel in their own territory. Moreover, the AMS could put doctors directly into the field, while the Health Commission could not directly employ doctors to do community work, relying instead on nurses and health workers. But as a government agency, the Commission was the preferred body for other government bodies to work with and to fund. Like attracted like, and the Commission received the bulk of the funding via an Aboriginal health allocation from the Federal government. By contrast, like many other Indigenous-controlled organisations, the AMS was poorly funded. Again, the Federal government used the State government apparatus to inspect and approve AMS projects before funding them. The existence of two different services — one self-managed Indigenous organisation responsive to community needs and the other a fully funded government institution — meant that any long-term planning by the AMS around the State was thwarted. The AMS was encouraging communities with significant Indigenous populations to establish their own community-controlled health centres, but there were many small communities which did not warrant a full-time doctor and these were poorly serviced. It has only been recently that any

Indigenous medical service has acquired the resources to adequately service the medical needs of a State. This is the Victorian Medical Service, which is based in a fully equipped medical clinic housed in a large building in Melbourne. Although this might be seen as an example of how Indigenous medical services might expand into State-wide operations this is not so, for with the exception of Tasmania, the other States are simply too big for main services to be provided from a single locality, and Indigenous medical services must remain decentralised out of necessity. The Victorian Medical Service from its Melbourne urban base was able to provide specialist services, and thus was at last fulfilling the objectives of the first Indigenous-controlled health organisation in Redfern.

With its close community ties, the AMS knew that there was a problem in dental health among the Indigenous people of New South Wales. The change of diet from natural bush foods to a high-starch and sugar diet, which were once the main staples of government rations, had continued into the post-mission and settlement period. Indigenous people, often a long way from the nearest town and in no position to visit the local dentist regularly, were suffering. As a consequence many middle-aged and older persons simply lacked sufficient teeth to ensure ordinary food consumption, and many younger ones suffered from decaying teeth which became sources of infection.

The AMS wanted to equip a dental van to travel around the New South Wales countryside. The plan was for the van to visit Indigenous communities, treat major problems and do some preventative education, and also to build a bridge, if possible, between the dentist travelling with the van and the local dental services. The State Health Commission decided that it could do a better job. It obtained funds from the Department of Aboriginal Affairs also to equip a van and put it on the road, but it was unable to attract dentists to work in the vehicle and was eventually forced to hand its operation over to the AMS.

The reasons why the AMS was more successful than its Government counterpart were that they could directly employ doctors and dentists to work in the field, and that they got better value for each dollar spent on staff because the people employed were attracted by the ideology and challenge of the service rather than high salaries and professional advancement.

Another area of conflict between the AMS and the Government service was ideological differences regarding the role of the latter. The State Government's Indigenous health programs and the AMS itself were similarly funded from the special Federal government allocation for Indigenous people. The AMS felt that this special funding should be spent on developing projects and not given to a State Government department to provide ordinary services which were the responsibility of the State. It argued that a portion of all State moneys should be spent on Indigenous communities, as they were permanent residents of that State, but the New South Wales Government refused to contribute any money towards services for Indigenous communities which had to rely on the Federal Government handout instead.

By 1982 the Government's Aboriginal Health Section had a complement of 104 staff located around the State, thirteen of them in head office. In January 1983 the then Minister, Laurie Brereton, abolished the section, leaving the Sydney office with only two 'Indigenous-specific' positions, which were not filled by Indigenous persons but by other staff whose responsibilities were to look after

Indigenous health. By contrast, the AMS had developed a range of programs, such as diabetes screening clinics, weight-control programs and care services for elderly Indigenous persons. This last project was hampered by complex financial arrangements requiring a mass of forms and applications to be filled in for three different funding bodies. In spite of this and other difficulties, the Indigenous health services in Redfern and in other centres continued to expand their programs.

These health services, like other Indigenous resource agencies, employ a holistic approach based on the Indigenous approach to life and community, which is one of caring and sharing flowing from a complex web of personal and social relationships. This means that health cannot be separated from other issues like housing, employment, education and even legal matters and politics.

This interrelatedness of health and all other Indigenous community concerns is of fundamental importance. Implicit in the subject of health is the question of general well-being. In the late 1970s the Department of Aboriginal Affairs decided to concentrate on improving housing for Indigenous people throughout Australia. With so many families living in shacks, car bodies and even under sheets of galvanised iron, there could be no objection to the DAA's policy direction. However, to implement this policy, it drained off funds from almost every other area, including health.

The provision of health services generates a certain amount of employment in Indigenous communities. Housing, however, was and still is of much greater benefit to the outside community in that it creates employment for non-Indigenous building contractors and tradesmen, as well as the purchase of huge quantities of materials from local businesses. For example, it has been estimated that over thirty per cent of the economy of the Northern Territory is directly reliant on Indigenous communities, and with any increase in Government funding to them there is a flow-on which benefits the entire local economy.

In regard to housing, the end product — an 'Aboriginal house' — is not made available to Indigenous families on the basis of need, but on their ability to pay. In many country areas, some Indigenous families have been lured away from reserves and missions to housing constructed for them in country towns, mostly by State housing departments with funds provided by the DAA. Indigenous families have been shifted from reserves into the nearby non-Indigenous townships. For a time it was thought that this was a deliberate policy to free up Aboriginal reserves so that they could be sold off. A problem with this population shift was that it also separated important Indigenous community members from their relatives, thus affecting the sense of community and individual well-being. This policy was deliberate and in the Indigenous settlement of Lake Tyers in Victoria, for example, houses were intentionally destroyed to prevent Kooris from moving back into them.

Apart from this, individual applications for occupancy of these houses were often submitted when one or more members of the family were employed. Many Indigenous persons, however, were in seasonal and short-term employment, so although there was a wage or wages coming in there was nothing like the financial security which comes from permanent work. Because of this, before long many of these families found themselves unable to pay their rent and were faced with eviction. Once evicted, they knew that their chances of being allocated another Housing Commission home were remote, so many hung on for as long as they could. Eventually, a number of these families were evicted and found themselves with nowhere to go. The reserve houses had either been bulldozed or occupied by other needy families, and so they made do with what they could find, such as wrecked car bodies. With this came health problems.

In other parts of Australia, the policy was for Indigenous people to be 'slowly' introduced to standard European housing. They received 'training housing', from which it was proposed that when they had become somewhat 'housebroken' they would move on to 'Stage Two housing', and finally to some sort of modified Housing Commission dwelling. This is still the case in Western Australia and the Northern Territory, with families continuing to work their way up the ladder. This plan saw the erection, at tremendous expense — from which, of course, the local non-Indigenous contractors benefited — of corrugated iron cells with concrete floors. No matter how large the family, they started off in one of these metal boxes. However, this may not be as bad as it sounds, for many Indigenous people still conducted most of their socialising out of doors, and thus to some extent they could adjust to them. Nonetheless, they were often so unsuitable that they took a fair toll of lives, since the previous Indigenous lifestyle had been more healthy than the one which involved living in such a 'house'.

Along with the drive for better housing, whatever the reasons, came a recognition of the need to improve Indigenous education and tackle such basic health concerns as hygiene. Unless

Indigenous people attained a higher level of education, they would forever be locked into low-paying and insecure employment, or no employment at all, unable even to pay rent or afford the necessities of life. Nor in regard to health would they be able to understand essential medical processes. Health and housing, especially in the western mode, involve an education in their use. There is no innate instinct which enables people automatically to understand the necessary culture involved in keeping up a house, and education is needed for such things as reading the dosage on a bottle of medicine, or even to believe in its efficacy. Without education, western medicine might remain a mystery, especially when illnesses arising from such things as a sedentary lifestyle and poor food habits acquired in mission days are outside the experience of the native doctor, or fail to respond to bush medicine.

However, good health is a prerequisite for benefiting from education. Students must be free from illness and have access to a sufficiently high standard of care to ensure that their bodies and minds are functioning properly, as well as an adequate diet. If poverty also prevents them from buying such things as school uniforms and other items they need, their academic performance will similarly suffer.

I well remember that when I was young I had bad eyes and had difficulty in seeing the classroom blackboard. To cope with this I had to try to put myself close to the board, or devise ways of working out for myself what was on it. What I did not do — which might reflect the alienation I felt from the schooling system — was to tell the teacher or any of the school authorities, or even get my eyes checked, as in those days there was no Indigenous health service in my home town. When Indigenous students have such difficulties in seeing or hearing or even interacting with other children, stereotyping often comes into play, and instead of realising that they may have physical or social problems the teacher merely puts it down to their Indigenality.

Thus poor health can result in a vicious circle of prejudice, alienation of the student and eventually trouble with the legal system, and so on. Of course, not all legal problems stem from bad health, but some do. The poor health of a mother has often provided the 'Welfare' with an excuse to intervene, to 'help' by taking her children into 'care'. Once children are caught up in the Welfare system they can be trapped on a path which leads from foster homes to more drastic correctional facilities, and on to an institutionalisation which affects the victim all through his or her life. Once started on this path, it is difficult to find another, and the journey might have begun purely because of ill-health which was not detected until too late.

Indigenous health services are in a similar position to the legal services in that there is a lack of a central coordinating body, and attempts to form one have floundered for a number of reasons. The National Aboriginal and Islander Health Organisation (NAIHO) was formed to facilitate greater cooperation between the services and channel expertise and material assistance to the weaker ones, as well as establishing branches in areas where they did not exist. It set about its tasks in an energetic fashion and was extremely democratic, making sure that all services and staff members knew exactly what was happening. Bruce McGuinness was the national coordinator, and leading Aboriginal activists such as the able organiser Denis Walker supported and worked for it.

Its ideological basis was 'community control', which involved among other things holding periodic seminars where the various services were located so that ongoing policy directions could be formulated by the communities themselves. The cost of such democracy was enormous and perhaps this was one of the reasons why NAIHO ultimately faltered. This is a constant problem for organisations endeavouring to play a national role, when the distances are vast, the costs immense and the funding haphazard.

NAIHO and the Victorian Aboriginal Health Service (VAHS) initiated a health workers' education program which proved extremely successful and became a model for similar programs set up by other services, including the Western Australian Aboriginal Health Service. It drew on other schemes such as the 'Barefoot Doctor' system in China to develop methods of its own. In line with its concept of community control it emphasised the need for the participation of Indigenous people in the design, development and delivery of health services, especially in the field of primary medical care, preventive and promotive services, and environmental health. Training and educating Indigenous health personnel to carry out these responsibilities had high priority.

The role of the Indigenous health worker, who is chosen by the community or family groups within it and who is trained to deliver basic primary medical care, had at that time no parallels within the existing health care systems in Victoria, or anywhere else in Australia. It is similar to that of the World Health Organisation's 'primary care worker' who in many developing countries provides the first contact with health care facilities and operates at a community level.

A 'new model' two-tiered scheme was proposed around this time for the delivery of Aboriginal health care. A 'basic unit' consisting of full-time Indigenous staff, augmented by part-time workers chosen by family groups, would be based at community-controlled health cooperatives and provided with basic medical supplies and equipment, while transport facilities would be made available for patients through the cooperatives. At a second level, an 'extended unit', based on the VAHS model, would operate with added facilities for training Aboriginal health workers.

I was a tutor at the Aboriginal Health Training Course in Melbourne in 1984 and I was impressed by how keen the students were to learn. The course, of eighteen weeks' duration for a class of thirty, was the major component of a community organisation series and had been conceived and designed by Indigenous people who had experience in health and education, in consultation with the Aboriginal community and medical professionals, under the overall guidance of the Victorian Health Service. The VAHS liaised with leading medical institutions in Melbourne to ensure that the methods were professionally correct and to find venues for field-work for the students.

The training program adopted a holistic approach, centring on health, education and employment. Its main premise was that health problems were related to wider economic, political and cultural problems. Health was seen as only one aspect of the overall development of the community. Rather than emphasising the acquisition of sophisticated high-quality medical skills for community treatment, it was felt that priority should be placed on using health as a way of motivating community members to improve their standard of living and quality of life through better nutrition, water supply, housing, education and transport, as well as tackling issues like permanent employment, the need for regular income and ultimately broader political questions. Nor could physical health be separated from mental and social health. The total well-being of the person and his or her community was the goal, with the recognition that the well-being of the community depended on that of the individual. Community involvement was necessary as it helped the community to regain control of its own destiny.

The course also included a community-based health program and a health workers' education program. The former was based on the principle that the community had to be responsible for its own general health as well as that of each individual, and to do this it had to tap its own resources — human, material, professional and traditional. Whereas previously health care had been centred only on taking care of sick individuals, this was now extended to include the family and the whole community. As a means of encouraging this approach the VAHS conducted a series of seminars in communities with the aim of setting up a Health Consultative Group in each community which would be responsible for appointing a suitable Aboriginal health worker, listing the community's health priorities and assisting the health worker to overcome these needs.

The health workers' education program was arranged to introduce students to a range of health problems likely to be found in communities and to teach them how to cope with the problems by treatment, coordination with existing health and social services and referral, how to understand the cause of such problems, devise ways of preventing them and analyse the personal, social and political aspects of community health.

The health workers' program reflected the same concerns that had led to the setting up of most Indigenous resource agencies. As regards medical services, these were that the traditional western health service model practised in Australia had been shown to be inadequate to meet the needs and demands of Indigenous persons in urban and rural areas. At that time existing public services made little effort to adapt to the needs of Indigenous persons, who found these services difficult to use, fragmented, elitist and costly. Complicated medical services, especially hospitals, are often alien and impersonal institutions, and not just to Indigenous people. Australian health services are geared to the relatively better-off and in some respects are organised more for the convenience of their professional staff than for the needs of the patients. For these reasons, Indigenous people tend to avoid using the services as much as possible, and this is a major factor in our continuing poor state of health.

The state of the health of the family is acknowledged to be very important in the general well-being of Indigenous society, so that those whose duty it is to promote health and prevent disease occupy key roles in the community. There is no doubt that, given the way respective Aboriginal communities have responded to a recent Health Commission inquiry into Indigenous health, the training of health workers is a high priority. It must not be forgotten that the whole program of NAIHO and the VAHS was devised with Aboriginal communities in mind, and it proved successful because of community support.

In many ways, the Victorian Aboriginal Health Service may be seen as an example of how an Indigenous resource organisation can succeed by taking a holistic approach to the problems with which it is confronted, rather than treating them as a set of isolated or unconnected phenomena. Following the lead of NAIHO, the VAHS operates from a position of community control, which ensures a number of checks and balances guaranteeing that such an organisation works for the good of the community it is answerable to. This has certainly worked for the good for the Koori community in Victoria, which now has a well-organised and well-equipped health service responsive to the people's needs.

Perhaps just as importantly, the Victorian Koori community has an educational program which has succeeded much more than similar programs run by non-Indigenous institutions. This is being carried out by a school bearing the Indigenous name *Koori Kollej*, which has now established itself and is proving popular among Indigenous students. It is not that the educational process has been made easier, but that it has been de-alienated and made Indigenous, as have health services for Kooris in Victoria.

FURTHER READING

Hawke, S. and Gallagher, M., *Noonkanbah: Whose Land, Whose Law?* Fremantle, Arts Centre Press, 1989.

Nathan, Pam and Japanangka, *Health Business*. Melbourne, Heinemann, 1983.

Saggers, Sherry and Gray, Dennis, *Aboriginal Health and Society*. Sydney, Allen & Unwin, 1991.

Seeing and Reading Us Mob
Lecture 9

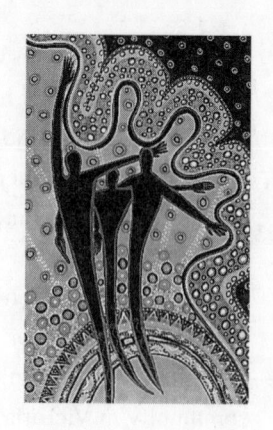

How are Us Mob portrayed in the media and how do people come to regard us from the images that are presented? Do they show us as part of this Australia, simply as people, or do they isolate us and sow discord and distrust? To many of Us Mob, the media do not seek to heal the wounds of yesterday and today, but too often re-open the wounds. Too many times they have produced programs and articles about Us Mobs which are patently untrue. Their methods and emphasis are often astray. Too often they refer to us as 'Blacks' or 'Aborigines' as if there were no differences in Us Mobs and our cultures, and even our environments and particular concerns. Too often the media are a simplifying mechanism, issuing a thin stream of so-called information often distorted and predigested for the consumer — pap for the masses, as it were.

Perhaps the problem with the media as viewed by Indigenous people is a particularised aspect of how the media construct and present their stories generally. Every group or class in Australia seems, sooner or later, to approach the various forms of the media with suspicion, or to learn how they are structured so as to use them for its own ends. From a naive position, people at first accept each form — press, radio or television — on its own terms, expecting it to be objective, or at least a reliable source of information. Then, when they learn otherwise, they think that by merely 'reforming' the media everything will be all right and that these streams of information will function objectively, almost like computers, so that the way in which the media structure information is left alone. So how should we approach the different genres of media production? Should our starting point be media ownership, or should it be the genres themselves — how news, for example, is framed, how programs are structured, how character devices are employed? The medium is the message, as much as the contents framed for our consumption.

What we face with the different mediums of information, so-called, is a massive restructuring of the representation of realities, not with objective information flows. A program is successful not because of its 'truth' content but how it has been structured for mass appeal. It might seem cynical or overly pessimistic to argue that no really acceptable portrayal of Indigenous people is possible when the mechanisms of media production ensure that images and events are presented in certain ways, and that these ways are paramount in determining how Indigenous people are seen and accepted by the viewers or readers of such mediums of so-called information. In fact, to gain information it may be better to find alternative sources outside the mass media rather than continuing to discuss and argue over what they present, especially when there is such a paucity of information which must be structured to give the greatest possible enjoyment to the maximum number of consumers, inevitably resulting in stereotyping to some degree or other. An instant recognition of the representation is aimed for, and this has little bearing on the 'truth' of the representation. What is necessary is to distinguish between the representation of the image and the image the reader or viewer receives. The transmitter and receiver should be on a similar wavelength, so that the closer the wavelengths the clearer the image received.

The Indigenous person who aspires to enter the media, to use one or other of their organs of representation, is faced with a dilemma. This is how to use the media efficiently, how to get a point across, or to establish an Indigenous presence in a non-Indigenous world which has been structured in certain ways, and one in which people are educated to present ideas and images in certain ways. In the case of television, it is structured by a certain use of time, by the mechanisms of the camera, by voice presentation, by lighting and so on, as well as by an ideology of representation which is there to be bought by the highest bidder. Prime time is not Indigenous time, and when a program such as *Blackout* is scheduled close to prime time on the national network, it presents Indigenous people according to the dictates of a centralised regime located in Sydney. The implication is that 'This is what is happening in Black Australia', and the emphasis is on the sameness of Indigenous people, rather than on acknowledged differences, and the political is eschewed for the topical. Sport is good, art is good, but any 'real' news or 'real' facts are eschewed, and a self-consciousness is engendered which reminds me of the old Australian newsreels of assimilationist days.

Koori people have agitated for a long time against being depicted in stereotypes like that of the Aboriginal warrior standing on one leg and clutching a womera and spear, an image which can still be seen in some advertisements, and which stems back to notions of the noble savage. They want the emphasis to shift from such scenes as drunkenness or violence, or shots of people sitting in the dust in the middle of a desert, to Kooris walking the streets of cities and doing their thing. Even when this happens, the aim sometimes seems to be to show the similarity of lifestyle of dark and white city dwellers, but the camera angles must be tightened to hide those Indigenous lifestyles which do not fit into this picture — lifestyles which are not close to the European, but as far away as the man standing on one leg. The problem seems to be that there is a gap between the urbanised Koori and the other more rural groups. While we are fighting for the differences between cultures to be recognised, perhaps some mediation is required, for, after all, many of Us Mob are not city folk and what is more do not want to be simply dark Australians.

Perhaps such a mediator might be the actor Burnum Burnum, who in his work portrays Indigenous people who have adjusted to both worlds. Thus he avoids both extremes, in a way which is unfortunately not found on the Special Broadcasting Service (SBS) television channel which is dedicated to presenting multiculturalism, though the effect of its representation of persons from other cultures is to place them in a uniformly bland European context. Multiculturalism in the Australian media means showing the various cultures engaging in the Australian way of life. The faces appearing before us are fine examples of the Australian Dream succeeding, of a multi-culturalism shorn of all nasty foreign habits from clitoridectomy to fanaticism. On a program such as 'Vox Populi' we meet up with nice ethnics. One of the presenters of 'Vox Populi' is Rhoda Roberts, a Koori actor from Sydney, who after enduring many career changes as Indigenous persons often do, has found a niche in TV on SBS. Along with other ethnics, she has acquired the correct accent — high British — and as she is light-skinned and has an English name, it is doubtful that many viewers identify her as a Koori, though she is definitely 'ethnic'. She is one aspect of the acceptable face of Indigenality. It is an Indigenality which is not evident, but then, that is the SBS way of ethnic representation, and the media's way of striving for an objectivity of representation which is non-threatening and non-confrontational.

On the other hand, there are other representations in the commercial media which do present an aggressive, confrontational image, of stirrers and troublemakers, and thus not good Australians. In fact, they are given media time in order to show the stereotypes they are, and also to show that they are not representative of the more accommodating stereotypes seen in simplistic public interest programs. The media, especially in Australia, rely on a straightforward construction of characters which leads to programs being criticised rather than the media as such, or to the discussion of issues being contained to self-righteous anger or bland commonsense with any theoretical or controversial ideas being almost totally ignored. I have never seen, for example, a Marxist analysis on Australian television, whereas in England I saw one on Channel Four, a very welcome change from the seemingly ideology-free discussions on Australian television. The mass media are based on accommodation and consensus. Their ideology is that of the status quo and what is attacked are those very things, people and events which disturb the status quo usually represented by the attitudes of the average Australian.

If Rhoda Roberts is the acceptable face of Koori Indigenality, what of the noble savage? The media often prefer representation of the Aborigine which is supposedly 'authentic', meaning being as black as possible, and as Other as possible. Many receivers of media images are not prepared to accept Indigenous persons being as assimilated as Rhoda Roberts appears to be. They want the 'real Aboriginal' and thus when Indigenous people are featured in news items the camera focuses on the most Indigenous face; that is, on the most Indigenous stereotype of the Other. This representation of the Other must be instantly recognisable by the viewers, or readers, as Indigenous. This is how the framing of images occurs in television. There must be instant recognition, otherwise the image will be lost in the cutting from shot to shot. This is similar to the roving camera at sports events, especially in cricket when it pans across the crowd to pick up a woman spectator. In Australian Rules football it is different, with fans being sought out who are instantly identifiable by their regalia, or an ethnic is shown to demonstrate that Australian Rules is truly an all-Australian game and even Vietnamese have fallen under its spell. Representation, as I have said, is ideology-laden, even down to a sex bias which is sometimes not immediately apparent because of the techniques used to present images of women as spontaneous and 'natural', whereas more often than not they are deliberately chosen and carefully composed.

It is strange — or perhaps not so strange — that the popular Indigenous actor Ernie Dingo has not been taken over and made a simple stereotype, but although he has on occasions been cast as the easily recognisable Indigenous person, he has generally managed to escape this fate. Perhaps this is because he is too articulate, too much aware of how he can be used, to allow himself to fit into a simple stereotype. He evades the stereotype by his talent, by being a person in his own right, and by being able to hold his own. He is nobody's Jacky but by switching from representation to representation he has not formed a solid 'personality' either to transmit or receive.

Ernie Dingo exists outside the the representation of the noble savage. I keep using the word 'representation' here because we must remain aware that what we are dealing with are representations, not realities, and in this process, especially on television, what is seen must be 'truer than true' and instantly recognisable. In other words, it must be stereotypical and, I would say, 'caricatural'. In this postmodern age, character or personality has become caricature, a prime example being Madonna, who is a composite of all that has gone before. In fact, she may be seen as an almost perfect example of this stereotyping, for we are never interested in discussing her worth as a singer, as an artist, but rather her worth as a personality. That is, she exists as a media event, and we accept her as this, as perhaps she does herself, for what is she after all but the result of a clever reading of how the media image is constructed.

My example of a similar but Indigenous stereotype is Burnum Burnum. He is instantly recognisable, dark-skinned, long-haired and long white-bearded, and usually in a suit which is nondescript enough so as not to take attention away from his face — for television is a framer of faces rather than of bodies — though Burnum Burnum can on occasion don his possum skin cloak if the need arises. With Burnum Burnum, the Aboriginal activist, the stirrer, the agitator, is removed to be replaced by a media image. The Other is presented as a tame Other, an Other in which you may read all those positive attributes you want Indigenous people to have without loss of their 'culture'. Thus all the dirt, all the misery, all the third-world conditions which are sometimes framed when you need a representation of the Indigenous person as victim, are removed and sanitised. Here is what the Indigenous person can be when he is restored his dignity. The Other is rendered non-threatening, though still a repository for the ancient wisdom which Indigenous peoples are supposed to have. The program 'Millennium', on SBS, was a fine example of just how 'noble' such a savage can be.

Representation on television is a conspiracy between transmitter and receiver to produce certain images with which both can be satisfied. There is a shift and displacement from a flow of information or any 'true' depiction of an objective reality to a stereotyping of images and characters which are given and read in certain ways, and placed in simplified stories or even series which may extend over some time. These events are composed and edited to elicit emotional responses, thus shifting or displacing reactions to the series of images themselves. Perhaps what is interesting is when two mutually exclusive representations such as police and Indigenous persons are used in the same sequence. How will we read them in the light of what we know of the police in Queensland and New South Wales, and of the Indigenous people after the Royal Commission into Aboriginal Deaths in Custody?

The police occupy an ambiguous place in Australian society. They are the thin blue line between society as a whole and the forces of darkness which threaten the Master and his possessions. I know that may read like a comic strip, but this is the level on which too often the media constructs their images. They, the police, are a necessary evil, the only ones allowed to go armed for the good of society, but because of their frontline position they may become contaminated. Indigenous people, in spite of the Rhoda Robertses and Burnum Burnums, share this ambiguity. They are members of a minority most likely to be incarcerated and they also embody the Other in all its otherness — violence, drunkenness and all the familiar negativities which lurk beneath all representations of Indigenous people. If this is indeed the way we are seen, it is but one step further to accept that we must be kept down, with force if necessary, and separated from the Master for his own security and well-being.

A few years ago, the ABC devised a simple but effective image to represent police and Indigenous people. The cap of a policeman, the symbol of his authority, was placed on the top of a police car with a flashing blue light. This was imposed upon an Aboriginal flag. The police car plus light plus cap evokes an emotional response, perhaps the feeling You Mob get when you are stopped by a police car for a traffic offence, and for a fleeting minute feel yourselves in the position of the criminal, or, as symbols are ambiguous, the relieved sensation you experience when the police come to your assistance. The Australian Indigenous flag is also a sign for many of Otherness, often seen by the media as a symbol of a resistance only held in check by a thin line of police constables. The police uniform partakes of the Australia flag with its subdued colours, against which is set the strong, and I could almost write 'anti', colours of the Indigenous flag, often called the Landrights Flag and thus a political symbol — red evoking blood, black a host of negative connotations, and yellow strong sunlight leading to cancer for sensitive white skins.

The event for which this image was composed was a TV story. In March 1992, an amateur video clip showing a charitable function in a country town in New South Wales was made by a police constable. When screened by the ABC it was greeted by viewers with outright revulsion. In the video clip, two policemen with blackened faces were shown with nooses around their necks, one declaring that he was Lloyd Boney and the other saying, 'I'm David Gundy'. These were two young Indigenous males. The first died in police custody and the second died at the hands of the police.

The following day the Prime Minister, Paul Keating, issued a statement calling on Australians to eliminate racism from the nation and condemning the police concerned for mocking the deaths of Aborigines in custody, adding that the episode should become 'a turning point in Australian attitudes to Aborigines'. Many other such comments were made condemning the video clip. The tone was one of 'outrage', outrage from 'decent' people over those considered racist and particularly the police, who it was declared must be educated out of their racism.

What is strange about this incident is that it happened only a few years ago, but now it is as if it never occurred. This again is how the media, and especially television, work. The flow of representations continues, but sooner or later the images are forgotten. For images to stay in our minds they must be shown again and again. Thus advertisements are repeated and repeated until they stick in the mind so much you may even dream them. News items, on the other hand, last only for a few fleeting moments before disappearing into the ether. For an image to make a permanent impact, paradoxically it must be instantly recognisable — in other words, a stereotype. So Burnum Burnum is instantly recognisable as an Indigenous person because he fulfils the necessary criteria — and perhaps so does the cap, the blue light, the top of the police car imposed on the Indigenous flag. As I've said, like Marshall McLuhan before me, the medium is the massage.

FURTHER READING

Bostock, Lester, *From the Dark Side: A Survey of the Portayal of Aborigines and Torres Strait Islanders on Commercial Television*. Sydney, Australian Broadcasting Authority, 1993.

Greenfield, Cathy and Williams, Peter, 'Bicentennial preliminaries: Aboriginal women, newspapers and the politics of culture', *Hecate*, 13 (2), 1987–8.

Hodge, B. and Mishra, V. *Dark Side of the Dream*. Sydney, Allen & Unwin, 1992.

Meadows, M. and Oldham, C., 'Racism and the Dominant Ideology', *Media Information Australia*, May, 1991 (60).

Media and Indigenous Australians Conference, *Discussion Papers, 15–17 February, 1993*. Brisbane, 1993.

Mickler, Steve, *Gambling on the First Race: A Comment on Racism and Talk-Back Radio — 6PR, the TAB and the WA Government*. Report commissioned and published by the Louis St John Johnson Memorial Trust Fund, Perth, 1992.

SELLING OUR CULTURE
Lecture 10

AUSTRALIAN INDIGENOUS CULTURE HAS BECOME INCREASINGLY well-known throughout the world, as the enthusiastic reception accorded Indigenous performers and artists overseas amply demonstrates. In its search for a national identity Australia too has come to appreciate our culture and its products. Our paintings adorn the walls of Australian embassies throughout the world and there are art galleries run by Australians in cities such as Amsterdam and Paris selling only our artworks. This expanding interest in our culture has another effect. Many tourists arrive in Australia wanting to visit Aboriginal communities. Tourism is a big money-spinner these days, and regions such as Queensland and the Northern Territory have begun featuring us and our culture. It is difficult to know if this is a good or bad thing for us.

The value of tourism is a debatable point. Some say that it leads to the wrecking of a culture, some that it preserves it, and others that people who get mixed up in it are living in two different worlds — that of the tourists for whom they put on a show and that of the community to which they return at the end of the day. But the main thing for us should be how we can use tourism, rather than letting it use us by turning our culture into a commodity for exploitation. It is to the credit of the Australian government that we have not been allowed to be completely exploited by the tourism industry and are still largely able to determine how and to what extent we should take part in it.

In an interesting article in the journal *Meanjin* a few years ago, Tim Rowse, who has lived and worked in Alice Springs, discussed the attitude of local Anangu people towards tourists. In 1985, the Commonwealth government transferred the title of the National Park which includes Uluru and Katatjuta to the traditional Indigenous owners, but under the terms of the agreement they had to immediately lease it back to the Australian National Parks and Wildlife Service. The conditions of the lease specified that they would be paid a percentage of the gate fees. A study of the living conditions of the Anangu people was conducted by non-Indigenous researchers, though under Indigenous control through such bodies as the Pitjantjatjara Council, the Central Land Council and the Mutitjulu community who live next to Uluru.

Rowse observes that the Anangu living in the region of the Uluru-Katatjulu National Park did not have the choice of accepting or rejecting tourism. There has been a huge increase in tourism to the area since the 1970s, but most of the industry is so tightly controlled that the Anangu have little input into what might prove a valuable source of income. In fact, when I visited Yulara, the resort complex, Uluru, the tourist attraction, and Mutitjulu, the Indigenous village, at the first two places Anangu people were most noticeable by their absence. But it was a different scene at Mutitjulu, where the most striking feature was the number of signs stressing privacy. It was obvious that tourists were not welcome in the village and on my visit the only non-Anangu there were community workers, or their visitors. Thus any influx of tourists appeared to be strictly controlled.

The Mutitjulu community had to earn its privacy by testing the terms of the leasing agreement, which proved that they were able to deny tourists access to that part of the park on which their village stands, and other small sensitive areas. This may not be such a restriction of the freedom of movement of tourists as it sounds, for at the time the whole system of management and environmental control in the National Park was being overhauled, with tourists being confined to certain areas. Previously they had used an area close to Mutitjulu and the Rock for camping and the Ininti store and a B.P. garage had been built there in 1972 to cater to their needs. Under the terms of the agreement and the administrative reorganisation, the motels and camping grounds were now transferred to Yulara, a site some distance from the base of the Rock but still near enough for tourists staying there to get a good view of it and Kutatjulu (the Olgas) eerily poking up on the horizon. With the removal of the rather unsightly camping grounds and buildings at the foot of the Rock, the monolith stood uncluttered as a truly majestic monument, much like other tourist attractions I have seen in other parts of the world. Tim Rowse does not discuss this management policy, but says that the proximity of Mutitjulu to the Rock is an example of the strength of the lease the Anangu had entered into, though it must be pointed out that the village is not nearly as close to the Rock as was the camping ground and certainly does not detract from the grandeur of the Rock.

Rowse claims that under the leasing agreement the Anangu-controlled company (Malpa Trading) owning the Ininti store and another company (Marulku) owning the Anangu arts and crafts outlet were 'given space at the new Ranger Station to sell refreshments, souvenirs and artefacts to tourists'. And he adds: 'By this spatial separation, Anangu further defined the Mutitjulu community living area as their enclave within the park.' This may be true, but I have no recollection of the Ranger Station, or of the businesses there, and as it is to Yulara that the tourist dollar goes it would have been good business to have the art and craft outlet there. In fact, alternative sources of income are becoming of increasing importance to Indigenous communities owing to the fact that the current high levels of government funding will not last forever, and if there is a drastic drop in such funding many communities will find themselves in dire straits. Thus, to ignore economics and leave business in the hands of non-Anangu is to leave the profits in their bank accounts, as well as control of the tourism industry in their hands.

In the report on the Anangu people's living conditions I mentioned previously, the researcher Jan Altman surveyed the Mutitjulu community's income and employment situation and concluded that the tourism industry only involved the Anangu indirectly. Very few people gained an income by selling goods or services personally to tourists (except perhaps casually) and Anangu investments in the tourism industry were managed and operated by non-Anangu. When Anangu were employed by Malpa Trading they preferred working at the Ininti Store which was seen more as a community facility, as was Malpa Trading, and only secondarily as a profitable tourism enterprise. Altman cautioned against this approach, owing to the fact that Malpa Trading as a community facility had to be subsidised by revenue from the gate receipts.

In regard to arts and crafts, a worker from the Marulka Company visited each Anangu camp in Pitjantjatjara country several times a year to collect products for the park shop. Most, if not all, of the craftspeople were on social service payments and engaged in craftwork to supplement their incomes, so that there was little pressure to maintain output. Of course this is an Anangu way of doing things, and possibly an Indigenous way as well, at least in the Northern Territory where most artefacts are produced in this manner. This manner of working to a great extent means that one is buying a quality, handmade product as against the machine-made. If production was organised to make as much as possible, then a different marketing apparatus would come into play. This seems to have happened in Queensland where machine-turned Indigenous artefacts are mass-produced for a large market extending from Sydney to Albany in Western Australia.

There is no escaping the fact that Indigenous people are mainly interested in tourism and tourists because of the profit motive. Tourism is essentially about money. Economics is the foundation of the tourism industry and it is to economists and their reports that governments pay heed when they discuss the viability of a tourism project. The tourism industry exists to service the needs of tourists, who are mainly interested in seeing and hearing things. In 1988, some of us put on a revue at the Belvoir Theatre in Sydney called *Not the 1988 Party* in which there was a skit about two American tourists who met up with a couple of Indigenous people. They came to Bennelong Point and their cameras began clicking. When they asked why it was called Bennelong Point, the answer came: 'It's bin a long time since Aborigines bin there.' The point is that tourists are all clicking cameras and the product must be packaged for them. Thus if the Anangu wish to take part in tourism all they have to do is become part of the package.

Some Indigenous people wish to learn to cope with it and turn a profit at the same time. Although Uluru in Anangu country is the premier tourist attraction of central Australia, the Arrenthe people, whose country lies on the southern and eastern side of Alice Springs, are eager to embrace tourism and its economic benefits. They have a 'keeping place' in Alice Springs rich in historical associations which they wish to make into a tourist destination, and they would accept a new road going through Hermansburg as long as it went to tourist sites in their country. Indeed, in my conversations with Arrenthe persons, I gained the impression that they rather resented the fact that Pitjantjatjara country — or Anangu land — dominated the local tourism industry through having Uluru and emphasised that they had wonderful places within their country. So again we see that there is more than one Indigenous viewpoint on things like tourism and many communities are prepared to participate in it. When I was in

Darwin for Aboriginal Week in July 1989, it was a local festival with Indigenous dancing each day in the centre of the city, numerous art exhibitions and a fair. In conjunction with Aboriginal Week an art exhibition and sale is held at Nauiya Nambiyu (Daly River) which brings crowds of people from Darwin. All in all, from what I have seen, tourism in the Northern Territory is handled in a much better and compassionate way than in a country like Thailand, a place with which I am also familiar.

Tourism has benefited Indigenous communities in many ways, especially by the part it has played in the widespread acceptance of Australian Indigenous art. Some decades ago now, Indigenous bark painting began to be influenced by tourism and the size of the painting was determined by the suitcase. This was called 'suitcase art'. Like tourism our art has come a long way since then and has grown into a regular industry which is in turn an important part of what has become an Indigenous culture industry, with, in some communities, a turnover in a good year running into hundreds of thousands of dollars. Of course, there might be objections to my seeing art as an industry with an importance placed on economic return. The artist starving in the garret is very much a stereotype of western tradition. There is an historical attitude which exalts what is called 'high' art as the most sublime expression of the human spirit, though this has not stopped art from becoming commodified nowadays to the extent that you may have art supermarkets and fire sales. Then the Indigenous art industry is firmly in the hands of art gallery owners and entrepreneurs such as Jenny Isaacs who through splendid publications and sheer business acumen keep up the price and interest in Australian Indigenous art. In Alice Springs and Darwin, the closest cities to the communities which produce what is readily accepted as 'traditional' art, there is a plethora of art galleries, few of which are owned by Indigenous people. Most Indigenous art outlets are run by mainstream gallery owners who have found it a profitable business, so much so that a number in the capital cities deal only in Indigenous art.

Today, in the western world — and this includes Australia — culture is seen as an enterprise which must produce a profit. An investment in culture is judged by the economic returns it generates. For example, in 1992 the Aboriginal Arts Committee of the Australia Council proudly declared: 'Today, cultural activities are a 7.6 billion dollar industry in Australia, making them a major employer, taxpayer and money earner for the nation.'

In its annual report three years earlier, the Australia Council itself said of the burgeoning Indigenous art movement:

> Fundamental to the development of Aboriginal culture are the arts and crafts centres established by Aboriginal communities. Board support for these centres has allowed Aboriginal artists to work and have access to markets which, at least in the initial transactions, are controlled by Aboriginal people.
>
> During 1988 there was an upsurge of interest in Aboriginal art and several centres, including Maningrida, Ramingining, Yirrkala and Warlukurlangu, were able to organise successful exhibitions on a commercial basis. Growing interest and popularity of the works of art from Papunya resulted in unprecedented sales by the Papunya Tula Artist Pty Ltd and allowed this centre, for the first time, to forgo its application for subsidy from the Board.

As can be seen from this, the growth and acceptance of Indigenous culture and arts are a recent phenomenon. Part of the explanation is that the Indigenous people's activism brought them to worldwide attention, as well as the impact of what has come to be called the New Age movement, which extols all things traditional, or seemingly traditional, and provides a ready market which is being serviced by a number of Indigenous people. New Agers do not eschew the profit motive and are prepared to pay for the services of Indigenous teachers. This market can be very lucrative. I know of one Indigenous woman who charges four hundred dollars for a weekend learning about Australian Indigenous culture.

This new market is part of a general upsurge of interest in 'traditional art'. Until recently, the products of Australian Indigenous culture found a place only in the collections of ethnological items in museums. They were considered to be mere relics, primitive artefacts for so-called experts to ponder over and theorise about. The Indigenous people of Australia have always been at the mercy of well- or ill-intentioned colonisers who came, entered Indigenous territory, left traces and departed. Rex Batterbee was one such person who came to central Australia and 'discovered' Albert Namatjira. In popular legend, it was he who taught Namatjira to paint landscapes using watercolours, while it was from the head of Hermannsburg Mission, from Pastor Albrecht that he received his first paint box. This was the impetus which supposedly gave him his start. Little account is taken of how Albert Namatjira was producing artwork well before his 'discovery'. The South Australian Museum has a 1934 ink and pencil sketchbook of his which predates his watercolours. By comparison with drawings made by other Arrenthe artists on the mission at the time, he was already advanced as an artist. It was only later, in 1936, that Namatjira accompanied Rex Batterbee on a painting trip to Palm Valley. During this trip, Batterbee saw examples of his work and arranged for him to travel to Adelaide in December 1936 for his first solo exhibition.

Although using watercolours to paint European-style landscapes, Albert Namatjira may be seen as the first Indigenous person to enter the art industry. The time was ripe for an Indigenous artist to receive recognition, as the Jindyworabak movement was advocating the use of Indigenous themes in the European-derived art of Australia. Later, other artists such as Revel Cooper of the Carrolup Mission in Western Australia, began using watercolours under the encouragement of mainstream artists such as Elizabeth Durack. But they failed to crack the art market and their work remained relatively unknown in comparison to that of Albert Namatjira.

At the time Albert Namatjira received acclaim as an artist, the Commonwealth government had instituted the policy of assimilation for Indigenous people. Namatjira was seen as an example of the success of this policy. He had his own income, house and truck and in 1957 was granted 'honorary Australian citizenship'. One of the conditions of this 'citizenship', however, was that he virtually had to forsake his own kith and kin and identity as an Indigenous person. He refused to do this and so stopped being a token to be seen instead as a victim. The same may be said of Revel Cooper, who met an untimely and violent death in Sydney. These pioneer artists, because they would not separate themselves from their families and people and comply with the policy of assimilation, became symbols of the Indigenous will to resist and are still seen as powerful role models by Indigenous people today.

The Indigenous art of Australia, as Namatjira's work shows, has the capacity to take aspects of non-Indigenous culture and make them its own. Often this is not to the advantage of art dealers, or the would-be discoverers of an authentic Indigenous artistic tradition, who want it to reflect a static culture which fits into the genre of 'primitive art' and is unsoiled by European influences. But even the very concept of art is a European construct and until recently the idea of 'art' and 'the artist' separated from the community did not exist in our thinking, any more than a work of art having a value in and for itself — though it might be said this latter concept was lying dormant waiting to be stirred by the right stimulus. It is said that Geoff Bardon provided this stimulus at Papunya and from this came the famous Papunya Tula art, those large canvases of dreaming landscapes which until recently did not exist in the form we see them today. As Ulli Beier has made clear in an article in the periodical *Long Water*, they were, from the first, painted for the art industry:

> Geoff Bardon soon realised that the men needed an outlet for their work. He loaded the paintings into his van and took them to the Arms Art Gallery. But while he felt totally in his element working with the painters, he found the business side of things extremely tough. He was not prepared for the difficulties he would encounter . . . the owner of the art gallery pressured him to give her exclusive Australian rights — even world rights — for the paintings because she understood the commercial potential of these works immediately.

Papunya was formed as a 'collection place', a concentration camp for many different tribal groups who were dumped there and left to live on rations under government supervision. Their tribal countries lay in all directions far away from the settlement, and the men of the different communities living there included the custodians of many dreaming myths centred on sacred sites and tracks in their homelands. This knowledge was encoded in lines joining concentric circles and connecting them into a terrain, the space of the canvas, which was a text filled with the narratives about their dreaming ancestors. Among these lawmen and custodians were men who became well-known artists, such as Johnny Warrangula Tjaparula, Mick Numieri, Bill Stockman Tjapaltjari, Clifford Possum and many others.

When they began painting it seemed only natural that they should turn to their countries and dreaming for inspiration. They regarded the surface of the earth as a skin similar to their own, which in ceremonies they marked with ochres and scars to symbolise this similarity. From birth they had lived in intimate contact with nature and had learnt to respond to its many moods and forces, to which they also paid homage in rituals of song and dance and body painting. In their ceremonies they stressed the interconnectedness of humans, creatures, plants and stones with the great mysteries of life, death and rebirth. These ceremonies blended together the physical, emotional and spiritual needs of the participants, and when they turned to the medium of the visual arts, it was on these sources that they drew for inspiration. Realising the richness of their traditions Geoff Bardon directed the Papunya artists away from any experimentation and towards what would catch the attention of the market. According to Ulli

Beier, he urged the men to remain traditional: 'I was breaking through a door into a completely adult artistic problem: how were these men to express themselves in an indigenous way?'

The men took heed of this advice, says Beier, and turned to their roots for inspiration. Papunya Tula art did not arise from a void, but from a deep tradition of visual art, especially expressed in sacred designs on boards. Although these were considered secret, they were inspirational, so much so that in an early work from Papunya I can remember seeing on a wall of the conference room of the Australia Council, the outlines of the boards have been drawn in. Eventually, as the artists' skill developed, any pictorial reference to the boards was dispensed with and the designs expanded to fill the whole canvas, though they remained true to the tradition in that the paintings were composed while singing song verses from the epics detailing the exploits of the ancestral beings and when completed were supplied with a written narrative which told the story contained within the artwork.

The paintings are highly symbolic, using traditional motifs from body and sand paintings, and can thus be 'read' if one has the knowledge. Fixed designs are used, such as a star in which six smaller circles about a larger one represent a constellation. A camp, or sitting down place, may be represented by two concentric circles with straight horizontal lines being fire sticks. A waterhole is depicted by concentric circles; a 'U' sign is a sitting man; spiralling lines or wavy vertical parallel lines can mean running water, a rainbow, a snake, string, cliffs, or the honey hive of the native bee, and horizontal wavy lines represent smoke, or fire, or blood. These are placed on a canvas, the spatial surface of which represents the landscape.

The Papunya Tula painters use a limited number of symbols to create canvases which portray the sacredness of their country. There is a clear ideology behind each work, for to paint the country is to assert your ownership of it, just as to 'sing' your country is to assert your ownership and knowledge of it. Thus, in a sense, it is impossible to copy these paintings, though people have tried by using the same symbols; but there is more to producing such a painting than arranging dots and concentric circles on a canvas. Without the spiritual essence, and the underlying knowledge of the connection between land and painter, land and work and the whole chain of land-painter-work-dreaming-land, such imitations are gauche and of little interest. The paintings from the Western Desert have this unifying vision which makes for works which, although traditional, are still striking and original.

Indigenous visual art is not confined to the standard dot paintings of the Western Desert and varies from culture to culture. When Cyclone Tracy struck Darwin and wrecked the city on Christmas Day 1974, it had a tremendous impact on Indigenous communities all across northern Australia. It was considered by many to have been a manifestation of the Rainbow Serpent deity showing his displeasure over Indigenous people who were forsaking their law and culture. Within a year, a cultural revitalisation movement spread across the north. Geoffrey Managalamarra, at Kalumburu on the northern coast of Western Australia, received in a dream the songs and dances of the *Cyclone Tracy Palga* (ceremony), which was performed for the next two years by Indigenous communities throughout the

Kimberley region. One of the emblems carried in this ceremony was a large plaque with a map of Darwin painted on it above which hovered the cyclone. About the same time as Geoffrey Mangalamarra had received his ceremony, Rover Thomas, at the Indigenous settlement of Warmun (Turkey Creek), was visited by the spirit of a woman who had died in a motor vehicle accident which had been caused by heavy rains. Water, rain and the Rainbow Serpent deity are connected, and in this visitation the woman said that her death had been caused by *Juntarkal*, another *Wungurr* or Rainbow Serpent. In later visits, Rover Thomas received details and songs about the travels of this woman after she died. One of these songs sang of how she saw from Kununurra, which is many hundreds of kilometres from Darwin, the destruction of that city. Her visitations resulted in a ceremony called the *Kuril Kuril*.

This ceremony was seen as tangible proof that the connection of the Warmun community with their culture was as strong as ever. As in the *Cyclone Tracy Palga*, a number of emblems or plaques were carried on the shoulders of the men in this ceremony, and as a result of being seen in public, performances of the ceremony gradually came to be recognised as real works of art. The demand for these plaques led directly to the production of paintings in the same genre. An important feature of the *Kuril Kuril* cycle of ceremonies is that, within certain limits, artists may select the subjects they wish to portray. Rover Thomas and his mother's brother, Paddy Jaminji, had painted the first plaques used in the ceremonies. Paddy turned to painting them on canvas and Rover Thomas soon followed suit.

Rover Thomas has gone on from strength to strength and is now considered a major artist. His work was chosen to be hung at the Venice Biennale, one of Europe's most prestigious art events. His paintings reflect a long tradition of Indigenous art in Western Australia, taking different forms in various parts of the State. The western coast and the adjacent regions inland are known for their fine engravings on wooden artefacts and pearlshells which were in great demand in the old days and were traded over a wide area. The Pilbara has many galleries of rock engravings and paintings which are second to none in Australia. The Western Desert dot style, similar to the Papunya Tula paintings, is produced in many Indigenous villages such as Balgo and is distinct from that of the Tula paintings in being much more detailed and elaborate. The Kimberley plateau exhibits a variety of styles, in one of which is seen the well-known *Wandjina* figures which are believed to have come from the Wandjina ancestral beings themselves. These have great spiritual significance and are tangible evidence to the Indigenous people of the Kimberley of the eternal presence of their ancestors. The original images are rock paintings which are touched up from time to time by the guardian of the sites. This restoration work is not only an expression of the bond between artist and ancestor, but also, if carried out at the appropriate time of the year, activates the dormant powers of the ancestral being and maintains the natural cycles of the universe. Thus the act of painting, apart from its acknowledgement of the powers resident in the earth, also has cosmic significance. It is not that art captures life, but that art contains life.

A distinctive quality of Paddy Jaminji's and Rover Thomas's work is the occasional use of particular human-made features of landscape, such as cave paintings to identify certain sites. These are not only signatures of ownership, but also references to the *Kuril Kuril* ceremony. The *palga* or ceremonial plaques also portray landscape in an extremely naturalistic manner, though the ancestral beings often appear in such landscapes. By depicting or referring to specific events, these images seem to freeze time and convey a sense of timelessness inherit in the living land. Dreaming and historical events that have shaped the perception of country endure in these paintings through into the present and then into the future. They evoke the land with an awesome and everlasting continuity, renewing faith in the enduring stability of the earth.

This stability is evident in a different way in the bark paintings of the artists of Arnhem Land. They display powerful, animated natural figures, the anatomical contours of which are crisply drawn against the red of the bark surface, while their bodies vibrate with dots or contrasting patterns of cross-hatched lines. They are sometimes depicted twisting in movement, or surrounded by swarms of diminutive spirits. The primary subjects are Dreaming ancestral figures, those who gave shape to the earth, the original artists from whom the present-day artists draw their inspiration. The paintings evoke the persistent energy of these beings who now rest under the earth or the sea, or have ascended into the sky. From their resting place they preserve the cosmos by continually discharging their power, which is tapped through the act of painting as well as by ceremonies.

The land is also important to these artists. Arnhem Land has a spectacular landscape of cliffs, gorges and hidden caves along a rugged escarpment. Virtually all the walls of the accessible caves and rock shelters in this escarpment are covered with very fine paintings of large human and animal figures, as well as fish. Some of these frescoes are very old, but others are of recent vintage, showing the influence of the modern world, with things like trucks and steamships painted into traditional scenes.

In the old days paintings were important in ensuring cultural continuity. Today this has changed and most, if not all, bark paintings are produced to be sold or given away. But there is still a continuity of cultural practices passed down through the generations, and most paintings are graded according to the religious importance of the subject matter, with different levels of knowledge encoded within the artwork.

Much of this knowledge is restricted and is not to be revealed to the general public, but there are other paintings which feature subjects drawn from the natural environment. Some of these, often of ordinary animals, show the internal organs of the body such as the heart, lungs, liver and intestines, in so-called 'X-ray' details. Others feature the thin, elongated figures of the *mimi* spirits, said to have been artists themselves who left their portraits on many rock faces. Some bark painters continue the tradition of the *mimi*, who are believed to have been very important to humans, teaching them how to hunt, cook and butcher game. Some *marrkidjbu* (indigenous doctors or shamans), such as the artist Mandarrk, see these spirits and draw them directly from life.

In the past, images were created as magic phenomena which were involved to inflict harm on enemies. The same artistic techniques are still used, but without the magical element. In contrast to the naturalism of the animals, so-called sorcery subjects are human, often female, and are drawn in contorted or unnatural poses, with the limbs disjointed, elongated or twisted as if to suggest malformation. Sometimes small barbs are shown lodged in the body.

But ancestral figures in scenes from the Dreaming are the most important subject matter of the artists of Arnhem Land. These paintings are distinguished by the incorporation of cross-hatching 'infill' techniques known as *rarrk*, which derive from the patterns painted on sacred objects and the bodies of initiates in the *Mardayuin* ceremony which is performed to regenerate the flow of energy from the ancestors of the Dreamtime. It is said that these ancestors passed down the designs to the appropriate clan whose present-day members 'own' them collectively and are their custodians. They cannot be reproduced without their permission.

Arnhem Land paintings operate through a polysemic system encoding many different levels of meaning, although the main element is an inherent connection with the land which enables the artist to creatively use images drawn from the storehouse of collective clan culture. Most of these features are evident even in commercially produced bark paintings today. As the artist George Milpurrurru puts it: 'Today we paint for ceremony and we paint bark paintings to sell. We can share our religious paintings, because that is what bark paintings are, with *balanda* (white people) and perhaps they will learn something about us from our paintings . . .'

The growth of the Indigenous culture industry and the entry of Indigenous artwork into the market place has aroused a variety of responses. It has resulted in a certain degree of jealousy between traditional and urban artists, the cynical copying of traditional techniques for commercial reasons without any regard for authenticity or quality and artists being ripped off by unscrupulous dealers and agents, though on the other hand many artists have done extremely well out of their work. Indigenous artists enter the high art market with a unique product to sell and in the main have been able to sell it at a fair price. This is only one aspect of the culture industry, for below the art galleries lies the tourist world of souvenirs which is managed by both Indigenous and non-Indigenous people. Then there are music and ceremonies, books and cassettes, clothing and designs. Even if we have reservations about the penetration of Indigenous culture by market forces, we must agree that the quantity and quality — both good and bad — of the products are proof of the strength of Indigenous culture. It has also been recognised that it is important to exercise some leverage over the market, and a national coordinating body, the Aboriginal Arts Management Association (AAMA), has been formed to safeguard and protect the rights of Indigenous artists, as well as to arrange exhibitions and shows. Its success so far augurs well for the future.

Further Reading

Beier, Ulli and Johnson, Colin (Mudrooroo), *Longwater: Aboriginal Art and Literature Annual*. Sydney, Aboriginal Artists Agency, 1988.

Pitjantjatjatjara Central Land Council, *Sharing the Park: Anangu Initiative in Ayers Rock Tourism*. Alice Springs, IAD press, 1991.

Rowse, Tim, 'Hosts and Guests at Uluru,' *Meanjin*, 51 (2), 1992.

Rutherford, Anna, *Aboriginal Culture Today*. Sydney, Dangaroo Press/Kunapipi, 1988.

Sutton, Peter (ed), *Dreamings: The Art of Aboriginal Australia*. New York, George Braziller Publishers, 1988.

Our Histories
Lecture 11

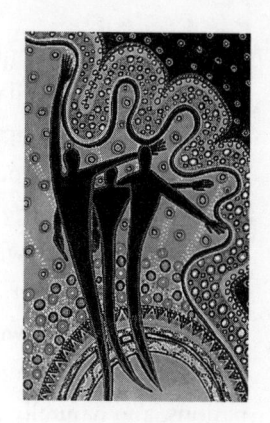

Can our mythologies and stories be rewritten into the dry narrative of a history text? Can the uneven branches, twigs and leaves of our Dreaming Tree of life and death gain meaning from being compressed in an account which ignores the spiritual and writes about Us Mob as victims? Do we want to be reduced to the blandness of an official report trying to reconcile us at the expense of our own structures and shapes?

History, after all, is a construct based on time, on a linear sequencing which deems those without a long classificatory system of managing time to be without such a history. It is only those societies which have sought out an objective time-system that have created history. Without such a timescale, without such a manner of sequencing events, what history can there be? History, in this sense, is a seemingly objective treatment of human (and perhaps planetary) events along a fixed time-line. Nations rise and fall; kings and queens strut their stuff and then depart. Such a history is similar to a novel, such as Tolstoy's *War and Peace*. It is only when the time-line, the sequence, is fleshed out and the past seems to live in our minds that we begin questioning whether we have been reading a fictional account, or not. If we question the text, especially when we find that we — that is, Us Mob — have either been left out of the story, or adapted to fit into the sequence of events, we might begin fashioning our own narrative with ourselves cast in the main role. 'Our' here means our race, our nations, and naturally from this we also begin creating an Other.

Our story, our history, will query what has been written by the dominant society, or the dominant power within that society, as the true record of a sequence of events along the time-line. From this rewriting of what was once considered an official or 'true' narrative, an equally 'true' revisionist version may result, which seeks to replace what is now seen as an outmoded narrative. This is the stage, especially with the efforts of the Reconciliation Council behind it, that the process of rewriting history in Australia has now reached.

Of course, although always seen as time-bound, history can be many things to many groups and classes, and when the official narrative fragments sufficiently, the discourses of ideology emerge to use the so-called facts of history as weapons. Still, these weapons are but language, discursive practices written down and bound to a system of time and a sequencing of the past which may be as artificial as many of the now outmoded historical narratives at which we smile, or snarl. History, once a matter of delving into musty records, placing one record against the other in a Masterly attempt to rescue the supremely 'true' narrative, is now seen to be a process tainted by gender and racial bias. The Australian historian Manning Clark was once the Master historian of the nation. Now he is dead. They have named a road after him, but his grand Master narrative became discredited even in his own lifetime. History has become fragmented and the fragments are claimed by different groups to be sifted through to rescue those bits we like. History has become a discursive practice running hither and thither. The past is found in many places and these are to be interpreted through discourse. It is because of this fragmentation, this suspicion of official records, that so-called 'oral history' has been given value. But even this has its deficiencies. History may be found in the minds of old men and women, but in many cases they do not remember things in an orderly sequence. An examination of oral narratives will often reveal that the mind does not operate in a linear fashion and so, in order to authenticate memories, recourse must again be made to those records — that is, if we wish to do away with the way the mind and memory structure past events and give them meaning.

Until recently, the Master's idea of history rested on a timeline with beads of events strung along it. But although this history always claims to be propounding the 'truth' about the past, free of any ideological prejudice, in fact it is in a constant process of being revised and updated to give the present a more satisfactory account of the past in accordance with new ideological conceptions. In other words, history is the past reconstructed for an ever-increasing series of presents. Its importance lies not in its exposition of 'truth', but as a device which orders society and gives meaning to a collectivity. Still, for all this denial of 'truth', at the risk of appearing to contradict myself, I must affirm that a people, a society, a community, or even a person without a past really has no culture and no deeper meaning or purpose. We Indigenous people are caught in the dilemma of having a past without having a 'true' past, and consequently no 'self'. This is why the past is important for us and why so many regional Indigenous historical narratives are being written. It is our past and only we can write it, for in a sense we need history and it is not 'ours' until we do the writing ourselves, giving importance to those stories which now matter to us.

Perhaps it needs to be asked whether there was a history in Australia before the invasion, before the Other were denied a subjectivity and rendered into objects about which things had to be written in books by often unsympathetic authors? This raises a further question, for as we had no methods of writing, does this mean that history can only be written, or are there other ways of rendering it? If we accept that there are in fact other ways of encoding history, then we must look for something else which connects with the past and establishes that past for the present. If we exclude such methods of inscription as rock art, then we find that what gave a sense of continuity with the past for the Indigenous people of Australia were songs, stories and ceremonies, both religious and secular, which passed down over the generations those events which were deemed to be of sufficient importance to be recorded in such forms. Even if these events cannot be read as narratives or be placed in a lineal time sequence, they still create a sense of the past and thus establish a historical continuity for Indigenous communities. An example of these sorts of events is the arrival of groups of people from the sea recorded in the Arnhem Land song cycles and ceremonies, and there are similar accounts in the Kimberley and New South Wales. How are we to read these records — as historical accounts of people arriving on the coasts of Australia, or as inventions of a mystical Indigenous mind?

People do not think in identical terms, as a cursory consideration of the different concepts such as that of 'self' found in languages bears out, as do the structures of languages themselves. People also encode their history in any number of ways and the present continues to reactivate these records, or perhaps I should say reinvent/re-empower them. Thus what are sometimes called 'myth' and 'legend' are but ways of recording 'history', of what a particular community thinks of as important elements of its past. They operate as much as the reinvention/reactivation of the past as seemingly objective historical narratives.

Instead of its importance to the Indigenous people in ordering their past to their present being acknowledged, pre-invasion Indigenous Australian history was seen as little more than idle fancy. By the time of the invasion of Australia, 'history' in the European countries had assumed the structure of a realist narrative based on time sequencing. Anything which did not fit this format was disregarded, or subsumed as 'myth' or 'legend' to be collated by ethnographers who analysed our beliefs only in terms of foreign ideas and European theories. Thus it may be noted that an Indigenous community was seen dancing a new ceremony which involved the miming of cattle, but there was no realisation that it was in effect dancing an event into its history.

Dance, after all, was not considered by the Master a legitimate means of encoding history. But as the noted historian Greg Dening has said about his particular field of study: 'History in the Pacific needs to be vernacular and vernacularly tolerant of great variety because it is in the variety of vernacular histories — legends, ballads, anecdotes, plays, dances — that we develop skills in the poetics of history — its reading — and its production.' Similarly, the German scholar Klaus Neumann has observed:

> First, there seem to be two good reasons for experimenting with a variety of styles: the potential corruptness of the conventional Western historiographical narrative, and the need to become more self-conscious about conventional and unconventional forms of representation. Second, particular varieties of vernacular histories, those the subjects of my history share with me when I enquire about their past, would bear on this production — to the extent they become part of it. Third, a writing of post-colonial Australian history would benefit from a close look at a peculiar variety of Aboriginal histories, representations of the past in post-colonial Black Australian literature.

Of course I do not agree with all of this. Neumann's 'conventional' and 'unconventional' forms of representation may be judged to be still reading the Other from a Master perspective, not an Indigenous one. It must not be forgotten that until recently the very fact of rendering something in writing was the uncon-ventional form of representation for Indigenous people. To put it bluntly, it was a method of recording which we did not particularly find worthwhile, and perhaps many still do not. In fact, it may be said that many Indigenous people are passing from a pre-literate to a post-literate culture in that although song is still being used, other means such as the video tape are being taken up.

Indigenous people did not turn their attention to their history until the 1970s, with one of the first historical works being James Miller's important *Koori: A Will To Win — The Heroic Resistance, Survival and Triumph of Black Australia*. This followed a linear time sequence and marshalled evidence mainly from British records to produce a counter-history of New South Wales. It reconstructed an Indigenous past since the invasion marked by oppression and heightened by Indigenous resistance. It sought to see the recent past from a Koori perspective (though we must keep in mind those British written documents lying beneath its narrative) and sought to empower Kooris by giving them a historical narrative in opposition to the British invader historical narrative. This text followed in the footsteps of other post-colonial histories seeking to reclaim the past from the colonisers, such as R.C. Majumdar's monumental *History of India*, which replaced the 'official' historical narratives written by British scholars. Miller's book is a similar example of the 'Native writing back', though within the parameters established by European historical scholarship.

The production of such academic histories by Indigenous people is still in its infancy and those which have been written often rely on the work of non-Indigenous academics, so much so that there is sometimes not even a reference to a book by an Indigenous person. This over-reliance means that too often we adopt the European academic practice of pitting European academic against European academic and in the process the Indigenous voice is muted, if not lost. I am not saying here that all European historians and histories should be excluded for purely ideological reasons, but that a balance should be sought and maintained. For some time now, for any number of ideological reasons, European historians have been writing Indigenous people back into the general Australian historical narrative, and we should ask why they are doing this. One of the reasons, and a strong one, is that for some time now, Europeans in Australia have been trying to construct some sort of national identity which separates them from their motherlands. When the immigrant population was reasonably homogenous, it was relatively simple to uphold an identity based on British imperialism, but with the numerous national and racial groups within the immigrant Australian population today this is difficult, if not impossible, and so elements which must be seen to be truly Australian must be separated out and commodified into a new Australian identity. In this process, the original inhabitants provide important items for a national identity. In fact, the Indigenous heritage has begun to be labelled the heritage of all Australians and by some adroit selecting and rewritings, all Australians have come to have a past extending back to the Dreaming. Of course, this history still shades off into the pioneers and explorers, but if the Reconciliation Council has its way, the Indigenous people will enter the 200-year-old invader history and the invaders will inherit a past going back to the Dreaming. The process is well under way, and if all goes according to plan, by the year 2001, when Australia decides to become a republic, much of the past when Indigenous people and invaders clashed will be redefined and the Indigenous people accorded their rightful place in a united Australia.

Of course, this will be a composite history duly written and authorised, but if an Indigenous history was constructed — if such a thing was possible — how might it be written when some of the earlier events taken from the song circles and mythology are undated? A possible time sequence might read like this, with the dates being supplied from the official invader records when needed:

Dhanggawul family land at Jelangbara after hazardous canoe journey.
    Wawilag Sisters enter Yolngu country from desert.
    Bugini people set up camp on northern coast.
    Bugini people depart after trading with Yolngu.
    Bugini song cycle performed.
    Macassans land to trade at Port Keats.
    First Macassan song cycle performed.
    Yolngu man travels to Macassar.
    The three brothers with their grandmother land at Yambaa on the Eastern Coast.
    Circumcision initiation ceremony reaches the Maia, Mandi and Inggardu communities on the west coast.
    Elders of the Maia, Mandi and Inggardu communities reject new ceremonies.
    Disaster strikes Eora at Port Jackson.
    Plague spreads from Port Jackson along the river systems. Many die.
    Bibbulmum elders debate origin of white-skinned arrivals.
    Large canoe wrecked on coast. Warawala people find strong knives.
    Bibbulmum elders declare strangers to be human not spirits of dead tribespeople.
    First *rangga* enters into ceremonial use among the Yolngu.
    Mouheneenga community in Tasmania attacked from sea.
    The Eora hero Pemulwy mounts resistance campaign against invaders.

> Mimi rock art discovered by elder. Theory advanced that it was painted by little people living in rocks.
> Yagan repudiates brotherhood with the invader Stirling.
> Bibbulmum reel under attack at Pinjarra.
> Bibbulmum hold meeting to discuss their future.
> Madlunga ceremony is traded south by the Wagaya community of northern Queensland. Received with enthusiasm.

And so on and so forth. As I have said, some of these events may be dated by recourse to British documentation while many others cannot be. It may also be said that some, as I have constructed them, never happened. Of course, once we begin debating whether or not such events ever took place, we are extending the historical process to include or exclude them and if the discussion remains Indigenous then, as it is our history we are discussing, who after all is to say that these events took place but we Indigenous people? Of course, if non-Indigenous historians enter the debate, the whole list might be dismissed out of hand as lacking credibility, because it did not come from recognised historical sources. However, if it was accepted as valid, then perhaps the conventional European chronology might be extended back to include such events, which would mean that any attempt to establish a timeless Indigenous history would be rejected. This may be legitimate, or may not, for there may be another time sequence which orders the Indigenous events of the past.

It has been said that Indigenous narratives or texts are organised around places, that places or sites are the most important classifiers of Indigenous discourse and not time sequencing. Many Indigenous texts appear to bear this out, such as those by Paddy Roe in *Gularabulu*, as edited by Stephen Muecke, but what appears to have escaped attention is how Indigenous texts from many sources are structured in a time sequence. I have earlier described how Indigenous people order their society and environment by kin and thus if we refuse to accept the timelessness of Indigenous narratives and seek some form of time-patterning, I think that we should look for it in the kinship system and the social classification of the generation levels, as well as the movement of generations through the section system, which sets out a measurement of time. I have already discussed in some detail one of the stories in *Gularabulu*, 'Mirdinan', which Paddy Roe declares is a true story and one which is pinned to place in the usual way. During the narration, Paddy Roe engages in a typical Indigenous exercise of running through a genealogy with his mate, Butcher Joe Nangan, which fixes Mirdinan himself in the kinship system and gives an approximate date for the story. The historical person Mirdinan is thus situated in time, but this section does not appear in the printed text, for in exercising his position as editor, Stephen Muecke excised it as being extraneous to the overall story. This, I feel, was an imposition on his part, for the discussion establishes Mirdinan's place in time and his relationship to Paddy Roe and Butcher Joe Nangan.

Place is important to lend authenticity to Indigenous historical narrative, but what is more important is the relationship of the historical person to those living and narrating the story. It is this genealogy which gives the narrative a time sequence from the present back to the past when the character lived. It is when persons are being located in a society that recourse is made to remembered genealogical records. In fact, if we re-examine James Miller's *Koori: A Will To Win* with genealogy in mind, what may at first have seemed a conventional historical text now appears to be a Koori text based on genealogy, thus having an affinity with other Indigenous histories such as *Gularabulu* and the numerous family histories which Indigenous people are now producing. Often, these texts are immersed in conventional calender time, but when this is removed, then we find ourselves in genealogical time. Thus I contend that Indigenous historical narratives are structured around place and family (community) and have a time sequence based on genealogy.

A historian these days constructing an Indigenous history cannot ignore the genealogical tree which shapes and gives a time sequence to our histories. It is hardly possible, either, to maintain a stance of impartiality, of European pseudo-objectivity. This alien way of constructing our history should be relegated to the past, for too often Us Mob were written out of contemporary accounts and what records were kept did not stem from us. In fact, there is a danger in using the records of the past in that they may be complete fabrications, something which does not come to light without an extensive investigation and documentary analysis. An example of this is G.A. Robertson, who in the 1830s made his name and fortune by 'bringing in' the Indigenous people of Tasmania and then deporting them to windswept Flinders Island on Bass Strait. He wrote glowing reports of how they were becoming educated and 'civilised', and also of living in well-built houses, but this was far from the truth and in fact the people were rapidly dying off. In her book *Black Robinson*, Vivienne Rae-Ellis has exposed the crimes of this man who successfully managed to cover up his misdeeds and, even worse, whose journals have been made the basis of the history of the Indigenous people of Tasmania by a historian who accepts them as 'true', though perhaps exaggerated in places. It is only the Indigenous people of Tasmania who continue to condemn both Robinson and his contemporary commentator. Further, the Indigenous people of Tasmania owe their survival to the white seal hunters in Bass Strait in the nineteenth century, who were condemned by the authorities of the time and are still criticised by some historians today. But it was these sealers, the outcasts of colonial society, who enabled the Indigenous people to survive. Perhaps our attitude to history may be seen as the problem, and not the attitudes of academic historians. History is not for them oozing with the secretions of the past. Their historical tree has little sap, but our Nyungar history is very much with us. If we touch the trunk of our past, memories vibrate through our beings and refuse to be treated as dry records or documents. History is delivered in a voice anything but neutral.

Those who collect oral histories often engage in a number of manoeuvres to lessen the non-objectivity of the past which is not to the Master's liking. They emphasise what they regard as factual content; they edit, rewrite and organise the spoken discourse into a written text. Often, the spoken record (on an audio cassette) is transcribed and filed away, to be drawn upon only when a footnote or an example is required. The spoken account thus becomes a source similar to other written sources. It becomes tamed and digested into a written text, a familiar commodity to be consumed by the historian. Craig Tapping writes about this ideological process in his *Oral Cultures and the Empire of Literature:*

> Our quest, returning to the repressed of oral culture, is to un-block, to learn to hear and see the cultures which exist not — as is currently fashionable — in or on the margins of, but actually outside our documents and archives . . . So-called primitive cultures — systems wherein shamans, historians, bards, or even ordinary representatives of another generation or time stage and recount communal stories and collectively shared narratives — value what is told, not for its content but rather for its form. Form is always a message, part of the content of narrative . . . A performative aesthetic operates: just as it does when we read the most up-to-date postmodern document or text.

And so it is to the elders of our communities, to the custodians of our past to whom we must go and listen, if we are to escape the trammels of conventional history and to learn what are the important events of our past. An example of an elder who has passed on his knowledge of the past is Tom Bennell of our Nyungar people, who in his book *Kura* has a section aptly entitled 'Oral History' in which he gives us a Nyungar account of place. It is an interesting text and could never be mistaken for a conventional historical account:

> when the white fullahs come (hand moving circular)
> that was the only two left
> out of their family
> You take for h'instance the Dinahs

well I don't know the Dinahs much
wasn't a big family of 'em
h'an' I don't think there's h'any left now
might'e one h'or two
Well you take for h'instance
the whasnames
Narkles
there was four h'or five brothers
that was the biggest family there was left
of our Nyungar lot
there was a few of 'em Narkles
um these
Narkle boys
that 'round 'live now
thas only their back fathers
grandfathers
there was only four h'or five
of them boys left
I know
they was ol' fullahs
h'an' they all died out
like our lot see
but there's no ol' men
you could take through now
h'an' for instance
our lot
like I say 'bout 'em
whasnames
Kearings
Nippers

Niyette
h'an' ah
Garlett
h'an'
Humphries
see ol' Ernie Humphries
'e married one of the Bennell's
thas only all Bennell family
thas left in Brookton now
there's nobody else there
Harold Collard married one (a Bennell)
Jim Collard married a Bennell
Norman Bennell married my mother (Kate Collard)
see
thas only the family
you may as well say
There is Norman h'an' Kates family
ah
h'an' McGuire's
h'an' ha
some of the Collards
but there weren't many there
'cause Uncle Fred h'an' 'em
come from our grandmother's side
well
I can bring h'it right back
to Nyungars
'cause they can't tell me
who they not
h'an' who they aren't

> h'an' who they are
> 'cause I know 'em
> I tell a lotta people
> I know a lot of people.

The value of texts like *Kura*, from which the above extract is taken, is that they stand apart and are not lost in the straightness of standard written English, though it can happen that our special voice may be absorbed into a historian's narrative. If this happens to our oral discourse, it becomes only a colourful thread of quaint quotations which supports the contentions located in the standard English written text. In the Nyungar text I have used, there is no enclosing standard of English written text or paraphrases or lengthy footnotes, explaining and placing the contents of the oral discourse into the standard time sequencing of the conventional historical written text. Tom Bennell is allowed to have his say and is treated as an elder of our people. This is a novelty in the treatment of Indigenous texts, which usually must be explained, and in the explanation the Indigenous voice is muted. Here the Nyungar voice is left to exist as Tom Bennell spoke and it is up to the reader or listener to engage in a conscious act of absorbing. In it you may find the elements which I have said mark the Indigenality of an Indigenous text. It is organised around place, its subject matter is family and, furthermore, time is treated in a genealogical manner.

The Indigenous people of Australia have a history which is different from that of Europe, and if we are to create an Indigenous history of Australia much more work must be done on form as well as content. It is no use just collecting the facts and fitting them into a conventional European historical framework. This does not make for an Indigenality of text, at least in the case of our Nyungar elders. If the authentic voice is lost then all that we have is just another attempt at assimilating Indigenous discourse into mainstream Australian English.

FURTHER READING

Bennell, Tom, *Kura*. Compiled by Glenys Collard. Bunbury, Nyungar Language and Culture Centre, 1991.

Dening, Greg, 'History in the Pacific', *The Contemporary Pacific*, Spring/Fall, 1989.

Miller, James, *Koori: A Will to Win — The Heroic Resistance, Survival and Triumph of Black Australia*. Sydney, Angus & Robertson, 1985.

Neumann, Klaus, 'A Postcolonial Writing of Aboriginal History,' *Meanjin*, 51(2), 1992.

Roe, Paddy, *Gularabulu* (ed. Stephen Muecke). Fremantle, W.A. Arts Centre Press, 1983.

Young, Robert, *White Mythologies: Writing History and the West*. London, Routledge, 1990.

Our Struggle for our Lands

Lecture 12

TO SEEK TO RECOVER OUR STOLEN LANDS; TO FIND THE room to grow with the resources necessary to ensure that growth. How Us Mob have struggled over the last 200 odd years for justice and our right to sovereignty. Still our story remains untold; still there are only fragments of the great struggle we have been engaged in against an enemy who has power, who has an army, who has the law, who has the government. It is difficult to consider our struggle without considering the heroism of those who have fought. We have had our casualties and traitors, we have had our plots and government agents, and still we have managed to advance. The great struggle for land rights appears to be over. We have been given 'native title' to some land, though even this is not much and we must go before tribunals to prove that we have the right to it. Now there is even talk of compensation, and so the whole struggle has changed.

Those of us who fought long and hard have become part of our history. Those of us who continue to fight seem to have been left behind as memories of those days of struggle. Times have changed and there is talk of reconciliation and justice in the air.

Kevin Gilbert fought for a treaty and was ignored. The Aboriginal Provisional Government fights on for sovereignty and is ready to negotiate, but this organisation which is representative of at least some of Us Mobs was shunted aside when the government created a Council for Aboriginal Reconciliation which is not representative. We do not need it, though it has the government's backing, and so again we make our demands known and they are duly placed once more before the government. We hope that good will come from it but, we wonder, will it be as before? Not so long ago, in 1988, there was the Burunga Statement which called for negotiation between the government of Australia and the Indigenous people. This was agreed to by the then Prime Minister Robert J. Hawke, who went back on his word as he floundered from Treaty to Compact to Reconciliation. This is how it was and is; but if the Council for Aboriginal Reconciliation's recommendations are truly listened to and acted on by the government of Australia, by 2001 we shall be concluding the end of our struggle for land rights in a just and lasting compact which guarantees our sovereignty with due constitutional safeguards. Denis Walker, the son of Oodgeroo, Elder of the Tribe Noonuccal and Custodian of the Land Minjerriba, once said that the Indigenous people of Australia and the invaders were in a state of war and that this war has continued since the convicts and soldiers landed at Port Jackson. It is this war that has seen many Indigenous people murdered and gaoled which must be concluded.

The land rights struggle has been going on for our lifetimes. I have been a participant in the struggle for quite a few decades now. Perhaps I might even be seen as a veteran. My face and figure can be seen in certain photographs, in certain films and news items which are now historical. In 1972, the Aboriginal Embassy was set up in Canberra to mark a new phase in the land rights struggle. Now, in viewing films and photographs from then, they seem of a long ago past. Then I too am becoming part of that past. A past of street demonstrations and slogans. Now Mabo and Native Title have shifted the battle from the streets into the courtrooms. It is too early to say what Us Mob will get from these tribunals which have been set up, but we must be aware that the Commonwealth Government has kept the right to overrule the decisions of the National Native Title Tribunal if the Minister determines that the decision is against the national interest, or the interest of a State or Territory. Again, the High Court decision stated that legislation can be passed which in effect ends native title; and so, in Western Australia, there was the *Land (Titles and Traditional Usage) Act 1993* which replaced native title with so-called 'rights of traditional usage' and the Indigenous protest went to the courts. In March 1995 the Act was struck out and we won more in the High Court of Australia than we had won in the streets. All in all, the land rights struggle has transmuted into the Native Title struggle in which there is little place for the old-style activist. Activism and the struggle on the streets are now over, or seem to be over, and so as a memorial to this period I offer the edited text of a document which was written in the early 1980s by a group of Us Mob to give some ideological underpinning in an overall context of Indigenality to the question of why land is so important to the Indigenous people and why we have been struggling so long for restitution of our lands.

Marcia Langton, now a member of the Council for Aboriginal Reconciliation, then wrote: 'The land, for Aboriginal people, is a vibrant spiritual landscape. It is peopled in spirit form by the ancestors who originated in The Dreaming, the creative period of time immemorial.' This quotation headed the document, which continued as follows:

FOR MANY YEARS NOW, activists within Australian society have been advocating Aboriginal Land Rights. To most people this has been perceived as some sort of social equality. This is not the case. Aborigines, in espousing Land Rights, have made a call to have non-Aborigines recognise Aboriginal rights to land in Australia as their traditional land rights. What has happened within this process is that non-Aboriginal people have perceived that some sort of tokenism needed to be made to Aboriginal people in order to satisfy land rights. This has happened not only at individual levels, but right up through the institutions as far as governments. This is particularly evident in the Woodward Report.

However, this is not what Aborigines have been on about. What we have in fact been on about is that we own this land and that nothing has been done, either in black man's law or white man's law, at a national or international level, to change the status. The reality is that Aborigines own this land and they have been denied use of it by non-Aborigines, for whatever reasons, and that non-Aborigines have done this for some two hundred years.

In this paper we discuss the significance of the land in terms of Aboriginal art and culture and the question of Land Rights in view of the relationship between land and culture.

In discussing the states of Aboriginal people in today's Australia — whether these be from the urban dispossessed or the endangered tribe — the basic importance of the spiritual and cultural ties to the land are at best ignored, and at worst dismissed by the European.

The whole question of Land Rights and the correction of injustice must be preceded by a recognition of the enormous damage done through spiritual deprivation.

The denial of cultural and spiritual heritage and lack of recognition of relationship to the land are the root cause of loss of identity, loss of health, and subsequent degradation.

Restoration of the opportunity to determine the future for themselves, and thus to re-establish their relationship with creation, are fundamental to the regeneration and good health of the individual, the family, and the community.

Aboriginal people view life in its entirety and resist categorisation, the breaking into parts, which seems to predominate in European thinking about the approaches to life.

No-one can have an appreciation of Aboriginal culture together with the importance of the relationship of the land to that culture without understanding the history and beliefs of Aboriginal Australia.

In 1981, in *The Aboriginal Heritage Act Recommendations*, The South Eastern Land Council stated: 'Aboriginal history is written — in the land around us!'

For this reason, in examining the question of the place of art and its relationship to the land in Aboriginal culture, it is essential to begin with the Aboriginal Dreamtime.

The well-known actor and dancer David Gulpilil has said: 'The Dreamtime is very important to Aboriginal people. It is the basis of our culture.'

The Aboriginal Dreamtime is the explanation of our existence; indeed, of the existence of all creation.

The vital significance of the land becomes apparent in examining these beliefs — which form the basis of Aboriginal religion.

In 1977, the artist Wandjuk Marika said:

> I am of the earth.
> I am a son of the earth.
> I am the trees, the rivers, the rock,
> I am kin to the earth's creatures.
> I am kin to the earth's creations.
> The earth is my mother.
>
> The white man is also of the earth,
> But he is mad,
> For what man in his right mind
> Would rape his own mother.

And in 1982, Bruce McGuinness of the Victorian Aboriginal Health Service lamented:

> We seek only humanity
> We are cursed with profanity
> White wants are pandered

> Black needs are slandered
> Your god's son up on a cross
> We and our god at a loss
> To understand
> Your rape of our land
> One day soon when all is well
> Your god and us will send you to hell
> Pay the rent!

According to Aboriginal belief, all life as it is known today — human, animal, bird, fish — is a part of one unchanging, interconnecting system; one vast network of relationships, which can be traced to the great spirit ancestors of the Dreamtime. The Dreamtime is our understanding of the world and its creation. It is the beginning of knowledge from which the laws of existence were derived.

In the beginning, the earth was flat and featureless. There were no mountains, no rivers, no plants or animals — not one living thing existed. Unknown life forms slept below the surface of the land. Then these great spirits, in both human and animal form, made their dramatic entrance on to the barren landscape. Some broke through the crust of the earth, others descended from the skies, or came from distant lands across the sea.

They made journeys across the land, digging for water, hunting and searching for food. As they searched, they moulded and formed the landscape creating rivers, mountains, trees and rocks. They made the plants, the animals and all living things — including the people who are the descendants of the Spirit Ancestors.

The Ancestors of the Dreamtime lived on the land in much the same way as us; they differ in that wherever they stopped, wherever any event took place in their lives, they left behind them features of the landscape which remain today.

Wearied from their activities, the Ancestral spirits sank back into the earth. The points where they emerged and re-entered the earth are described as sacred sites. It is from these places that we Aboriginal people of today derive our existence. They are the foci of our personal identity and they lie at the heart of our religious beliefs and our attachment to the land.

We Aboriginal people believe that in the Dreamtime our traditional way of life was established by these ancestral spirits; this way is still followed by those of us still following the old ways. We believe that our ancestors were taught about our tribal lands by the spirits, and were told how they should behave.

For us Aboriginal people, the land has special meaning, for all over the land, rivers, gorges, rocks and mountains are reminders of the great Spirit Ancestors of our Dreamtime creation.

When the Dreamtime ended, we were left with a social and cultural heritage which came from our Ancestors. Our Ancestors of the Dreamtime also gave us possession of tribal lands, and hence tribal land and all forms of life contained within it are regarded as a sacred trust.

Land to us Aborigines is not a possession in material terms, as the white man looks upon land, but a responsibility held in sacred trust.

> We do not say the land belongs to us, but we belong to the land.

The bonds with the Spirit Ancestors of the Dreamtime are such that we believe in a united world of body and spirit for every form of life in the land, both living and non-living. This means that the rocks, rivers, mountains and waterholes are more than just a reminder or a symbol of the Dreamtime. They represent reality and eternal truth.

The Dreamtime continues as the Dreaming in the spiritual lives of Aboriginal people today. The journeys and events of the Dreamtime creative beings are enacted out in our ceremonies today by dancers elaborately painted and decorated with special symbolic designs. Song-poetry narrates the story events of the Dreamtime and brings the power of the Dreaming to bear on life today.

Therefore, the core of our tribal culture is music, dance, ceremonies and story-telling. All these are closely bound up with the land and nature in sacred ceremonies and rituals.

These ties with the land and nature are strengthened by our Spiritual Ancestors who established the code of life, which today is called *'the Dreaming'* or *'the Law'*.

Each of us has or should have a totem or special symbol representing our spiritual attachment to our own Ancestral Spirit. This is in accord with our belief that each tribal group is descended from Ancestors of the Dreamtime. These totems are important because they demonstrate the unity of the people with nature and all living creatures and life forms. All are part of nature including men and women: only appearances differ.

Life came from and through the land and is manifested in the land. The land is not an inanimate thing: it is alive.

The late Larry Lanley, Chairman of the Mornington Island Council referred to the land as a *mother* — a mother who provides us with everything we need. He said an Aborigine cannot survive without his land — he will die without it.

Our Aboriginal societies are based on a powerful all-encompassing religion. We believe that our children are born of women but conceived by a spiritual source whose font is the land. The land has two kinds of landscapes — one physical which all human beings can view; the other spiritual which only Aboriginal people can see. For Aboriginal people there is only one way to own land and that is to be conceived of it. Land is a parent. It is this principle that prevents any kind of land aggrandisement, which has been the scourge of the rest of the world.

This principle of land as parent is clearly described by Djiniyini Gondarra from Galiwinku (Elcho Island). He says:

> The land is my mother. Like a human mother, the land gives us protection, enjoyment, and provides for our needs — economic, social and religious. We have a human relationship with the land: Mother, daughter, son. When the land is taken from us or destroyed, we feel hurt because we belong to the land and we are part of it.

This relationship between the land and Us is explicitly explained by Marcia Langton:

> The land, for Aboriginal people, is a vibrant, spiritual landscape. It is peopled in spirit form by the ancestors who originated in the Dreaming, the creative period of time immemorial. The ancestors travelled the country, engaging in adventures which created people, the natural features of the land and established the code of life, which we today call 'the Dreaming' or 'the Law'. The Law has been passed on through countless generations of people through

remembrance and celebration of the sites which were scenes of ancestral exploits. Song, dance, rock and sand painting, special languages and oral explanations of the myths encoded in these essentially religious art forms have been the media of the Law to the present day.

White anthropologists Catherine and Ronald Berndt speak strongly of the harmony and balance between our lives and our total environment:

> The Aborigines were intimately acquainted with their environment, knowing personally the land, and all its natural species, and the regularly changing seasons. Within their special limitations their life was full, and they obtained virtually all they desired. They grew, loved and died believing themselves to be part of a comprehensible and universal scheme arranged primarily for their benefit. There was no real strangeness; no grappling with essentially unknown elements, nor unforeseen conditions. They were sure of themselves, and of the culture in which they had grown; they could cope with all they met, all they saw and all they heard. There was no real struggle for survival, even in the most arid regions, of the kind that we ourselves know in our own mechanised and highly complex cultures; no extreme poverty, nor monopolisation.

As the Berndts describe, we Aborigines throughout Australia developed a particular way of coping with our environment. We make the environment part of our own social perspective, seeing as human its non-human ingredients. Thus we come to terms with it, placing it within a particular social context and providing it with meaning in relation to ourselves: the unknown can be made known, and the unfamiliar made familiar.

This mantle of meaning is especially important in regard to the visual arts. What we represent in our paintings on bark or stone, or though sculpture, has symbolic significance. What we depict is explicable in terms of itself — it can be identified as a particular natural species, or natural phenomenon, but also it can be identified as having symbolic meaning because a socio-cultural belief system has been superimposed upon the natural world. People see themselves associated with different aspects of nature — often, but not always in mythological terms. In our art, the symbolism has been developed to such a degree that it has become a visual landscape. We are part of the world about ourselves, and what we produce expresses that essentially harmonious relationship between our people and our environment.

Art for us is a functional part of the social order, with a defined role to play. Most Aboriginal art may be classified as sacred. It conveys, through its symbolism, aspects of myth. Most myths concern the great Spirit Ancestors of the Dreamtime. Aboriginal art, as a medium of communication with the spirit world, remains today as a living force in our communities. It is indeed a two-way communication, or perhaps, relationship.

These Spirit Ancestors and their adventures in the Dreaming are the subject matter of myth, song and ritual. They are also manifested in tangible, material form. A wide range of representational art is made in the shape of mythic beings, or things connected with them — symbols of them, or evocations of them.

The preparation of these works is in itself a ritual act, often accompanied by particular songs relevant to them. This symbolic form of a particular being is regarded as a vehicle for its spirit. Hence the artist is a re-creator, and is responsible for reactivating the spiritual powers of the Dreaming spirits, bringing them into direct relationship with the artist and his or her community so that they can draw on their powers. It is important to note then that the artist performs a crucial role, not so much as an artist, but more as a reactivator of the spirits. Almost everything he or she paints or carves or constructs is an act of creation, regenerating the spiritual.

Neither is it simply a matter of an artist painting or carving any object of mythic significance; the artist has to carve what is spiritually relevant to them, either because of their conception or birth affiliation, or because they are linked spiritually in a special way, through the Dreaming, with what they have produced. Being born or conceived at a particular mythic site implies that that part of the spiritual substance of the supernatural being resident there has entered the foetus and animated it. This makes the person a potential custodian of the sites, myths and songs associated with the spirit beings there.

Aboriginal art is land-based. Almost every painting or piece of sculpture is an item, is a charter relating to land, to ownership and possession of specific tracts of country. More than this, almost every painting and piece of sculpture is interpreted through a mythology in which Dreaming characters are the eternal actors. The land is vivified and made socially relevant through these Dreaming characters — in their own right, and also in the right of living Aborigines.

The rivers, rocks, gorges and waterholes are all reminders of the great Spirit Ancestors of the Dreamtime. The land, therefore, is dense with meaning — with song and story. Most Aboriginal art is then a statement concerning land: not just any piece of land, but specific stretches of land substantiated through identified mythological associations. At the same time, it is a statement of personal and social ownership by virtue of the connection of a particular person or persons with those Spirit Beings.

Galarrwuy Yunupingu, former Chairman of the Northern Land Council [now a member of the Reconciliation Council] years ago in a speech to the National Press Club in Canberra called the land his 'backbone' — he said that he only stood straight, happy and proud because he had his land. He referred to the land as an art, allowing him to paint, dance, create and sing as his ancestors had done before him. He saw the land as the history of his nation, declaring that it told Aboriginal people how they came into being and by what systems they must live. He called the land 'my foundation', and said: 'Without the land I am nothing'.

We have used a number of terms like 'land' and 'ownership', and before we approach the subject of 'Land Rights' it is important to point out that there are assumptions in the English meaning of these English words which are alien to Aboriginal people.

Mr Wesley Lanhupuy, Manager of the Northern Land Council, has stated:

> For Aboriginal people there is no separation between land and resources: there is no separation between us and what was our country and there never will be because of our spiritual belief and understanding. The English word 'land' has narrow connotations of economics and geography. The implications are dramatically broader for Aboriginal people when talking about their country, *Yirralga* (traditional land), by traditional owners. It encompasses all things.

Thus to us Aborigines, there is a combination of ownership and responsibility which is derived from Aboriginal law, ceremony and customs. All this breaks down and broke down when we are and were forcibly evicted from our land.

The South Eastern Land Council mourned the loss of their land in these words:

> Wokarjee winnek tjar ngark
> Tjar ngark winnek ark yarreearr
> Wokarjee winnek Marm Yungrrarrk
> Marm Yungrrarrk winnek ark yarreearr.

> (Return to me my land
> My land weeps
> Return to me my Spirit
> My Spirit weeps!)

It is from such a deep abiding sense of loss that the struggle for Land Rights was conducted.

The elements involved in the Aboriginal system are land, human beings and all other things that dwell with them. This system is a harmony and balance, and this is perfection.

The problem is that if any element of the system is destroyed, this circle of perfection is broken. One hundred and ninety four years ago this cycle was broken and in the southern areas of our continent our society was all but destroyed.

The balance and harmony was lost but the strength of it lived within the survivors and gave rise to the identity that Aborigines will carry with them into the twenty-first century and beyond. It is this identity which distinguishes us from anyone else who lives in our place. It is this identity which makes us what we are, and accounts for our continuing struggle.

'We are Aborigines, we are desert winds, we are the sunlit plains, we are the bright waters, we are Australia. This land is our birthright. In this new world, in our new society, we have but a single principle. We are our brother's keepers,' writes Aboriginal woman Marcia Langton.

Whatever historical timescale one may use, the fact remains that Australia is the land of the ancestors of us present Aborigines. We are dispossessed of our land, along with our human and historical rights. We are deprived of the most basic heritage by a technologically superior, alien-military culture.

The additional instructions to Lt James Cook, appointed to command His Majesty's bark the *Endeavour*, when he left England in 1768, are well known. After his observation of the transit of Venus he was to search for the eastern coast of the imagined southern continent and explore and chart it.

> . . . You are likewise to observe the genius, temper, disposition and number of natives if there be any, and endeavour by all means to cultivate a friendship and alliance with them, making them presents of such trifles as they may value, inviting them to traffic and shewing them every kind of civility and regard, taking care however not to suffer yourself to be surprised by them, but to be always upon your guard against any incident.
>
> You are also with the CONSENT of the natives to take possession of convenient situations in the Country in the

name of the King of Great Britain, or, if you find the country uninhabited, take possession for his Majesty by setting up proper marks and inscriptions, as First Discoverers and Possessors. [Emphasis added.]

The alienation or dispossession from one's heritage does not erase the memory of the robbery. It is often passed on in an oral tradition from generation to generation. It is natural, therefore, for the Aboriginal people to clearly point to their land, sacred sites and sites of significance, despite the fact that we were forced to give up and break our links with our land. The oral traditions contained well-known and understood, though unwritten, rules and regulations governing land relationships and duties, and responsibilities attached to it. The spiritual nature of the relationship between Aborigines and our lands, fortified by sacred worship, rituals and ceremonies, have helped to preserve historical memory and links with our ancestral lands. We Aborigines know the land to be ours by virtue of this memory.

The land is the Aboriginal people's spiritual heritage, it is part of our being a people. Land is the basis of all relationships with Aboriginal human and physical environment. Land defined the clan, its culture, its way of life, its fundamental rights, its religious and cultural ceremonies, its patterns of survival and above all its identity. Land was synonymous with Aboriginal existence. It could not be defiled, desecrated or cheapened. The expropriation, erosion, plundering, misuse or spoiling amounts to cultural genocide. Therefore, recovery of the land has a deep spiritual meaning for Aboriginal communities and forms the basis of cultural revival and survival.

It may be difficult for people of European descent to comprehend the holistic approach to life-death-life and to the totality of creation which comes so naturally to the Aboriginal people. In fact, it is difficult for Europeans to accept Aboriginal people.

The first non-Aboriginal descriptions given of the Black Nations of *Terra Australis* were derogatory, of this there is no doubt! To reiterate those racist terms here would only contribute to the already abundant tomes of phrases, words and terms that are coined with only one purpose, and that is to put us, The Black Nations, down. We will not repeat them — even as examples — for fear that we may be teaching some non-racist person words, phrases and terms that they, being non-racist, may be oblivious to.

However, there are words that were used to describe us, The Black Nations, which we believe were factual, but used out of context. These words are 'savage', 'hostile', 'dirty' and 'unreliable'.

Allow us the opportunity to now set the record straight.

Firstly, the word *savage* was coined to describe us, The Black Nations, as animalistic. That is to say, that we were less than human, and therefore it was cool to dispossess and oppress us. Those early 'pathfinders' were obviously acting under orders from their 'bosses' to make these descriptions, even before they had seen us. It is clear to us — the oppressed — that all that has happened over the past two hundred or so years is part of a carefully contrived plan to deprive the Black Peoples of the World of their humanity first, and their priceless resources second.

The second word we wish to deal with briefly, is the word *hostile*. The early pathfinders used this descriptive noun to indicate that we, The Black Nations, were not happy with their presence in our country — our land — even though they purported to be friendly and meant us no harm. It was difficult for us to think or act differently with a gun pointed to our heads. That gun is still pointed.

The third word needing some attention was/is the word *dirty*. Mr Dampier used this word ad nauseam to describe our Sisters and Brothers of the Western Australian part of *Terra Australis*. He could not have been speaking or writing about our clothing — we weren't wearing any. He could not have been speaking about our personal bodies — he did not get close enough to see or smell. He could not have been speaking about our eating habits — he did not break bread with us. He must have been speaking about our attitudes to him and what he represented. Dampier was only one of a multitude of 'trailblazers' . . . some with guns, some with bibles, all with evil intent . . . intent only on dispossession and oppression.

Last but not least, a word used to abuse was the gem, *unreliable*. How this particular gem came into vogue is anybody's guess. We somehow think that perhaps one or more of the intrepid trailblazers had organised a meeting with one of The Black Nations and were grossly disappointed when no-one arrived. Yet the word has persisted as a supposedly true characteristic of all Aboriginal peoples.

The National Aboriginal and Islander Health Organisation does not refute these words: we in fact encourage their use, not ab-use.

Let us now, by way of explanation, state what we mean:

Firstly, we are very much savages. We are savage for our land and for the back rent that is owed to us.

Secondly, we are very hostile because you people who owe that rent won't pay up.

Thirdly, we are unbelievably dirty. We are dirty on non-Aboriginal misuse and abuse of our land and its precious resources.

Fourthly, we are certainly unreliable because we cannot be relied upon to acquiesce to non-Aboriginal demands on us to relinquish our rights of sovereignty.

We the Aboriginal community — The Black Nations — of Australia exist in a state of undeclared war. Our rights have never been relinquished. Non-Aborigines constantly declare that our struggle is with the 'elected governments' while they — the non-Aborigines — continue to abuse and misuse our land. The weapons used to keep us down are guns, bibles and words. This war, in recent times, has been fought by us with words, while the governments and the non-Aborigines who put them there use guns and bibles as well as the ab-use and mis-use of words.

If you, your organisation or government, feel real contrition for your unholy sins — THEN PAY THE RENT!

I do not know of any collection of Indigenous documents which puts forward our case but there are numerous collections of documents and essays by non-Indigenous people who discuss and dissect us. If there are to be Indigenous Studies courses, they should make use, as much as possible, of Indigenous documents and records. This is only one such document I helped to put together, and there are many more which set out the Indigenous position on any number of subjects and tell it as it is. The above document is important in that it is not only a political tract but also a cultural one, in that much of it is stressing the ideology of Indigenality and the need for cultural revitalisation programs. Our views on Indigenous matters are often disregarded, while those of so-called experts are embraced. This is very apparent in some of the glossy booklets which have been produced by the Council of Aboriginal Reconciliation. They are not Indigenous documents and as far as myself and other Indigenous people are concerned do not put forth the Indigenous position, but only the views of non-Indigenous academics who think they know what our position is. Reconciliation is supposed to involve consultation with Us Mob, but many of us have not been consulted.

No-one has bothered to collect the documents and records of the Land Rights struggle. No-one has yet told how we pored over White Papers and Green Papers, over draft legislation after draft legislation and held public meetings in our communities in which we broke down the legal jargon sentence by sentence so that we could all understand it. Many times our work has been in vain, but each stage of our struggle has been documented by us and these documents wait to be collected. Then, apart from these documents, there are the writings by Indigenous people such as Kevin Gilbert which offer solutions to our problems, though like all else they are ignored when government initiatives are undertaken supposedly after consultation with us. There is an abundant Indigenous literature in this country which awaits collection and use. It is about time that it is used in this post-activist period of reconciliation.

The Land Rights struggle was and is more than a slogan, as the above document shows. But it remains a slogan unless it is explained, and this is the reason why I wrote 'Song Eleven' in my volume of verse, *The Song Circle of Jacky*:

> Our demands you negotiate: we want our rights!
> Our traditional lands to be ours for ever.
> Our sacred places ever sacred under our lawful keepers.
> Our ancestors stood and fought: mark those places!
> Our mission homes, where you put us: ours!
> Our losses must be paid for: compensation
> To those forced off their lands by alien hands.
> Compensation to the lost and forsaken.
> Pay, so that Australia may be made whole:
> Pay, for old crimes never tried or justice passed.
> Pay, part of the money you made from our land,
> We never surrendered, or sold to you;
> Pay with no conditions or political tricks;
> Pay, negotiate the terms with us,
> Free our land from blood debt,
> And festering wounds of discontent.
> Pay and free us from welfare cheques,
> And hat-in-hand and condition-laden grants.

A simple demand held by many Indigenous people is for Land Rights and compensation. Compensation as we worked out in those heady days of activism was for a fixed percentage of the National Gross Product, and perhaps this should be in the submission to the Australian Parliament by the Council for Aboriginal Reconciliation who do seem, at least, to be aware of one important document, perhaps because it was widely publicised at the time. In 1988, Indigenous elders of representative communities presented the then Prime Minister, Robert J. Hawke, with a statement which came to be known as the *Barunga Statement*. This read:

THE BARUNGA STATEMENT

We, the indigenous owners and occupiers of Australia, call on the Australian Government and people to recognise our rights:

- To self-determination and self-management, including the freedom to pursue our own economic, social, religious and cultural development;

- To permanent control and enjoyment of our ancestral lands;

- To compensation for the loss of use of our lands, there having been no extinction of original title;

- To protection of and control of access to our sacred sites, sacred objects, artefacts, designs, knowledge and works of art;

- To the return of the remains of our ancestors for burial in accordance with our traditions;

- To respect for and promotion of our Aboriginal identity, including the cultural, linguistic, religious and historical aspects, and including the right to be educated in our own languages and in our own culture and history;

- In accordance with the universal declaration of human rights, the international covenant on economic, social and cultural rights, the international covenant on civil and political rights, and the international convention on the elimination of all forms of racial discrimination, rights to life, liberty, security of person, food, clothing, housing, medical care, education and employment opportunities, necessary social services and other basic rights.

We call on the Commonwealth to pass laws providing:

- a national elected Aboriginal and Islander Organisation to oversee Aboriginal and Islander affairs;

- a national system of land rights;

- a police and judicial system which recognises our customary laws and frees us from discrimination and any activity which may threaten our identity or security, interferes with our freedom of expression or association, or otherwise prevents our full enjoyment and exercise of universally recognised human rights and fundamental freedoms.

We call on the Australian Government to support Aborigines in the development of an international declaration of principles for Indigenous rights, leading to an international covenant.

And we call on the Commonwealth Parliament to negotiate with us a Treaty recognising our prior ownership, continued occupation and sovereignty and affirming our human rights and freedom.

In reply there was an immediate statement from the Prime Minister.

1. The Government affirms that it is committed to work for a negotiated treaty with Aboriginal People.

2. The Government sees the next step as Aborigines deciding what they believe should be in the Treaty.

3. The Government will provide the necessary support for Aboriginal people to carry out their own consultations and negotiations: this could include the formation of a Committee of seven senior Aborigines to oversee the process and to call an Australian-wide meeting o nvention.

4. When the Aborigines present their proposals the Government stands ready to negotiate about them.

5. The Government hopes that these negotiations can commence before the end of 1988 and will lead to an agreed treaty in the life of this Parliament.

At last, we Indigenous people thought that we had reached an important stage in our struggle which would lead to a healing of the rift between us and the Invaders; but our hopes were dashed. The Prime Minister returned to Canberra and his statement was disregarded. The word 'treaty' became an 'accord', or 'compact' and then quickly became 'reconciliation'. How often in the past had similar promises been made and been quickly broken but what could we do but continue our struggle? As I wrote in 'Song Eight' of my *Song Circle of Jacky*:

> They give Jacky rights,
> Like the tiger snake gives rights to its prey;
> They give Jacky rights,
> Like the rifle sights on its target.
>
> They give Jacky the right to die,
> The right to consent to mining on his land.
> They give Jacky the right to watch

His sacred dreaming place become a hole —
His soul dies, his ancestors cry;
His soul dies, his ancestors cry;
They give Jacky rights —
A hole in the ground!

Justice for all, Jacky kneels and prays;
Justice for all, they dig holes in his earth;
Justice for all, they give him his rights,
A flagon of cheap wine to hide his pain.
Justice for all, they give him his rights —
A hole in the ground to hide his mistrust and fear.
What can Jacky do, but struggle on and on,
The spirits of his Dreaming keep him strong!

So how many Land Rights campaigns and demonstrations have there been? Who knows? The history has not been written; the documents lie uncollected; only our oral records circulate and often these are only regional. And what was achieved? Not much politically, and when I was in Sydney for the 26 January 1988 rally and march, I came to the conclusion that such gatherings had become mere rituals. In fact, I thought that my days of demonstrating had come to an end. Then, in 1991, I found myself in another which was against the projected *Queensland Land Rights Act*, although again it did not achieve much as the Bill soon became law. Still, the demonstrations did keep the struggle going and now new weapons are being used, not in the streets but in the law courts where the great victory was gained of having the doctrine of *Terra Nullius* destroyed and Native Title accepted under common law.

Then there is the Council of Aboriginal Reconciliation which at least has recently submitted an important report to the Australian Parliament. So now, for better or worse, we have moved away from the grand Land Rights struggle. It has become history, and we are in what has been described as a post-Mabo period in which we are being given some justice and some rights. But the treaty? . . . Well, we will have to wait and see what the Document of Reconciliation they are talking about will be.

FURTHER READING

Bennett, Scott, *Aborigines and Politics*. Sydney, Allen & Unwin, 1989.

Gilbert, Kevin, *Aboriginal Sovereignty, Justice, the Law and the Land* (includes Draft Treaty). Canberra, Burrambinga Books, 1987–93.

Johnson, Colin (Mudrooroo), *Song Circle of Jacky and Other Poems*. Melbourne, Hyland House, 1986.

Libby, R.T., *Hawke's Law*. Nedlands, University of Western Australia Press, 1988.

Woodward, Justice A. E., *Aboriginal Land Rights Commission, First and Second Reports*. Canberra, Australian Government Publishing Service, 1973 and 1974.

Reconciling Us Mob
Lecture 13

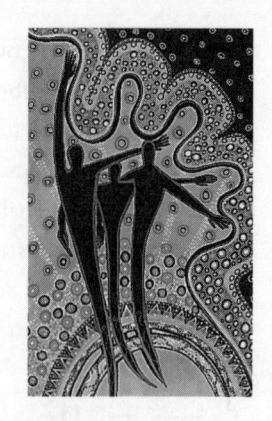

Inevitably, one is compelled to acknowledge the role played, in the dispossession and oppression of the Aborigines, by the two propositions that the territory of New South Wales was, in 1788, terra nullius in the sense of unoccupied or uninhabited for legal purposes and that full legal and beneficial ownership of all the lands of the Colony vested in the Crown, unaffected by any claims of the Aboriginal inhabitants. Those propositions provided a legal basis for and justification of the dispossession. They constituted the legality of the acts done to enforce it and, while accepted, rendered unlawful acts done by the Aboriginal inhabitants to protect traditional land use. The official endorsement, by administrative practice and in judgement of the courts, of those two propositions provided the environment in which the Aboriginal people of this continent came to be treated as a different and lower form of life whose very existence could be ignored for the purpose of determining the legal right to occupy and use their traditional homelands.

Mabo v Queensland, Deane, Gaudron JJ

TERRA NULLIUS IS PERHAPS THE ONLY LATIN THAT INDIGENOUS people know, except perhaps for a few more obscure legal phrases gained in experience of the courts. To us it was an ongoing insult and a painful reminder that from the first we had been denied existence, that in 1788 we had been rendered a no-people and our land a vacant land without us. We were an anomaly, a living and breathing nothing with no past and no future. Of course, we fought against this feeling of utter worthlessness, and what were our demonstrations but a way of proving to the invaders that we were in Australia and that Australia was ours. As the band No Fixed Address sang: 'We have survived the whiteman's will and you know you can't change that.'

The greatest step towards reconciliation occurred on 3 June 1992 when the High Court of Australia decided for the Meriam Islanders and their claim that they had 'native title' to the majority of the land of their islands and by doing so, and in their lengthy and convoluted decision, destroyed the doctrine of *Terra Nullius* once and for all. The news caused euphoria in Indigenous communities, which was quickly dispelled by a racist backlash spurred on by the media. Indigenous people were not the only ones under attack but even democratic institutions such as the High Court itself. It was difficult to understand these persistent attacks except as racist, for all the Court had done was to do away with a legal fiction while making few concessions to the aspirations of Indigenous people for sovereignty. In fact, the resulting uproar about what was essentially a timid decision showed the need for constitutional guarantees and perhaps a Bill of Rights to be enshrined in a new Constitution which would protect us from racist onslaughts.

It is clear from a study of its lengthy judgement that the High Court's decision means simply that Native Title does exist and can be protected by legal action, and that it may be held by an individual, group or community depending on traditional laws and customs, which according to the court are to be determined by the Indigenous people, not Australian law. This Native Title can be extinguished in several ways: when the traditional owners have moved or died; when a valid grant of freehold title has been given; most cases when a lease has been granted, including a mining lease (though not, it seems, an exploration lease); when the Crown has used land for roads, railways, or public facilities. A further ruling means that most claims for compensation for alienation of land, except under certain terms of the *Racial Discrimination Act 1975*, can be entered into. There is a further point which was stressed in the High Court decision, though with provisos which most likely have to be defined in further court actions, or as it was stated:

> Like other legal rights, including rights of property, the rights conferred by common law Native Title and the title itself can be dealt with, expropriated or extinguished by valid Commonwealth, State or Territorial legislation operating within the the State or Territory in which the land is situated. To put the matter differently, the rights are not entrenched in the sense that they are, by reason of their nature, beyond the reach of legislative power.

I assume that it was under such provisos that the Western Australian legal challenge to the new Commonwealth Act on Native Title was mounted and was also the legal basis behind the Western Australian Act which in effect abolished Native Title and replaced it with native traditional land usage. In March 1995 the High Court declared this Western Australian Act discriminatory and hence null and void. Thankfully, this showed that there was a will by the Court of Australia to defend the Native Title ruling.

The Court's ruling that the Meriam Islanders possessed Native Title to their offshore lands created an unprecedented uproar in the media, which quoted one supposedly eminent person after another to the effect that Indigenous people could lay claim to the whole of Australia and even that it was a racist decision which supported the separation of the Indigenous people from the rest of the nation and endowed us with special rights and privileges. The answer to the first assertion is that theoretically we could claim the entire continent, but under the High Court ruling it was very unlikely that that our claims would be heard, let alone allowed to go through the whole court process. As Native Title had been held to have been sold off as freehold or granted under lease, the only such claims which were likely to succeed were in the case of vacant Crown land with which Indigenous people had had a continuous association. This issue of vacant Crown land was seized on by the Western Australian government, but again, owing to the concentration of many Indigenous people on missions and government stations, it is highly unlikely that many claims could be proved — or those claims which could be proved would be for Crown land on which Indigenous people were living and thus would merely change the ninety-nine year lease which had been given to Indigenous people in lieu of Land Rights into Native Title. Thus most of the scare tactics were based on little more than mere supposition, and Indigenous people, if they were to contest Native Title, might find themselves locked up in the court for long periods of time with a continuous outlay of money to lawyers.

The prolonged furore resulted in the Commonwealth Government seeking to frame special legislation which would bring some order into the whole business. They began a round of consultations with the various State governments and immediately found themselves embroiled in mutual recriminations, with the Liberal premiers of Victoria and Western Australia in particular grabbing the headlines with outrageous assertions that not even the family backyard was safe from Indigenous claims, and the like. Eventually, after a long hard slog under fire from both political opponents and Indigenous organisations, the Commonwealth government framed a Bill which pleased no-one. Intense pressure on Indigenous organi-sations caused them to support the Bill, but with less leverage on the conservative State governments, the Commonwealth could do little to stop Western Australia passing counterlegislation which in effect did away with the whole common law concept of Native Title and replaced it with 'traditional usage'. This was passed before the Commonwealth Bill and was law for almost two years before being declared null and void.

The *Commonwealth Native Title Bill* of 1993 was born from compromise and tried to be all things to all sides with the less powerful Indigenous minority receiving much less than they demanded. It is similar to other legislation concerning Indigenous people in that there is a proviso for the Minister to overrule the decision of the special tribunal set up to decide on Native Title if there is an overriding need, though the issue can then go to the Federal Court for adjudication.

The Bill was hastily drawn up and rushed through Parliament, and it is doubtful that this was of any benefit to the Indigenous people. Political decisions are never what they seem, and it should be noted that the government's moralistic stance on civil rights internationally, especially in the case of China, Malaysia and South Africa, was often met with jibes about Australia's treatment of its Indigenous people. This was stressed when the Bill was being debated. The government argued that it would bring Australia in line with other countries and thus fulfil its obligations under such agreements as the *International Convention on the Elimination of All Forms of Racial Discrimination*.

There was a further reason for the haste with which the legislation was passed. The High Court decision on Native Title might have rendered invalid grants of land or leases on land made after 31 October 1975, which were now in conflict with the Commonwealth *Racial Discrimination Act 1975*, which seemed to require that Native Title be treated in a non-discriminatory way. It was thought that where a grant of interest in land would extinguish or impair Native Title interests without compensation, the effect might be considered in a court of law to be discriminatory. Thus speedy legislation was necessary to remove this uncertainty which might have seen productive tracts of land tied up in the courts while title was adjudicated. This was no idle threat, as it was under the *Racial Discrimination Act* that the *Western Australian Native Land Usage Act* was declared invalid.

The Commonwealth legislation protects Native Title from being extinguished on any pretext, although it does validate freehold grants, residential, commercial, pastoral or agricultural leases and

Crown actions involving permanent works. What can be claimed under Native Title is vacant Crown land and national parks which are Crown Land under the control of the Commonwealth.

One of the most vociferous opponents of Indigenous land rights and of Native Title is the mining industry, whose economic strength makes it a powerful lobby group. It wants unfettered access to land, which it declares is in the national interest — though some might claim otherwise — and was able to get a good deal under the legislation. One of the demands of Indigenous people in the Land Rights campaign was the right to veto mining on Indigenous land and recognition of their ownership of minerals underneath. Many Indigenous people are not against mining if they are allowed to protect their sacred sites and also to have a share of the royalties to ensure a degree of economic independence. As many Indigenous communities are in remote areas with little economic prospects besides mining, control of any minerals under their land and the revenue from them are very important, but the proposed legislation did not consider this. It was decided that mining grants would not extinguish Native Title, but merely suspend it, and they might again be exercised after the the minerals had been dug up. In addition, Native Title rights would be subject in the same way as other titleholders' rights, which meant that the government kept control of all the minerals under the ground and could grant mining rights almost at will. It is little wonder that, after a time, the mining industry decided to support the legislation.

Without going into detail, the Act as finally passed allows that Native Title land may be acquired by governments under normal compulsory acquisition laws for purposes such as essential public use. But its most important provisions relate to the creation of a National Native Title Tribunal (NNTT) and empowering the Federal Court to determine Native Title and compensation claims. The NNTT deals with uncontested claims for Native Title and compensation and is able to enquire into any issue referred to it by the Commonwealth Minister. It also has the power to negotiate with relevant State or Territorial bodies to determine if grants can proceed over Native Title land if negotiations have broken down. The Federal Court is given the power to hear contested claims to either determine Native Title or compensation.

Another clause in the Act, in keeping with other legislation dealing with Indigenous land and heritage claims, provides for the appointment of a Native Title Registrar to whom all applications under the Commonwealth system have to be made. This Registrar is responsible for the establishment of a Register of Native Title Claims and a National Register recording all land held under Native Title, but may delegate these powers and duties to a recognised State or Territory body. States and Territories may also establish their own bodies to hear Native Title and compensation claims, under strict controls and with the Commonwealth Minister having the power to revoke their recognition if they operate in an arbitrary manner.

The *Native Title Act* of 1993, in spite of all the uproar it aroused, on the whole benefits only a small minority of Indigenous people who can prove a continuing association with the land or whose claims are uncontested. This leaves a considerable majority who have no chance to claim, or gain, Native Title. In order to assist these dispossessed people, a few clauses in the Act set up a National Aboriginal and Torres Strait Islander Land Fund. Details of this Land Fund are only now (1995) being worked out. It rightly belongs to the process of 'reconciliation', which is part of the Commonwealth Government's strategy to bring all segments of the nation together by 2001.

The Council for Aboriginal Reconciliation, with twenty-five members, fourteen of whom are Indigenous, is formulating and forwarding the processes of reconciliation. Even after three years, it still seems something of a mystery to many people in Australia. From what I have seen, every now and again the chairperson of the Council attends some function and this is reported in the media. Its first submission to the Government in 1995 did receive some publicity and it has placed some of its literature in mass circulation magazines. Thus, its methods are improving. One of the problems it has is that of credibility. Many Indigenous people see it as yet another government body imposed on them from above. The Indigenous writer and activist Kevin Gilbert, in one of his last interviews, refused to accept not only the Council but the very idea of reconciliation. He stated:

> We have to look at the word 'reconciliation'. What are we to reconcile ourselves to? To a holocaust, to massacre, to the removal of us from our land, from the taking of our land? The reconciliation process can achieve nothing because it does not at the end of the day promise justice. It does not promise a Treaty and it does not promise reparation for the taking away of our lives, our lands and of our economic and political base. Unless it can return to us these very vital things, unless it can return to us an economic, a political and a viable land base, what have we?

A handshake? A symbolic dance? An exchange of leaves and feathers or something like that?

It is not possible, and the people who comprise the Reconciliation Council are not the indigenous representatives from the Aboriginal communities. The eminent white people are from the mining industry, they are selected from the churches, they are selected from the business council. So immediately the white people (who are these eminent Australians on that body) are people who come from areas of very deeply-vested interests and these interests are certainly not pro-Aboriginal ownership of land.

The Aboriginal people who are on there (the Reconciliation Council), many of them are employees of the government. They work in government departments. They have a vested interest in following the various programs or policies of government and there can be no representative voice. It is a ten-year period for this process to occur. Now that means to us a further ten years of being deprived, a further ten years of dying, and a further ten years where there is nothing promised at the end of the day.

Justice, in fact, is not even the objective within this. The object is reconciliation, which means to educate people to the Aboriginal condition — and heaven knows they must be educated — and to wash their hands, virtually, of the obtaining of justice for Aboriginal people.

The Aboriginal Provisional Government — which perhaps should have been asked to be on the Reconciliation Council, as it has more grassroots support than the Indigenous members on the council (and more ideas as well) — in an article published in *Koori Times*, asked the following questions:

> Nobody really knows what is meant to happen when the
> process of reconciliation is complete. Is there meant to be
> a social policy document capable of being implemented by
> governments? If so, how could that possibly be better than
> the 339 recommendations of the Black Deaths in Custody
> Commission, under consideration by state and federal
> governments? And if the council is meant to enquire into
> the circumstances of Aborigines, has that not already been
> done, over and over again?

The unfortunate thing about these questions is that the answer to them is 'Yes', and if this springs readily to mind, what use is the Reconciliation Council and what is it for? Is it just another government initiative which is going terribly wrong right from the start? For as I write there is much dissatisfaction with it from the Indigenous communities.

When the Minister for Aboriginal Affairs, Robert Tickner, moved the second reading of the *Council for Aboriginal Reconciliation Bill 1991*, he declared:

> It is the intention of the Government, backed I hope by
> the unanimous commitment of the Parliament, that the
> formal process of reconciliation initiated by this Bill will
> signal the beginning of a decade of reform and social
> justice for Aboriginal and Torres Strait Islander people and
> for building bridges of understanding between Aboriginal
> and non-Aboriginal Australians.

The Bill became law and the Council was established and began producing and distributing glossy publications. In one of them, *Council for Aboriginal Reconciliation, An Introduction*, its aims were stated as follows:

> Reconciliation is about improving relations between
> Aboriginal and Torres Strait Islanders and other Australians.
> It is summed up in the Council's vision which is: A united
> Australia which respects this land of ours; values the
> Aboriginal and Torres Strait Islander heritage; and provides
> justice and equity for all.

These are laudable aims but the question must be asked: how is this to be accomplished? And then, shouldn't it be non-Indigenous people who should seek reconciliation and not Indigenous people, a majority of whom comprise the Council? The publication then details what the Council considers to be the key issues crucial to reconciliation. These include a greater understanding of the importance of land and sea to Indigenous people; better relationships between all Australians; recognition that Indigenous culture and heritage are a valued part of the Australian heritage; a sense of shared ownership of history; a greater awareness of the causes of disadvantage of Indigenous people; a greater response to addressing the underlying causes of the high levels of custody of Indigenous people; greater opportunity for Indigenous people to control their own destinies; and, lastly, whether the process of reconciliation would be advanced by a document of reconciliation. This last issue is quite interesting and reminds me of the Indigenous joke that each Minister of Indigenous Affairs has his own pet project. One had 'assimilation', another 'integration' and now we have 'reconciliation'. It may also be said that once we were promised a treaty, then a compact, then an accord and now a document of reconciliation.

Overall, the Council may be seen to be pretty innocuous and at the best is duplicating work which has been performed for some time by other non-Governmental organisations and individuals. Being a Government organisation, the Reconciliation Council is also constrained by Government policy, leaving no other option but for Indigenous people to be assimilated into what is termed multicultural Australia as good citizens. If any other political solution is acknowledged, it is given short shrift in favour of reconciliation.

I may be seen to be somewhat negative in my approach to the Council for Aboriginal Reconciliation, at least in my comments on their first three years in existence. More needs to be done to give teeth to the Council. Perhaps one way to do this is to broaden its membership to include more representative Indigenous individuals and members of the mainstream who are not so politically middle-of-the-road. Perhaps if we are to achieve reconciliation we should get all the extremists together and let them get to know each other. As it is, the members have been selected to cause the least amount of stirring and I am sure that they are extremely well-mannered at their meetings. Then perhaps the Council's membership should be broadened to include representatives of students, single mothers, the unemployed and prisoners' groups, for these too might benefit from the reconciling process. Still, whatever reservations I have expressed about the Council, it might be argued that if it does help to bring the people living in Australia together in some sort of accommodation, it will be doing some good. As Pat Dodson, the chairperson of the Council, is reported to have said, the aim of the exercise is to get Indigenous and non-Indigenous persons to pass each other politely in the street.

To this, I might retort that it is not enough and that the Council for Aboriginal Reconciliation has been set up to do more than to bring the population of Australia to some sort of tolerance, that with the recognition of Native Title there is a role for the Council to play in furthering the needs of Indigenous people and thus fill the void which has occurred in Aboriginal politics with the passing of Land Rights from the political to the legal domain. This, it appears from their latest and often surprising document, may be exactly what the Council, with some newly appointed Indigenous members such as Marcia Langton and Jackie Huggans, is now seeking to do.

Going Forward: Social Justice for the First Australians was submitted to the Australian government in 1995. It is a sweeping and positive document commenting on, criticising and recommending changes in the policies governing many Indigenous lives in this country. It urges changes in the Australian Constitution to outlaw racism and to protect the rights of Indigenous Australians. It broadens the political debate by urging regional self-government for the Torres Strait Islands, reserved seats in Parliament for Indigenous Australians, an Indigenous Bill of Rights and, lastly, compensation for those peoples forced off their lands. In fact, many of the recommendations in this submission to the Government are what Indigenous people have been struggling to attain for years, and it is gratifying at last to see them in a document officially presented to the Government. If goodwill is forthcoming from the Commonwealth Parliament and some of these recommendations given substance, it is possible that 2001 might see the end of the healing process with the Indigenous people accepting their place in a Republic of Australia.

Further Reading

Brennan, Frank, *Sharing the Country: The Case for an Agreement Between Black and White Australians*. Melbourne, Penguin Books, 1991.

Commonwealth of Australia, *Native Title Bill 1993*. Canberra, Commonwealth of Australia, November 1993.

Council For Aboriginal Reconciliation, *Information Kit*. Canberra, Australian Government Publishing Service,1991

Council for Aboriginal Reconciliation, *Addressing the Key Issues for Reconciliation: Overview of Key Issues Papers No's 1–8; Understanding Country (No 1); Sharing History (No 4); Agreeing on a Document (No 7)*. Canberra, Australian Government Publishing Service,1993–4.

Council for Aboriginal Reconciliation, *Going Forward: Social Justice for the First Australians*. Canberra, Australian Government Publishing Service, 1995.

Gilbert, Kevin, ed., *Aboriginal Sovereignty, Justice, the Law and Land*. *Canberra*, Burrambinga Books, 1993.

Hewat, Tim, *Who Made the Mabo Mess*. Melbourne, Wrightbooks, 1993.

'Mabo v Queensland', *Commonwealth Law Reports*, Vol. 107, Sydney, Law Book Co., 1992.

Mickler, S., *Gambling on the First Race: A Comment on Racism and Talk-Back Radio — 6PR, the TAB, and the WA Government*. Melbourne, Murdoch University, Centre for Research in Culture and Communication, May 1992.

Stephenson M.A. and Ratnapala, S., *Mabo: A Judicial Revolution*. Brisbane, University of Queensland Press, 1993.

Conclusion

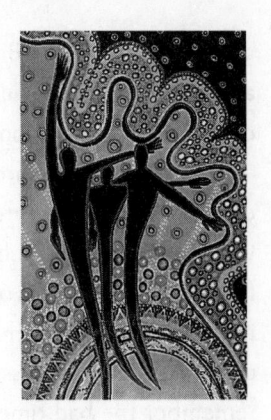

IN KOORI VICTORIA THERE IS A CORPUS OF MYTHS DETAILING the epic adventures of the Bram Bram Bult brothers. This long, involved and convoluted mythology spreads over a considerable distance. Dreaming trails or song lines pass through any number of communities whose local ancestral heroes entered into a relationship with these two brothers, who came bearing the gifts of ceremonies, songs and new ways of thought. One of the myths connected to the Bram Bram Bult concerns the Dreaming Tree of life and death and how through jealousy it was burnt down. The huge tree, the connection between the sky world and the earth world, crashed down and lay across all of what is now Victoria. There are present day landmarks — impressions in the earth which are the indentations made by the impact of the branches, twigs and leaves hitting the earth. The place where the huge trunk fell became a river and the hole of the root system a great depression in the ground, to which the Bram Bram Bult came. They watered the ashes at the bottom of the depression and there sprang up a shoot which continued on the Dreaming Tree of life and death.

This is where we are at present. Our Dreaming Tree of life and death is growing into a sturdy sapling under the shade of Grandfather Tree which is Australia. It will continue to grow as it is fertilised by the ashes of our past. And as they did to our ancestors in the Dreaming, others still come bearing us gifts which they urge us to take. They profess goodwill and seek goodwill from us, but we remember the bad times and hold back. It is not our fault that we appear suspicious, for when the invaders came to our land, they too professed goodwill. It was then that the killing times, the kidnapping times and the incarceration times began. We suffered and bear the marks of the suffering on us today. But then many other Indigenous peoples bear the scars of history. Should we then finger our scars and hold back from at least approaching You Mob.

Australia is Grandfather Tree and many trees and shrubs grow in his shade. There is plenty of room still in our forest, but we do not wish to belong to a plantation in which each tree is of the same species. No, every community, every group in Australia, should be sovereign and be allowed to grow, keeping to the things they hold dear. Is it too late to put aside the dominance of the majority group who once pruned and hacked and burnt and cleared, then planted trees from alien seeds? If this is to be an Australia in which everyone is to be the same, then there is really no place for Us and our Dreaming Tree of life and death.

We as Indigenous people can only hope for a future which will be fruitful and good for all of us living in Australia. There is talk of a Republic of Australia, a reshifting of focus away from Europe to a safety under the Grandfather Tree of Australia. There is to be a new beginning, an Australian beginning, or rather a shifting of your alliances to our land in which we all can live in safety and security. What can we do but hope that the new Republic will be a just and peaceful nation for us, that it will be a nation holding on to our Indigenous ideals of caring and sharing, of putting old wrongs aside and concentrating on the future. You have been here for a little over two hundred years and even in that little time Grandfather Tree has begun to reshape you to fit into our land. There are a few problems and these can be resolved if we talk to you as equals rather than being talked down to, if we can negotiate with you as equals rather than having solutions imposed on us. We know what we want and it is up to you to listen to us.

As one of our elders writes: 'What I'm saying, you listen. You'll feel your string, you feel your body, you'll feel yourself. Might be morning, you feeling . . . Arrh, I want to understand that. I want to listen.'

Perhaps we do need a new Constitution and a Bill of Rights which will enshrine our freedom as a sovereign people who never surrendered, or lost our identity. We declare that we have been in this land of Australia since time began. We say that we have been here since the Dreaming and that is why we continue to struggle for acknowledgement of this. Once we were declared not to be, our land was said to be a *terra nullius*, a land vacant of people. We did not plough, or build tall buildings. Our life was a constant pilgrimage over the land and we visited our holy places and followed the way of our ancestors. It must have been a good life, for we have been here since the Dreaming, or as your archaeologists say, for over

40,000 years. Even if you do not accept our presence from the Dreaming, at least you must accept that 40,000 years is so long a period that it is impossible to hold it in the mind.

Generation after generation of Kooris, Murris, Nyungars, Nangas, Yolngus, Yamadjis, Wonghis and other communities continued down in an unbroken line. We with the blood of those first people in our veins feel for our land because we have been here for so long. And over this length of time, our ancestors bequeathed to us the Law to follow. A law which ordered us to take care of our land and our families. We have tried to do this, but the newcomers had different ideas and ways of using the land. Our land suffered and we suffered and it is only now that there seems to be a hope that we are entering a time of healing, a time of prosperity in which we all can share. Our Grandfather Tree is sturdy and strong; our Dreaming Tree of life and death continues to grow strong and we will continue to endure and grow strong.

And so, perhaps, this book, these lectures, mark an end to the old hurtful times, and mark an entrance into the healing times. It is up to all of us to make this healing time a reality. If we do not do so, Us Mob and You Mob will continue to bicker and fight and contend and contest and never enter into a respect for one another. If this happens it will be a sadness and a worry to all of us and never will there be an acceptance of our Grandfather Tree, Australia, and how he sheds his shade over us without favouring one or the other. There is plenty of room beneath his boughs and around his trunk for all of us to live and grow in a diversity of cultures under which is a spiritual oneness. In our culture our ancestors were many and met and exchanged gifts. Today, in

Australia, we all are many and from many lands, but we can all meet and exchange gifts and dance out ceremonies acknowledging our diversity and our underlying spiritual unity. In 2001 the era of reconciliation will come to an end and perhaps there shall be a Republic of Australia. This gives us only about five years or so to finalise things and enter into the next century with rejoicing that the bad old days have finally been put to rest and a new and better Australia has come into being.

Index

AAMA (Aboriginal Arts Management Assocation) 173
ABC 150–151
'Aboriginal' 7
Aboriginal and Torres Strait Islander Commission 76, 88–89
Aboriginal Arts Management Association 173
Aboriginal Associations Act 78
Aboriginal Development Commission 81, 84–88
Aboriginal Development Commission Act 85, 88
Aboriginal Embassy 195
Aboriginal Health Section (Health Commission) 128, 131
Aboriginal Land Fund Commission 84
Aboriginal Legal Service 98–108
Aboriginal Legends of the North West (Edwards) 95
Aboriginal Loans Commission 84
Aboriginal Medical Service 128–132
Aboriginal Men of High Degree (Elkin) 44
Aboriginal Organisations Act 101
Aboriginal Provisional Government 194, 229
ADC (Aboriginal Development Commission) 81, 84–88
AIAS (Australian Institute of Aboriginal Studies) 120
AIATSIS (Australian Institute of Aboriginal and Torres Strait Islander Studies) 9
alphabet 59
Altman, Jan 157–158
AMS (Aboriginal Medical Service) 128–132
Anangu people 155–158
anthropology 9, 40, 50
Arrernte people 159
arrests 100
art
  industry 157, 158, 160–173
  and the land 204–206
assimilation 82, 107, 163
associations, incorporated 78
ATSIC (Aboriginal and Torres Strait Islander Commission) 76, 88–89
Australia Council 161
Australian Film Commission 16
Australian Institute of Aboriginal and Torres Strait Islander Studies 9
Australian Institute of Aboriginal Studies 120
Australian National Parks and Wildlife Service 155
Australian Stations of the Cross (Ungunmer-Baumann) 50

Baijini 2
Bardon, Geoff 164, 166
bark paintings 160, 170–172

Barunga Kriol 60, 63–64
Barunga Statement 215–217
Batterbee, Rex 162–163
Beier, Ulli 164, 166
beliefs *see* spirituality
Bennell, Tom, *Kura* 188–191
Berak, William 45
Berndt, Catherine 203
Berndt, Professor Ronald 70, 203
Biami (deity) 46–47
Bill of Rights 76, 222, 237
Black movement 8
Black Robinson (Rae-Ellis) 187
Blackout (TV program) 144
Bram Bram Bult brothers 235–236
Brereton, Laurie 131
Briscoe, Gordon 128
Bryant, Gordon 83–84
Bulletin magazine 70
bureaucracy 22, 77–83
Burnum Burnum 145, 149
Burunga Statement 194
bush, European response to 67

Cake Man (Merritt) 16, 99
Capital Fund 86–87
caricatures 148–149
Central Australian Aboriginal Legal Aid Service 106
ceremony as history 179
Chaney, Fred 84–85
charity 28
child-rearing 26
children
  court 106–107
  education 112–113
  separation from family 21–22
Christianity 33, 44–46, 54
cities 14–15, 29
Clark, Manning 177
Clarke, Marcus 67, 68
classificatory relationships 23
Coe, Paul 100
colonisation 2–4
commonality of interests 77
'community' 14, 76–79
community health nurses 128–129
compensation 214, 222
conception 27
Constitution 237
construction of Indigeneity 6–10
Cook, James 208–209
Coolangatta Statement on Indigenous Rights in Education 119
Coombs, Dr H.C. 'Nugget' 81
Cooper, Revel 163–164
Council for Aboriginal Reconciliation 75, 176, 182, 194, 213, 214–215, 219, 228–233
Council for Aboriginal Reconciliation, An Introduction 231
Council for Aboriginal Reconciliation Bill 1991 230

Creation Spirituality and the Dreamtime (Hammond) 34–35
Creoles 60–65
Crown land 223, 226
culture
  and the land 201
  sale of 158–173
curriculum 120–121, 124
Cyclone Tracy in art 167–168
Cyclone Tracy Palga 168

DAA (Department of Aboriginal Affairs) 77–81, 83–84, 132
Daly River community 35
Daly River language 61
dance 179–180
Dark Side of the Dream (Hodge and Mishra) 40
Darwin, Charles 67
Day of the Dog 26, 31
deaths 127
Dening, Greg 180
dental health 130–131
Department of Aboriginal Affairs 77–81, 83–84, 132
Department of Internal Affairs 83
Dexter, Barrie 83
diabetes 132
diet 130
Dingo, Ernie 147–148
'dirty' 211–212
diversity 20
Djaringalong story 95–97
Dodson, Pat 232
Doolan, Liz 128
dreaming 41–44
Dreaming Tree of life and death 235–236
Dreamtime 34–40
  in art 72
  land 198–201, 204–206
  law 94–95
drunkenness arrests 104–105
Durack, Elizabeth 163

Earth Mother 47, 51, 53
Economic Development branch (DAA) 84
economic English 58
education
  effect of 2–4
  health 134–136
  health workers 137–140
  Indigenous languages 69–70
  Indigenous methods 14, 112–125, 116
  Kriol 62, 64–65
Edwards, Hugh, *Aboriginal Legends of the North West* 95
elderly 132
elections 76
Elkin, A.P., *Aboriginal Men of High Degree* 44

INDEX

Embassy, Aboriginal 195
employment 135
English language
　Indigenous 59
　Kriol 59–63
　standard 56–59, 62
extended families 1–2, 24–26, 27–31

family 18–33
　broken up 21–22
　European 20–21
　extended 24–26, 27–31
　moieties 23–25
　nuclear 29
　pre-European 1–2
fatherhood 26–27, 29
Federal Court 227
films 16–17
flag 151
Fleming, Robert 114
Fraser government 84
funding
　health 129, 131
　legal services 101

genealogy 186, 191
genocide 92
Gilbert, Kevin 15, 71, 194, 213
Going Forward: Social Justice for the First Australians 75–76, 233
Gondarra, Djiniyini 202
government 75–91
　health programs 129–131
　Native Title 224
Gularabulu (Roe) 96–97, 185
Gulpilil, David 198

Hammond, Catherine, *Creation Spirituality and the Dreamtime* 34–35
Hawke, Robert J. 194, 215
Hawke government 88
health 126–141
Health Consultative Groups 139
health workers, Indigenous 129, 137–140
High Court 195, 221–222, 225
history 175–192
Hodge, Bob, *The Dark Side of the Dream* 35
Hollows, Professor Fred 128
Honey Ant Dreaming 71
'hostile' 211–212
House of Representatives Standing Committee on Aboriginal Affairs 80–81, 89–90
housing 132–135
　grants program 86
　public 29
Howitt, A.W. 45
hygiene 134

In the Beginning 113–119
incorporated associations 78

Indigenality 1–17
Indigenous English 59
Indigenous languages 65–73
Indigenous Playwrights' Conference 16
Indigenous Studies courses 113, 116
infants 26
initiation rites 116
International Convention on the Elimination of All Forms of Racial Discrimination 225
Isaacs, Jenny 160–161

Jacob, Trevor K. 114
Jaminji, Paddy 168–170
Jindyworabak movement 163
job-production schemes 28

Kalgoorlie 127
Keating, Paul 151
Keeffe, Kevin 120
kinship 18–31, 79
Kneebone, Eddie 34–35
knowledge transmission 90
Koori: A Will to Win (Miller) 181, 186
Kriol 59–63
Kura (Bennell) 188–191
Kuril Kuril ceremonies 168, 170

Lake Tyers (Victoria) 133
land 196–210
　confiscation 25
　dispossession 209–210
　European depredation 92
　and health 126
　importance 18–19
　Native Title 193, 195, 221–228, 233
　spiritual significance 51–53, 53–54
Land Fund Commission 85
Land Rights 81, 193–219, 233
Land Rights Act 1983 (NSW) 13
Land Rights Act (Queensland) 218–219
Land (Titles and Traditional Usage) Act 1993 (WA) 195
landscape, European response to 67–68
Langton, Marcia 196, 202–203, 208
languages 56–73
　in education 121
　English 56–59
　Europeans' response to 68–69
　Indigenous 65–73
　Kriol 59–63
　ownership 72–73
Lanhupuy, Wesley 206–207
Lanley, Larry 201
law
　ALS 98–108
　European 92–93, 97–98, 108–110
　Indigenous 93–98, 108–110
lawyers 100, 102, 105
legal services 98–108
legend 179

literature
　codifying the law 94–96
　as history 178–180

Mabo 195
Macassans 2
McGuinness, Bruce 136, 198–199
McKenna, Ross 128
McPherson, Shirley 85
madlunga 73
magic 49
Malpa Trading 157, 158
Managalamarra, Geoffrey 167–168
Marika, Wandjuk 198
marriage law 23–25
massacres 25, 92
matriarchy 27
media 142–153
medical services 128–132
medicine 135
Meriam Islanders 221, 223
Merritt, Robert J., *The Cake Man* 16, 99
Millenium (TV program) 149
Miller, James, *Koori: A Will to Win* 181, 186
Milpurrurru, George 172
mimi spirits in painting 171
mining industry 226
Ministers of Aboriginal Affairs 84, 88–89, 231
min-min lights 42–43
Mirritj, Jack, *My People's Life* 115
moieties 23–25
Morgan, Sally 27
mortality 127
Muecke, Stephen 96, 185
multiculturalism 145–146
Murdoch University 69
Murray, Les 70
Mutitjulu 156–157
My People's Life (Mirritj) 115
myth 179

NAC (National Aboriginal Commission) 86
NAIHO (National Aboriginal and Islander Health Organisation) 136–137
NAILSS (National Aboriginal and Islander Legal Services Secretariat) 101
Namatjira, Albert 162–163
names 11
National Aboriginal and Islander Health Organisation 136–137
National Aboriginal and Islander Legal Services Secretariat 101
National Aboriginal and Torres Strait Islander Land Fund 228
National Aboriginal Commission 86
National Aboriginal Education Committee 120
National Aboriginal Sports Foundation 86

National Aborigines and Torres Strait Islander Studies Project 119
national identity 182
National Native Title Tribunal 195, 227
Native Land Usage Act (WA) 225
Native Title 193, 195, 221–228, 233
Native Title Act 1993 227–228
Native Title Bill 1993 224–225
Native Title Registrar 227
Neidjie, Bill, *A Story About Feeling* 33, 47–49, 51–52, 53–54
Neumann, Klaus 180
New Age movement 162
New South Wales Health Commission 128
 Aboriginal Health Section 128, 131
Newman, Eddie 128
Ngiyambaa language 66
Ngukurr Kriol 60, 64
NNTT (National Native Title Tribunal) 227
'noble savage' media image 147–148
Northern Territory Supreme Court 106
Northern Territory Welfare Branch 83
nostalgia for Europe 4
Not the 1988 Party (theatre piece) 159
nuclear family 26–27, 29
Nungan, Butcher Joe 41
nurses 128–129
Nyungar language 69–70
Nyungar marriage laws 23–25

offensive behaviour arrests 104–105
Office of Aboriginal Affairs 83
On Aboriginal Religion (Stanner) 35
Oodgeroo of the Noonuccal 47–49, 53
Oral Cultures and the Empire of Literature (Tapping) 188
oral history 177, 178–180, 187–191
organisations, incorporated 85
orphanages 21
Our Future Our Selves 89–90

Pama Nyungan (language) 56–73
Papunya Tula art 164–167
Perkins, Charles 83–84, 86
philanthropy 28
Phillip, Governor 20
Pinjarra massacre 25
Pinupi education system 120–123
poetry 70–71
police 92–93, 99–100, 105–106, 150–151
politics 75–91
population shift 133
Port Keats community 35
powerlessness 127
prison 15, 93, 109
public housing 29
Public Servants' Act 85

Racial Discrimination Act 1975 222, 225

Rae-Ellis, Vivienne, *Black Robinson* 187
Rainbow Serpent 49–50, 53, 167–168
Rainbow Serpent, The (theatre piece) 47–49, 51
reconciliation 75–76, 213, 228–233
Reconciliation Council *see* Council for Aboriginal Reconciliation
Redfern
 community 14
 legal service 99–100, 104
 medical clinic 128, 130, 132
religion 33–34
 see also spirituality
 Christianity 33, 44–46, 54
Republic 237
Roberts, Rhoda 146, 147
Robertson, G.A. 186–187
rock engravings and paintings 169
Roe, Paddy, *Gularabulu* 96–97, 185
Rowse, Tim 155, 157
Royal Commission into Aboriginal Deaths in Custody 106
Russell, John 128

sacred sites
 desecration 126
 origin 200
sameness 20
'savage' 3, 7, 147–148, 210–212
secret business
 art 171
 Rainbow Serpent 49
self-determination 77–82, 89
self-management 89
shamans 44
singularity 20, 69
Smith, Shirley 128
snake deity (Rainbow Serpent) 49–50, 53, 167–168
Song Cycle of Jacky 214, 217–218
Songs of Central Australia (Strehlow) 70, 71
South Eastern Land Council 207
Special Broadcasting Service 145–146
Spirit Ancestors 199–200, 204–206
spirituality 33–54
 and the land 209–210
 and the law 94–95
 rock paintings 169
Stanner, W.E.H., *On Aboriginal Religion* 35, 49
stereotypes in the media 147–148
Story About Feeling (Neidjie) 33, 47–49, 51–52, 53–54
Strehlow, *Songs of Central Australia* 71
'suitcase art' 160
Sydney ALS 100

Tapping, Craig, *Oral Cultures and the Empire of Literature* 188
Tasmania 187
taxis 30
television 144, 145–146, 149–151
terra nullius 220–221, 237

textbooks 113–119
theatre 16
Thomas, Rover 168–170
Tickner, Robert 230
time sequencing 117–118, 175–176, 179, 183, 185–186, 191
tourism 154–158
Towards a National Philosophy ... 119
'traditional land usage' 223, 224
transport 29–30
Treasury 86
Treaty 76, 194, 216–217

Uluru-Katatjulu National Park 155–156
Ungunmer-Baumann, Miriam-Rose, *Australian Stations of the Cross* 50
Unipon, David 46
unity 19
'unreliable' 211–212
Uttemorrah, Daisy 41, 48

VAHS (Victorian Aboriginal Health Service) 137, 138, 141
Victorian Aboriginal Child Care Agency 107
Victorian Aboriginal Health Service 137, 138, 141
Victorian Medical Service 130
Viner, Ian 84
'visiting relatives' 14
vocabularies 66–67
Vox Populi (TV program) 146

Walker, Denis 136, 194
Walmatjarri language 63
'walu' 66–67
Wandjina figures 169
watercolours 163
weight-control programs 132
Welfare system 87–88, 136
Weller, Archie, *The Day of the Dog* 26, 31
Western Australian Aboriginal Health Service 137
Western Australian Department of Education 113–114, 121
Western Australian legal challenge to Native Title 222–223
westernisation 82
Whitlam government 101
women
 European 27
 Indigenous 8
Woodward Report 196
World Indigenous People's Conference on Education (1993) 120
Wright, Judith 67
writing 180
written language 59

Yanangu 121–123
Yolngu society 114–115
Yulara (resort complex) 156
Yunupingu, Galarrwuy 206